A Bouquet of Black Orchids

A Bouquet of Black Orchids

ROXANNE CARR

BLACK
lace

Black Lace novels are sexual fantasies.
In real life, make sure you practise safe sex.

First published in 1994 by
Black Lace
332 Ladbroke Grove
London
W10 5AH

Copyright © Roxanne Carr 1994

Typeset by CentraCet Limited, Cambridge
Printed and bound by Cox & Wyman Ltd, Reading,
Berks

ISBN 0 352 32939 4

Chapter One

The soft purr of the engine barely impinged on Maggie's consciousness as she turned off the M6 and headed south. Changing down a gear as she saw the traffic slowing ahead, her bare thighs moved against the soft, supple hide of the bucket seats and she shivered.

She was naked beneath the short, lycra miniskirt which barely skimmed her slender thighs. As her feet moved on the pedals, the soft, tender skin at the apex of her thighs was brought into contact with the warm leather. Denuded of hair, there was nothing to protect her sensitive flesh from the fleeting stimulation, and tension knotted in her abdomen.

Glancing at her watch she saw it was just after five. Six o'clock, Alexander had said. Knowing he would interpret lateness on her part as disobedience, Maggie nosed her way out of the queue of traffic and, ignoring the angry symphony of car horns around her, she used the hard shoulder to reach the nearest exit, praying that the back roads would be less congested.

* * *

Antony glanced at his watch and looked out of the apartment window, across the rapidly darkening carpark. To all intents and purposes, the women who were coming and going from the Black Orchid Club were making use of the gym or the sauna, or any of the other facilities offered by the high class health club. Only the elite, chosen few, like Maggie, knew what really went on in the inner sanctum. And those that knew couldn't get enough of the virile young men he employed to service them.

Behind him, Alexander was lounging on the white leather couch, leafing idly through a magazine.

'Sit down, Tony, you're like an anxious husband,' Alexander drawled without taking his eyes from the page.

'It's not like Maggie to be late,' Anthony fretted, though he turned away from the window and sat down.

Alexander flipped the covers of the magazine together and threw it carelessly on the glass-topped coffee table. Antony watched him as he stretched out, full length on his back and folded his hands behind his head, an action which made his white gymnast-style vest stretch across his well-toned pectorals and frame the golden fur beneath his arms.

Antony surreptitiously ran the tip of his tongue along his top lip which had grown suddenly dry. He wanted to go over and run his hand from Alexander's bare feet, up his hard, unyielding thighs, but he did not dare. Though the cold blue eyes were closed, the smooth-skinned symmetrical geatures relaxed, there was something about the way Alexander held himself that told Antony he was in a mood where he could not be trusted.

Alexander seemed almost glad that Maggie was late. Antony bit his lip. That could not bode well for Maggie.

'Why have you called her back in the middle of a

2

trip?' Antony asked, knowing, even as he said it, that the question was a mistake.

Alexander opened his eyes and passed a hand through his short blond hair in a gesture of irritation which made the hairs on the back of Antony's neck rise up.

'She's checked out three possible hotel locations already,' said Alexander. The comment seemed innocuous enough, but Antony had the feeling that there was something he was missing. The feeling intensified as Alexander sat up and flashed Antony a smile of such piercing sweetness that warning bells began to sound in his mind. It was always when he was at his most endearing that Alexander was at his deadliest.

'You miss her, though, don't you, Tony?' he said, his head cocked to one side as he studied Antony's face.

There was no point in denying it, Antony knew that he was an open book to Alexander.

'I'd rather got used to her being around,' he admitted, reluctantly.

'Which is precisely why she had to go.'

Alexander was brisk, jumping onto his feet and going over to the window himself. 'Ah! Here she is. Lovely as ever.'

His voice was a low caress as Antony joined him at the window. The two men watched in silence as Maggie's long legs appeared through the open car door, closely followed by the rest of her long, lithe body.

She had changed since the first time she had visited the Black Orchid Club, mused Antony. She had been introduced by Janine, a petite blonde with a voracious sexual appetite and a determination to seduce Maggie. Antony felt a sweet, dragging warmth in his groin as he recalled his own part in Maggie's initiation.

Visions of Maggie seared through his mind – her

naked flesh, white against the uncompromising black leather of her bodysuit as she was tied to the couch in the Exhibition Room . . . the sounds of her surrender and the sweetness of her shame . . . ah, how he had missed her!

On her first visit to the female only club, though, she had been tightly strung, her dark hair rolled neatly on her head, her business suit coldly sexy.

Now her hair reached her waist, falling in a long, unrestrained curtain across her narrow shoulders. Her perfect, curvy body was shown to advantage in the clinging red minidress, her brown, bare legs tapering into the impossibly high-heeled sandals Alexander liked her to wear.

Antony thought of her driving all the way from Cumbria in those sandals and felt a stirring in his groin. He sighed as Alexander's hand brushed the front of his jeans, the tightly restrained flesh leaping in response to the knowing caress, so casually given.

'What will she think of Carla?' he mused aloud, his voice unnaturally hoarse.

Alexander smiled.

'I look forward to finding out. Come, Tony. Let's welcome Maggie home.'

Maggie paused at the wide, glass entrance doors. It had been over a month since she had been here at the Black Orchid Club. She was supposed to be finding a suitable location for an hotel, but so far nothing had been quite right. She was glad to be allowed to come home before she had accomplished the task set for her.

The receptionist on the desk was new, but she greeted Maggie warmly and showed her straight through to the private lift. Hesitating for a moment before pressing the button to summon the lift, Maggie wondered again why she had been called back. There had to be a reason; Alexander never did anything without some ulterior motive.

Goodness knew, she had dreamed of this moment, thought of it as the end of her banishment from the club and, more importantly, the big bed upstairs. Yet now she was here, she felt . . . almost . . . *regretful*. It wasn't as if she had left anyone special behind on her travels. There had been partners aplenty, of course, but no one who reached inside her soul as had the two men who were, even now, waiting upstairs for her.

Giving an impatient shake of her thick, dark hair, she pressed the button firmly and waited for the discreet whirr of the lift mechanism which announced its arrival.

They were waiting for her in the lobby upstairs. Both so tall and blond, like heavenly twins about to embrace her. Maggie's heart leapt at the sight of them, as it always did. Her bare skin under the thin covering of her dress tingled as Alexander's eyes passed from her toes up to her head. There was no underwear to mark the smooth, clinging line of the dress and the shape of her naked body was clearly visible beneath it. Presumably, she passed the inspection, for his firm, well shaped lips curved in a small smile.

Antony's arms came about her and she was enveloped into his welcoming hug. But it was Alexander's light touch on her hair that made her shiver in anticipation.

'Go and put your case in the bedroom, Maggie,' he told her. 'I've left something on the bed for you to change into. Don't be long – dinner is almost ready.'

She hurried to obey him, her empty stomach reacting to the delicious aroma seeping from the small kitchen. Standing for a moment on the threshold of the room, Maggie took her time looking around it, a small frown creasing her forehead. The bed was the same, and the dressing table and the mirrored wardrobes, but something was different. She couldn't quite put her finger on what it was.

Slowly, Maggie walked around the room, running her fingertips absently along each surface that she passed. It wasn't until she reached the dressing table that she saw it. A cut-glass flagon of perfume. He eyes flew to the hook on the back of the door where, to her dismay, they encountered a filmy blue negligée draped symbolically over Antony and Alexander's towelling robes.

There was another woman living here. Maggie was surprised by how much that realisation hurt her. Of course, she hadn't expected them to stay away from other women while she was away, but to install someone here, in this room, in her place, this was too much. She felt usurped, cast aside.

Throwing down her bag in the middle of the bed, Maggie whirled on her spiky heel and prepared to confront them.

They were sitting side by side on the sofa, talking in low voices. The conversation stopped as she appeared and both men looked up at her. Antony looked troubled, but the expression in Alexander's eyes was unfathomable, making Maggie stop in her tracks. She got the feeling he was expecting her outrage, had orchestrated events to precipitate it.

'You're not dressed, Maggie,' he said softly.

Maggie forced herself to relax, to let her rage subside. Past experience had taught her that it was pointless to try to play Alexander at his own game. Whenever she had tried she had failed, usually painfully, and since he was the only one who knew the rules, Maggie knew she could never win. But she was determined not to let him have it all his own way.

Forcing her lips over her teeth in a semblance of a smile, she returned to the bedroom, her head held high.

Once inside, she found her limbs were trembling.

She hadn't been able to read the look in Alexander's eyes, but she was quite sure he had something planned for her, something which he anticipated she would not like.

'Five minutes, Maggie,' Antony's voice beyond the door made her jump and she made a conscious effort to put her growing misgivings aside, turning her attention to the boxes on the bed.

Opening one up, she peeled back the matt black tissue paper to reveal the contents. Her lips formed a silent 'O' of surprise as she lifted out the cobweb fine, black lace panties and matching suspenders. How unlike Alexander to be so . . . predictable!

The stockings were black silk, the miniscule, sheer lace bra underwired for maximum uplift. Peeling off her tight tube dress, Maggie eased the underwear over her slender limbs. Glancing in the full-length mirror, she smiled at her reflection. With the briefs barely covering her hairless sex, and the suspender belt sitting comfortably on the gentle swell of her hips, she realised she looked like every man's common or garden fantasy girl.

Easing the bra straps over her shoulders, she fiddled with the underwired cups until they stayed in position, gripping her breasts almost painfully as they were lifted and separated. In the second box, she found a plain black, jersey dress, fastened at the front from throat to calf-length hem with dozens of tiny buttons. In contrast to the relatively modest dress, a bright pink feather boa completed the ensemble. Maggie wound it loosely round her neck, leaving the end to trail down her back.

Alexander had dressed her as a stag-night stripper! A small smile of amusement curved her lips as she applied deep, ruby red lipstick and smoky grey eyeshadow to complete the look, and brushed her long hair into a gleaming waterfall. She was still smiling when she emerged from the bedroom.

The table was set for three. Antony looked up from where he was lighting the incense sticks dotted around the room and smiled at her.

'You look lovely, Maggie,' he said softly.

Maggie returned his smile and went across to the table, fingering the silver cutlery which gleamed in the soft candlelight. Knowing that they would not be alone for long, she seized the moment, turning to Antony and whispering urgently, 'Why am I here?'

Antony glanced warningly towards the opening which led to the kitchen before shaking his head.

'I'm not sure. Be careful.'

'Ah, Maggie! Sit down.'

They both jumped guiltily as Alexander appeared bearing a tureen of cream of watercress soup. He turned one of his rare, golden smiles on each of them in turn and they sank into their seats, Maggie in the middle.

The soup was cool as it slipped down Maggie's throat. All three ate in silence. No music came from the stereo system in the corner, no one spoke and Maggie felt tension mounting steadily inside her.

As he passed her a plate of smoked salmon wrapped in dainty filo pastry parcels, the back of Alexander's hand brushed lightly against her breast and Maggie jumped visibly. Meeting his eye, her breath caught in her throat at the raw, unguarded expression she saw there. Desire, certainly, but there was something else, some awful, dark emotion there which frightened, yet excited her.

The expression was only there for the merest second before Alexander deftly hid it, staring blandly back at her so that for a moment she wondered if she had imagined it. But no, she was quite sure of what she had seen and the sudden, palpable tension coming from Antony told her that he had seen it too.

Her food tasted like dust in her mouth and Maggie

8

gulped gratefully at the crisp, dry wine Alexander had poured her. The scent of the incense floated around them, enclosing them in a sweet, sickly fug which, combining with the wine, made Maggie's eyelids droop. The candlelight flickered across Alexander's face, casting demonic shadows beneath his cheek-bones.

Every time Maggie looked up from her plate, Alexander was watching her, his expression unreadable. Without thinking, Maggie sought Antony's hand under the table and squeezed it. He squeezed back, reassuringly, but quickly let her hand drop as Alexander glanced quickly across at him.

The fluffy lemon mousse was sharp on Maggie's tongue, coating her mouth with its sickly sweetness so that she had to wash it down with more wine. Alexander's leg pressed insistently against her to one side as she felt Antony's fingers work their way under her hair to the sensitive nape of her neck. She leaned into his hand as he began to massage the taut muscles there.

Alexander took her spoon from her limp fingers and pressed it between her lips. The lemon mousse smeared across her lips and Antony swiftly dipped his head to lick it off, his tongue sending delicate little thrills through her.

Maggie was aware of a heaviness creeping into her limbs as she felt Alexander's hand on her jersey covered thigh. Through the barrier of the fabric, he began to describe small circles, working upward to where her secret places already tingled in anticipation of his touch.

She almost cried out in dismay as the caress abruptly ceased and Alexander rose from the table.

'Tony – go and fetch the coffee. We'll have it on the sofa. Maggie?'

Maggie's legs shook as she followed Alexander into the living area. Her high heels clicked on the stripped wood floor, sinking into the lambswool rug which lay

9

in front of the sofa. Alexander went to put music on the stereo and Maggie's head jerked up as the strident beat of Robert Palmer's music blasted through the room.

Antony lay a tray of coffee on the low table and Maggie noticed there were only two cups. She frowned and went to sit down, only to be stopped by Alexander's hand on her arm.

'Dance for us, Maggie,' he whispered urgently.

Maggie stood awkwardly in the middle of the room as the two men made themselves comfortable on the white leather sofa. Behind her, the wall was all glass, the vertical blinds only half drawn. Yellow light from the street outside cast muted stripes over the room, competing with the flickering of the candles.

The smell of the incense lay heavy in the air, mingling with the strong aroma of freshly brewed coffee. Maggie's eyes moved from one to the other. Antony's jeans were stretched tight across his groin, evidence of his arousal. Alexander, as always, was inscrutable, merely waiting patiently for Maggie to begin.

After all the things she had done, the indignities she had endured at the hands of these two men, it was ridiculous to feel shy about dancing in front of them. Between them they had taught her to plumb the depths of shame, shown her the sweet piquancy of surrender. But her arms and legs felt wooden as she forced them to move to the beat, her balance precarious in the spiky heels.

Gradually, her self consciousness ebbed away and she began to enjoy herself, the steady throb of music moving through her limbs, loosening them. Moving her body sinuously, she elicited a cry of delighted encouragement from Antony.

Lifting her arms above her head, she lifted her hair and whirled in front of Alexander, revelling in the gleam of appreciation in his eyes as she swept a thick tress around his neck and down his shoulder. She loved it when she managed to affect him like this. By penetrating his reserve even by this tiny amount, she felt she had regained a modicum of control and the thought intoxicated her.

She laughed as she twirled away, her hips rolling seductively in time to the music, giving the two men on the sofa an irresistible view of her taut behind. By the time the disc had reached 'Addicted to Love' she was ready to go that one step further she knew Alexander was looking for.

Holding his eye, she slowed her movements and began, slowly, to unbutton the dress. His breathing was shallow, his eyes overbright as the dress fell away to reveal the lacy underwear beneath. Maggie inched the sleeves down her arms, finally discarding the dress in a heap and kicking it aside.

Antony's hands came up to mould her tightly restrained breasts as she leaned over him and she let out her breath on a gasp. Holding Alexander's eye, she leaned against the sofa as Antony's hot, wet mouth enclosed one lace covered peak, teasing it to a hardness which bordered on the verge of pain before he turned his attention to the other one.

Her skin felt hot, burning with a desire the like of which she had not experienced for weeks. It did not matter what diabolical plans Alexander might be dreaming up, all she wanted was to feel his tightly muscled arms come about her, his clever, knowing hands bringing her the glorious gift of pleasure which only he could bestow.

Knowing that her eyes pleaded with him, Maggie eased herself over the arm of the sofa so that she was half lying across Antony's lap, reaching towards Alexander. Alex tucked a stray tendril of hair behind her ear in a gesture which was almost tender.

11

'Oh, Maggie,' he said softly, 'How sweetly you return to us! Perhaps we should send you away more often?'

He laughed at her instinctive whimper of protest.

'What do you think, Antony? Should we give her what she so obviously craves?'

Maggie felt Antony's hand stroke the softly rounded globes of her buttocks through the filmy black lace, his other hand steadily kneading her swelling breasts.

'I'd like to,' he murmured, his lips against the back of Maggie's head.

'Of course you would,' Alexander's words were scornful even though his voice was soft, 'but you're forgetting how late she was. You *were* late, weren't you, Maggie darling?'

'It was the traffic,' she said, her voice thick as Antony's nimble fingers slipped under the elastic of the briefs and found the moist centre of her sex.

'Excuses, Maggie? You disappoint me!'

Alexander smiled, almost kindly at her, and began to unbutton his fly. Maggie gasped as Antony reached the burgeoning core of her and the waves of warm, liquid pleasure began to flow through her limbs. He knew just how much pressure to apply to bring her to the brink, yet not tip her over into orgasm too early.

As Alexander's long, slender cock sprang up, erect, from his open fly, Maggie's tongue pressed through her lips in anticipation. All she had to do was strain forward slightly and she would be able to take that smooth skinned, bulbous head into her mouth, but she held back, knowing that to move before Alexander gave her the word would result in the agony of deprivation which she dreaded.

Watching her carefully, Alexander read the desire and the frustration in her eyes and smiled. He reached over and cupped her chin in the palm of one hand, raising her head so that he could watch her reactions.

Maggie saw him glance at Antony, and Antony squeezed the throbbing tip of her clitoris between his finger and thumb.

Her climax was almost upon her and she stretched out her legs, her inner thighs quivering with tension. Alexander allowed the top of his penis to brush invitingly along her closed lips, yet when she opened her mouth, he pulled back, leaving her slack jawed, her eyes closed in anguish, gasping as she reached the brink.

Just as the lights began to explode behind her eyelids, Antony withdrew his hand. Maggie's eyes flew open in dismay as her body withdrew from the ultimate peak.

'Please . . .!'

Alexander laughed.

'Oh, Maggie, did you really think it would be that easy? Don't you know me better than that?'

Maggie felt like weeping, her body, denied its final release, trembled as it lay, limp now, across Antony's lap. She could feel his arousal pressing into the softness of her stomach through the stiff denim of his jeans and she realised that he was just as uncomfortable as she was.

Her head snapped round as she heard the soft click of the outer door being opened.

'Carla! Come and join us, my love.'

Alexander's voice was tender as he addressed the girl who stood, staring at the tableau before her in disbelief. Maggie tried to get up, but Antony held her down so that she could only see the girl from an angle.

She looked very young with her short blonde hair and petite figure, but as she drew closer, Maggie could see there were fine lines around the light blue eyes which aged her. She was wearing a simple sky-blue silk shift which clung to her modest curves as she walked.

As she reached the couch, she stopped in front of Alexander, as if she was awaiting instructions.

Maggie could feel the angry tension emanating from the girl and she admired her self-control. She flinched as Alexander brought the girl's unresisting hand to his erection and closed his eyes for a second as her slender fingers closed around it.

'Carla, this is Maggie. Would you remove her briefs, please?'

The girl stopped caressing him and obediently went to do as he asked. She never once glanced at Maggie, performing her task with swift efficiency. Her hands were cold as they touched Maggie's heated skin, and as she dragged the panties down Maggie's legs, her sharp nails snagged the skin, making her wince.

Carla handed the briefs to Alexander, who brought them up to his face, breathing in the heated woman-scent of her before casting them carelessly aside. Smiling at Maggie, he waved a hand at Carla, who immediately stripped off the sky-blue dress.

She was naked underneath, her pale skin lent a pearlised tint by the guttering candles. Maggie found it increasingly hard to breathe as she waited to see what would happen next.

'Maggie was very late to arrive, Carla,' Alexander's voice was low and hypnotic. 'I'm hurt that she was so reluctant to join us. Spank her, Antony.'

Maggie gasped as the flat of Antony's hand came down on her bare buttocks. She gritted her teeth, knowing that soon the stinging pain would turn into a deeper, warmer agony and she willed the transition to take place quickly.

Alexander watched her, his expression impassive. Maggie groaned aloud as Carla dropped to her knees and took him into her mouth. Lifting her buttocks a little to meet Antony's punishing hand, Maggie felt the glow spreading through her and tears started in your eyes.

Staring pleadingly at Alexander, she saw that he was still watching her, only now his eyes were glazed with pleasure as Carla's busy mouth worked on him. His lips were slightly parted, his eyelids half closed as he neared his climax.

Maggie was barely aware that Antony had stopped spanking her and his fingers had returned to the burning nub of her desire. As soon as she realised his intention, Maggie fought against the encroaching release, dismayed beyond all reason that she should allow herself to come while the other woman was enjoying Alexander so thoroughly.

For she *was* enjoying him. Her eyes were tightly closed, the muscles in her throat rippling as she relaxed them to allow him to penetrate deeper. Maggie could see the hot flush spreading across Alexander's chest as he reached the point of no return. His head arched back, his body convulsing as his seed pumped into Carla's greedy mouth, just as Antony applied enough pressure to Maggie's straining bud.

She cried out as her orgasm burst from her, seconds after Alexander's. Wave after wave shook her reluctant body until she collapsed, sobbing, over Antony's lap.

The music had stopped playing, unnoticed by them all and for several seconds the only sound in the room was of Alexander's and Maggie's ragged breathing. When at last she lifted her head, the first thing she saw was Carla's face, flushed with triumph, a smear of semen streaking her cheek. The look in her eyes as she stared at Maggie made her shiver.

Alexander recovered first. Stroking his hand down Carla's head, he smiled as she turned her face into his palm, her expression one of blind devotion.

15

'You must be very uncomfortable, Tony,' he said conversationally. 'Lie down, Carla.'

Maggie moved so that Antony could stand, watching dully as he quickly stripped off his clothes. His cock sprang free as he released it, swelling before Maggie's eyes as he lay down with Carla on the rug. The girl welcomed him eagerly, obviously well used to his strong, familiar body, wrapping her legs around his waist as he entered her with a grunt of relieved pleasure.

Sagging back against the sofa, Maggie welcomed the coolness of the leather against her burning buttocks. She closed her eyes as she felt Alexander's hand against her cheek, tracing the tracks of her drying tears with one finger. Slowly, she opened her eyes and turned her head towards him.

He smiled at her, one of the rare, golden smiles which made her glow, ensuring her enslavement to him. Then, to her surprise, he leaned forward and kissed her, gently, on the lips.

'Welcome home, Maggie,' he whispered against her mouth.

Maggie stared at him, wanting to believe that he meant she was to stay here, yet knowing that she could not trust him. Fresh tears started in her eyes and he caught one with his tongue as it overflowed.

Gently turning her head towards the couple on the rug, he drew her into the treacherous circle of his arms.

Chapter Two

*I*t soon became clear to Maggie that Carla was not prepared to give up her place in Antony and Alexander's bed. Her elfin face was alight with malicious triumph as Alexander gave Maggie the key to the flat downstairs.

'You'll be more comfortable there, darling,' he told her. As if he were truly concerned for her comfort!

Maggie swallowed down her humiliation and quickly wrapped her discarded dress about her. She couldn't meet Antony's sympathetic glance as she took the key and slipped through the door. Like a dismissed employee! she fumed as she let herself into the flat.

Alexander had obviously planned ahead, for there were toiletries in the small *en suite* bathroom and a night-dress folded neatly on the pillows. Someone had turned back the covers on the bed and switched on the twin bedside lamps so that a tawny glow fell across the satin bedspread.

No one had mentioned the proposed hotel, she realised as she brushed her teeth. Surely she hadn't been sent on a wild goose chase? She wouldn't put it past Alexander to have no intention of setting up a hotel at all, to have sent her to look at likely properties to get her out of the way so that he could introduce Carla to Antony.

As if Alexander ever needed to find an excuse to do anything! It didn't make sense, if Alex had merely wanted Carla, he wouldn't have bothered to spare Maggie's feelings by removing her from the scene.

Maggie wrapped the covers round herself and curled into a ball. She felt used after tonight's little scene, and she didn't like it. Not one little bit.

Neither Antony nor Alexander were about when Maggie emerged from the flat the following morning. She worked off some of her aggression in the gym, pushing her already well toned body to its limits so that she became aware of every muscle and sinew.

Since moving in with Antony and Alexander and ostensibly becoming a member of the Club staff, she had become so fit, now exercising was second nature to her. It gave her a very personal satisfaction to challenge her body and she liked the feeling of control exercise gave her. For the hour she spent there, it was almost possible to forget that the feeling of self-control was an illusory one; it would only take a word from Alexander and she knew she would surrender up her will with an ease born of months of training and practice.

Shivering, Maggie wished that she had some idea of what Alexander's current game entailed. But then, she reflected as she meandered in the direction of the steam room, if she knew his objectives, that would remove half the pleasure – for both of them.

Lazing for a while in the thick, fragrant steam, Maggie wrapped a towel around her nakedness and wandered through for a massage.

She was pleasantly surprised to recognise Con, the

well-built West Indian whom she had interviewed for the job of trainer herself.

'You've learned massage then, Con?' she smiled as she dropped the towel and lay face down on the table.

'That's right. It's good to see you back, Maggie – I'll give you a special!'

Maggie closed her eyes as Con's large hands slipped knowingly over her oiled skin. He was good, but no one could touch Alexander for massage. Maggie shivered as she recalled previous occasions when she had lain on this couch while Alexander's sensitive fingers had sought out every taut muscle, each aching crevice.

'You okay?'

Con's voice was soft in her ear and she realised she had groaned aloud.

'Don't stop, Con,' she whispered, 'You're good at this!'

He chuckled, a low sound, deep in his throat.

'You're tense, Maggie. I know what you need.'

Maggie opened her eyes and swivelled her head so that she could see him.

'Oh?' she said, raising an eyebrow at him, 'and what might that be?'

Con's hand unexpectedly reached out and cupped her cheek, the pad of his thumb brushing over the sensitive skin beneath her eye. Maggie stared into the velvety brown depths of his eyes and felt her womb cramp with sudden longing.

Reaching up, she stroked the palm of her hand over the smooth, soft skin of his shaven scalp, running her hand down the back of his head to the nape of his neck. Pulling herself up so that her face was close to his, she breathed, 'Well, Con? Tell me what I need.'

Con smiled slowly, his perfect white teeth flashing against the ebony perfection of his skin. His voice, when he replied, was low and treacly.

'You need loving, Maggie – some good, sweet loving.'

His breath was slightly minty as it whispered over her lips. Maggie's eyes felt heavy lidded as her nerve endings recalled the last time she had made love with Con. He was right; what she needed right now was some old-fashioned, uncomplicated love-making after her sexual performance of the night before.

'And you're the man to give it to me, I suppose?' she whispered, her lips brushing lightly over his.

'*I* think so.'

His free arm came around her waist and drew her closer to him, so that her breasts were flattened against the broad, inflexible wall of his chest. His skin was hot, the warmth seeping through the thin, white cotton singlet and into the pores of her cool, naked skin.

Maggie's eyelids drooped as he kissed her, his lips drawing on the sweetness of hers, coaxing her tongue into the warm, wet cavity of his mouth. A delicious langour invaded her limbs and she whimpered into the back of his throat as his hand left her face and cupped her breast.

'Wait,' she moaned, breaking away, 'not here. I want . . . Come with me.'

Con wrapped a soft towelling robe around her shoulders and followed her silently out of the massage room. Maggie half ran on bare feet along the corridor, towards the privacy of the flat. There was no reason to her desire, she was driven by an overwhelming urge to be alone with Con, to make love with him in the mundane comfort of a bedroom.

Maggie had left the room neat and tidy that morning, but she had forgotton to pull back the curtains. In the half light, it was easy to forget the brightness of the day outside where ordinary people were going about their everyday business.

She turned slowly as she reached the bed. Con stood

in the doorway, tension evident in the way he held himself as he watched her. Maggie smiled and allowed the towelling robe to slip slowly from her shoulders.

Con's eyes flickered down the length of her body. His face was impassive apart from the throb of a pulse in his jaw and Maggie exulted in this small indication of his desire. Throwing back her head so that the long, soft sweep of her neck was exposed, she ran the palms of her hands down the sides of her body, revelling in the softness of her skin, the gentle undulation of her feminine curves, finally bringing her hands up to her breasts. Cradling them in her hands, she looked Con straight in the eye and offered them to him.

At last he moved, crossing the bedroom in two strides. Placing his large hands at her waist, he lifted her as if her weight were nothing to him. Manipulating her body as he would a doll, he brought her tumescent breasts level with his face and licked first one, then the other straining nipple with the very tip of his tongue.

Maggie shuddered as sensation, almost painful in its intensity, darted from those two hard tips to the centre of her desire. She bent her head over Con's as he lifted her higher, flicking his tongue into the tender dip of her navel. Her toes curled as she heard him inhale the musky, female perfume of her hairless sex before lowering her, running her naked body slowly down the hard, heavily muscled length of his own.

Her legs would not support her as her feet hit the ground and she clung to him, loving his strength. It made her feel uncharacteristically weak, this over-whelming sense of masculine power, appealing to a deep, subconscious part of her which longed to play Jane to his Tarzan. There was an erotic satisfaction in the sense of helplessness which assailed her as Con swept her up into his arms and laid her gently on the satin covers.

Knowing that, this time, nothing was expected of her, Maggie closed her eyes and waited for Con to make love to her.

Con's loving caresses were so far removed from the casual humiliations inflicted on her by Alexander last night that Maggie felt her whole body relax and open up to him. The heavy musk of his skin intoxicated her, the tight, coarse wool of his chest hair rasping teasingly over the sensitised peaks of her breasts as he moved down her body.

Maggie sighed as his tongue swept delicately along the closed fold of her naked sex-lips, feeling the flesh of her vulva expand and open in response to his touch. Automatically, her thighs parted and the warm air kissed her moist skin before Con's probing tongue tickled a wet path from her sheathed clitoris to her feminine opening and back up again.

She moaned softly as the hood slipped back and the small, hard nub of her pleasure centre rose up to meet his reverent tongue. Her eyes flew open and she gasped as Con's strong teeth closed over it and he bit, very gently, sending an unexpected orgasmic ripple through her entire body.

'Oh, not yet!' she cried, feeling cheated.

Con laughed softly, almost to himself before swiftly dispensing with his clothes and covering her body with his. Maggie's nails raked across his shoulders as the thick, determined tip of his penis edged its way between her welcoming inner lips. Her entire sex seemed to open out to accommodate him as he sank into her, filling her secret passage with the power of his masculinity.

Legs wrapping round his waist of their own volition, Maggie urged him further inside and she felt him shudder as he drove into her. Once he was resting at the entrance to her womb, he was still, contenting himself with kissing her face; forehead, eyelids, cheeks and chin, his strong fingers moulding her skull and tracing the outline of her ears.

Maggie stirred beneath him, wanting the urgent thrust of him as he strove for his own climax, but Con clasped her buttocks in his hands, keeping her still.

Drawing the upper half of his body away from her slightly, he watched her face through hooded eyes as he slowly withdrew, then sank back into her soft flesh. He moved so slowly, with such control, so that Maggie was aware of every centimetre of her inner flesh as his invading cock rubbed against it.

Ripples of pleasure shivered along her nerve endings so that, very soon, she was aware of his every thrust – in her fingertips and in her toes, even the muscles of her forehead expanded and contracted with every surge.

Breathing shallowly, Maggie watched Con's face, fascinated. His eyes had glazed, sweat standing out on his glossy skin with the effort of restraint. Maggie could feel a heated flush creeping across the skin of her chest and into her face as the constant, rhythmic friction on her innermost point of pleasure began to take effect.

She was floating, weightless, divorced from reality as her body began to shake, virtually buzzing with sensation. She felt as if she were on an upward spiral, propelled by Con's skilful love-making to the peak of satisfaction.

Unable to control herself, Maggie gasped aloud with every quickening stroke. Con's heavy breathing kept time with her breathless grunts, his large hands squeezing her buttocks, separating the rounded globes so that the puckered rose of her anus brushed against the cool, slippery satin of the bedcover with each downward stroke.

Vaguely noticing Con's fingers edging closer to her

forbidden passage, Maggie was ready for the intrusion of his fingertip as he rimmed the entrance to her anus. The light pressure of his fingertip against the pursed mouth was enough to tip her over the edge and she cried out.

Writhing beneath Con on the bed, Maggie lost control of her body completely, intent on nothing but wringing every nuance of feeling from the orgasm that crashed through her. The man swiftly reaching his own climax within her was, at that moment, outside the reality of her own experience, a mere tool by which she could extract the maximum pleasure from her own pulsating body.

Slowly, very slowly, Maggie stirred and became aware of Con's weight smothering her. His penis still lay inside her, slack now with exertion. They were stuck together, their perspiration mingling, rapidly cooling in the air.

Feeling her sigh, Con rolled slowly to one side, slipping out of her soundlessly, leaving her bereft. Maggie smiled sleepily at him. Her limbs felt lead lined, her eyes refusing to open fully. She was so unutterably weary that she never said a word as Con got up and dressed.

She watched him through heavy lidded eyes as he fastened a black G-string before pulling on his regulation track pants. His white singlet stuck to his damp chest, a deep 'v' of sweat staining the fabric minutes after it touch his skin. As he raised his arms, his characteristically musky odour was stronger than before, though not unpleasantly so.

Turning her face into her own shoulder, Maggie could smell him on her skin. He smiled at her, almost fondly, unexpectedly reaching across to tuck the covers round her shoulders. Maggie curled into a ball and snuggled into them, smiling at his tenderness.

Bending down, he kissed the soft, sensitive spot beneath her ear.

'Good, sweet loving,' he whispered.

Hearing the smile in his voice, Maggie's lips curved, but she was rapidly losing the struggle to keep her eyes open. Giving up the battle, she slipped into sleep, leaving Con to slip quietly out of the flat.

There was something warm, something warm and wet moving slowly round her face. Maggie opened her eyes cautiously and met Antony's laughing blue gaze.

'Awake at last! I was beginning to wonder whether a cold flannel would work better!'

Maggie was instantly awake and alert, glancing round her to see if Alexander was with him. Reading her mind, Antony chuckled and pushed her gently back down onto the pillows.

'Alex is busy. He sent me to help you get ready.'

Busy with what – or whom? Maggie wondered jealously. Then the meaning of Antony's words reached her.

'Get ready for what?' she yawned, sitting up in bed and stretching.

The covers fell away from her naked breasts and Antony's eyes rested briefly on them. He smiled.

'Had a good afternoon?'

Maggie looked down and saw the tell-tale red marks on her breasts before glancing warily at Antony.

'Don't you know?'

Antony laughed and perched himself on the end of the bed.

'The intercom wasn't switched on today. Alexander hasn't been himself. I know *you*, though, Maggie. In spite of all the lessons you've learned, you'd still risk everything if you thought it would be worth it.'

Maggie raised her eyebrows at him.

25

'Wouldn't you?'

Anthony's eyes slid away from hers.

'We're different people,' he replied evasively. 'So was it?'

'Was it what?'

'Worth it?'

Lying back on the pillows, Maggie smiled and stretched like a satisfied cat. Antony laughed.

'Maggie, you are incorrigible! Come on, it's time to get up. We're all going out tonight.'

Antony refused to be drawn about their outing as he ran Maggie a bath while he washed her long, dark hair in the sink. With her wet hair piled up on top of her head and wrapped in a warm towel, Maggie sank into the fragrant water and sighed.

'Mmm, this is bliss!'

Antony was silent and she opened her eyes to look at him.

'You've missed us, then?' he said casually, though he avoided her eye as he worked up a creamy lather on a huge natural sponge.

'A little,' Maggie teased, frowning when Antony didn't smile. 'What's wrong?'

He looked at her then and she caught a glimpse of the fleeting sadness which crossed his frank grey eyes. Then he smiled and Maggie was left wondering if she'd imagined it.

'It's good to have you home, Maggie.'

He said it so softly, with such complete sincerity, that Maggie felt a rush of tenderness for him. Lifting one wet arm out of the bath, she reached around his neck and drew his head to hers. His lips were tender as he moved them over hers, his kiss slow and leisurely. More friendly than lover-like.

Remembering the passion they had shared in the past, Maggie coaxed a response from him, the blood quickening in her veins as she sensed the need that he was keeping in check. She gasped as he pulled roughly away from her.

'Antony . . .?'

She watched from her bath as he leapt to his feet and paced to the bathroom door in agitation, raking his fingers through his thick blond hair. Half rising from the bath, Maggie sank back down as he turned on her, dropping to his knees at the side of the bath and tangling the wet hair escaping from the towel at the nape of her neck in his fingers. Maggie winced as he tugged her head back, forcing her to look at him.

'Why won't you ever learn?' he grated. 'Still you think it's a game, that you only need to pretend to submit to Alexander.'

Maggie had never seen him so angry, though even through the suppressed violence of his rage, she could see the underlying anguish.

'Don't you want me?' she whispered.

Antony swore violently under his breath and let go of her hair. Looking away from her for an instant, his eyes were calm as he brought them back to her face.

'Of course,' he said quietly. 'But I love Alexander and his pleasure is my pleasure. I might desire you, but I will only act on my desire if Alex agrees. I thought, by now, you would understand.'

Maggie felt embarrassed, like a chastened child as she lay in the now rapidly cooling water. It wasn't that she did not understand, it was that she did not want to comply with the rules. It was only the fear of banishment which persuaded her to follow Alexander's directives. The idea of never again experiencing the delight of the particular brand of pleasure only he could bestow was unthinkable, and it was this which generally ensured her obedience.

Her interlude with Con had been a risk; normally

Alexander knew everything that went on in the Club. Undoubtedly, he would have punished her for the digression. She was pleased to have outwitted him, and therein lay the difference between her and Antony. Whilst she merely gave lip service to obedience, Antony was loyal to the last. And frightened. Not of Alexander's wrath, which could be considerable, but of the withdrawal of his affection.

'Poor Anthony,' she said softly, 'you really do love him, don't you?'

Antony's jaw clenched, but he did not answer her, merely picking up a large towel to wrap around her as she stepped out of the bath.

'Doesn't it make you angry when you know Alex is with someone else? Especially a woman?' she pushed as Antony combed through her wet hair.

Anthony caught her eye in the mirror and, unexpectedly, he smiled.

'Women are no threat,' he said.

Maggie raised an eyebrow at him, but knew he was right. In all the time she had known him, she had never known Alexander make love to a woman, he rarely even used them as he would a man. Alexander's pleasure was mainly in the control he exerted over those he held in this thrall. He might torment and abuse him, but his love was reserved for Antony.

Suddenly, Maggie felt ashamed for having teased Antony. Turning in her seat, she touched the back of the fingers against his cheek and smiled ruefully.

'I'm sorry. Can we be friends again?'

Antony caught her hand and pressed his lips against her knuckles.

'Always, darling Maggie. And there will be other times when we can be together – for as long as you stay here.'

Maggie frowned at the last, but a glance at Antony's

hooded eyes told her it would be useless trying to question him. She felt uneasy as she applied her make-up and dried her hair into a smooth, dark curtain.

Antony produced a new dress, a long, black velvet affair, adorned by jet beads sewn around the deep 'v' of the neckline. The dress fitted perfectly, skimming the gentle roundness of her hips and falling into a slim sheath around her ankles.

'We're going somewhere classy then?' she said, turning this way and that in front of the mirror.

Antony came up behind her and put his hands around her waist. Resting his chin on the top of her head, he surveyed her appearance with satisfaction.

'Wait and see,' he smiled infuriatingly.

Maggie was none too pleased to find that Carla was to accompany them. The other woman was also dressed in black velvet, though her dress was short, showing off the prettily sculpted shape of her legs and clinging to her petite figure. Her short blonde hair had been scrunch dried to give it more volume and it framed her small, angular face like a halo, softening it. The light blue eyes gazed calmly at Maggie, a small, self-confident smile playing around her pink-painted lips.

She looks like a doll, Maggie though viciously. A walking, talking, Barbie doll.

Alexander was driving and he opened the passenger door for Carla. Maggie was left to climb into the back with Antony. As before, she felt relegated, a has-been. Carla must have felt her resentful glare on the back of her heard, for she turned to look at Maggie. Gazing at her with wide-eyed insolence, she passed her a smile which was as meaningless as it was dazzling, before she turned away again.

Maggie was intrigued when Alexander turned off the main dual carriageway and drove along a series of gloomy backstreets. She began to wonder why their destination had been shrouded in secrecy. Before, she had merely assumed it was one of Alexander's little games to keep her in the suspense he deemed was necessary to command her obedience, but now she began to wonder.

Antony's fingers unexpectedly closed over hers and she glanced across at him. His smile was reassuring, triggering warning bells in her mind. What if Alexander had something unpleasant planned for her this evening? he knew her so well, she had no illusions about his ability to persuade her to take part in any number of situations that she would normally have refused.

She need not have worried. Maggie almost sagged with relief as they parked and she saw the discreet neon sign of the Island Casino.

As a smartly dressed cloakroom attendant took her cloak, Maggie reflected that the four of them must look like any regular quartet, two couples meeting up for a night out. After the men had given their membership cards to the inscrutably polite Italian on the counter, they each signed in one guest. Carla linked her arm through Alexander's, leaving Maggie and Antony to follow them up the stairs.

'Look's like you're stuck with me tonight,' Maggie murmured as Antony offered her his arm.

He chuckled, not at all put out and, with a slight shrug, Maggie took his arm, telling herself she would just have to go with the flow.

As they ascended, Maggie was gripped with a burgeoning excitement in spite of herself. The one and only time she had been to a casino was at the tender age of eighteen when she had accompanied her father. Even now she could remember the pride she had felt at being considered grown up enough to be taken out to such a sophisticated place by the tall, grey-haired man she had idolised throughout her childhood.

They had played roulette for a while, she guessed for her benefit, for her father could not wait to get onto the blackjack tables. The evening had become a very long and, yes, she had to admit it, boring one for her as her father's attention was claimed by the cards and she was left to stand, like an overlooked ornament, at his elbow.

She was jolted back to the present as they stepped through the heavy double doors which led into the lounge.

A bar, all wood panelling and gold coloured chrome, swept in an arc around the corner of the room, raised slightly above the marble topped tables which were dotted about on the thick, patterned carpet. Antony walked with Maggie and Carla to a free table on the balcony and he and Carla sank into a low soft cushioned sofa.

Maggie leaned on the gold-chrome rail which overlooked the gaming tables below. Across the other side of the room there were several enormous, gold-framed mirrors which reflected back the activity in the room below so that Maggie could see it from every angle.

Looking down, she studied the heads of the players as they bent over the roulette and blackjack tables. There was an air of muted excitement, a murmur of voices which did not rise above the soothing music piped through the public address system.

Maggie studied the croupiers. Most were young, awkward in their shiny green evening dresses and formal black suits and dicky bows. Inspectors stood, one to every two tables, their faces taut with boredom, their hands folded neatly in front of them as if they needed to be kept under control.

Every now and again, uniformed waiting staff wheeled in silver trays laden with tea and coffee and plates full of complimentary sandwiches, cut into dainty, bite-size triangles. As she watched, a woman in a long blue dress took a sandwich and popped it into her mouth without taking her eyes off the spinning roulette wheel. Maggie's mouth watered. The woman's shoulders sagged as her chips were cleared from the board and she moved away from the table.

Directly below her, Maggie could see the restricted area where several card schools were in operation. From her vantage point on the balcony above, she could see some of the hands dealt and guessed they were playing poker. These were the serious gamblers, not playing for fun.

It was all very civilised, she thought to herself, very . . . sanitised. The whole place had an air of a gentleman's club, a discreet, stylish meeting place where one could have a flutter if so inclined. An illusion of rakishness, cushioned by discreet comfort.

She was about to turn away when a movement across the other side of the room caught her eye. A door she hadn't noticed opened and a man stepped through. She wouldn't have thought anything of it except that there was something about the man that drew the eye. Something . . . familiar, though she was quite sure that she had never seen him before.

He was tall, well over six feet and the formal tuxedo did nothing to disguise the power of his build. He stood by the door and surveyed the casino with a distinctly proprietorial air, one hand shoved carelessly into a trouser pocker. From where Maggie stood, several feet above him and across the room, she could see his hair was thick and dark, the glittering chandeliers suspended from the ceiling lending it a blue-black gloss.

As she watched, someone stopped to speak to him, a middle-aged woman in a pink satin suit which strained across her substantial rear in a series of horizontal wrinkles. He leaned attentively towards her, his mouth curving into a polite smile at something she said. As the woman moved off, the smile slipped off his face, his mouth clenching in a grim line.

Maggie found herself wondering what it was that had annoyed him. She could not take her eyes off the man as he surveyed the room one last time before turning back towards the door. As he reached for the brass handle, he seemed to pause, then slowly, so slowly Maggie felt herself holding her breath, he turned and looked up towards the balcony.

His eyes, startlingly blue even from this distance, scanned the balcony before coming to rest on her. Maggie found herself caught by his gaze, unable to move, a strange, atavistic tingle zigzagging along her spine.

She knew this man, she was sure of it. And yet she did not, could not, for she would have remembered, had he been introduced to her. His gaze pierced the distance between them, zeroing in on her as if drawn by a force beyond his control. He frowned, his eyes narrowing as she continued to stare at him, unable to tear her eyes away.

Under his almost hypnotic appraisal, she felt naked, vulnerable, unbearably needy. His lips curved slightly at the corners, almost cruelly before he slowly and deliberately turned away.

Opening the door, he slipped through it, leaving Maggie staring breathlessly at the empty space where he had stood.

Chapter Three

'Your drink, Maggie,'

Maggie jumped as Alexander appeared at her elbow. He raised an eyebrow at her as he passed her a glass of dry white wine and she smiled tremulously at him.

After the dark haired stranger, Alexander's blond perfection seemed almost insipid, certainly unthreatening. Maggie frowned at the thought, knowing the strength of Alexander's will.

'Sit down, Maggie,' he said quietly, and she sat, ignoring Carla's spiteful glance and Antony's quizzical regard.

She had to get a grip on herself. If Alexander suspected how she had reacted to the sight of the stranger he would not hesitate to use that knowledge against her. In spite of herself, Maggie shuddered. She had a feeling that, thwarted, Alexander would make a formidable enemy. She jumped as she realised the others were all rising.

'We're going downstairs,' Antony murmured close to her ear as she turned bewildered eyes on him. 'Leave your drink – it's not allowed in the gaming hall.'

Maggie followed like an automaton. The last thing she wanted was to play the tables. It was ridiculous, but she could not get the stranger out of her head. Perhaps it was merely the fact that he had had such an effect on her? For the past few months, since she had been introduced to the Black Orchid Club, it was rare for her to spot anyone to whom she was remotely attracted unless Alexander had hand picked them.

Did this mean that he was losing his control over her? Noticing Antony's grey eyes resting thoughtfully on her, Maggie pulled herself together and took the chips Alexander offered her with a smile.

Antony watched Maggie as she placed her chips across the board. There was a tension in the way she held herself that hadn't been there before. Alexander caught his eye and he smiled faintly at him. So Alex had noticed it too.

Poor Maggie. She had no idea how close she was to losing everything for which she had strived. Battling with a sudden, unexpected weariness, he passed his hand across his eyes.

'Tony?'

Alexander touched his elbow lightly. His pale blue eyes were concerned as Antony looked at him.

'It's OK, I'm just tired.'

Alexander's eyes narrowed as he passed them over Antony's face. he shook his head quickly, as if irritated.

'Come on, Tony, this is me you're talking to. What is it.'?'

Anthony shrugged, glancing nervously around him to check that they weren't drawing attention to themselves. All eyes were on the tables, including Maggie's and Carla's.

'I wish I knew what was going on . . .' he bit his lip.

He hadn't meant to say that and he half expected Alex to laugh. The look in Alexander's eyes surprised him, and he sucked his breath. There was no laughter there, no mockery. Alexander's eyes were soft, loving even, and Antony felt a cramping dart of longing deep in the pit of his stomach.

The backs of his fingers touched discreetly against Alexander's hand and their fingers locked, intertwining in a rare moment of tenderness. As their eyes held, Alex smiled at him, a rare, brilliant smile which bathed him in warmth.

'Alexander, I've lost all my chips!' Carla joined them, pouting, and the moment was lost.

Antony stared at the pint-sized bird brain and imagined the pleasure it would give him to kick her out when Alexander tired of her.

'Come and show me how to play blackjack.'

He blinked as Maggie's voice sounded low in his ear. Turning to her he saw the empathy in her hazel eyes and he smiled, ruefully. Taking her by the hand, he squeezed it as they moved off.

Whilst he would be heartily glad to see the back of Carla, the idea of dispensing with Maggie was not something that gave him pleasure at all. After Alexander, Maggie was the person who meant most to him in his clandestine, twilight world. She had the spirit and courage which he knew he lacked. Unlike him, she would survive without Alexander.

She sat beside him on the blackjack table, glancing at him for guidance as the croupier dealt her first a four, then a five. The dealer's hand totalled seventeen, so she was required to stand.

'Double your stake,' Antony told Maggie.

The croupier waited for her to pile up her chips before dealing a third card – a Jack. Antony smiled as Maggie gathered up her winnings, amused by the almost child-like pleasure which lit up her face.

His earlier sadness receded as he shared in her

pleasure, and he reached forward to cut the pack of cards offered to him before the dealer put them in the shoe.

She could see now why her father had forgotten her that long ago night when he had played the tables. Maggie laughed as she won a third time, delighting in the small mountain of chips she had stacked neatly by her elbow.

Antony seemed happier now, she noticed, stealing a glance at him. For a moment there she had caught the murderous look he had passed Carla and had been worried for him. Carla's high-pitched, childish laughter reached her from the roulette wheel and Maggie winced. Poor Antony, no wonder he resented her!

When Alexander and Carla appeared at the table, Maggie was surprised to find that more than an hour had passed. She left the table reluctantly and went to cash in her chips. Alex raised a sardonic eyebrow at her as she carefully counted out the stake he had advanced her and she laughed as she folded her winnings into her evening bag.

'Where to now?' she asked, in far too good a mood to allow Carla's petulant presence to subdue her.

'This way.'

The smile slid from her face as Alexander led them all towards the discreet door she had watched the dark haired stranger use earlier in the evening. The blood seemed to slow in her veins as he knocked, twice.

She hadn't noticed the stranger come out, so presumably he was still in the room behind the door. For some reason, she was reluctant to see him again. It had unsettled her before and she was not confident that she could hide her reactions from her companions.

Alexander seemed edgy as they waited for a response. That in itself was unusual and Maggie raised a questioning eyebrow at Antony. He merely smiled blandly at her before looking away again.

The door was opened by a uniformed steward. Seeing Alexander, the man nodded and stood back to let them pass. Stepping through the door was like walking into a different world. Behind them, the Casino glittered like a parody of Monte Carlo. Beyond the carefully guarded inner door, the only light was provided by the low hanging ceiling lights which illluminated each player round the only one of the two tables which was in use.

A heavy fug of smoke hung in a pall across the table. One of the players struck a match and the sound of igniting phosphorous seemed loud in the heavy silence of the room. There were no chips in this card school, only a papery pile of notes in the middle of the table – tens, twenties and fifties.

Maggie's eyes scanned the players. There were five with their backs to her, four men and a woman, two in profile at either end and five facing. She saw the stranger immediately. He was sitting so that he had a clear view of the room. His face, lit from above by the low hanging spotlight, was a mass of shadows, his eyes glittering black from under lowered brows.

Maggie's mouth ran dry as she stared at him, watching his hands as he repositioned his cards in their fan. They were large hands, the veins prominent on the backs. Yet the fingers were long and slender, the nails, illuminated by the light, neat, clean and strong.

Whereas most of the men present had removed the jackets of their tuxedoes and loosened off their ties, he looked cool, unharrassed, his black bow-tie still neatly fastened at his throat. In Maggie's view, many men looked effeminate in formal evening wear, but not this man.

The pristine whiteness of his shirt where the cuffs protruded from his jacket sleeves emphasised the strength of his wrists. A glint of gold on the left wrist, discreet, yet unmistakably expensive was his only jewellery.

Antony, Alexander, Maggie and Carla stood quietly at a respectful distance as the man considered his hand. At last, he laid three cards on the table. Glancing at each of the players in turn, he smiled, slowly, without humour, before drawing the pile of money towards him.

The tension which had been palpable in the room eased. A general murmur of conversation began and several staff who had been hovering in the shadows moved forward to dispense sandwiches and coffee. As one or two of the players moved away from the table, Alexander stepped forward.

'Still winning, then, Tourell?'

The man looked up and the strangest expression crossed his eyes. Then he smiled, and it was gone.

'Good evening, Alexander,' he said smoothly.

He had a smoker's voice, deep and gravelly. It ran over Maggie's sensibilities, making goose bumps rise on her skin. She watched curiously as Alex reached across the table and shook the man's proffered hand. It had been a shock to know that Alexander knew him, it intrigued her to realise that there was something between these two men, something vaguely threatening.

'Are you joining us?'

Alexander smiled and shook his head.

'Thank you, no. I hadn't thought to see you here. Allow me to introduce Antony, Carla and Maggie.'

Maggie could see that Alexander's uncharacteristic formality was puzzling Antony and Carla too, though both of them shook the man's hand politely. Maggie steeled herself for the contact of his hand with hers, but he did not offer it. Instead, his sharp blue eyes narrowed as they appraised her, moving from her face to her bare arms and lingering on her nervously parted lips.

'Come, Alexander – have a seat. You'll play just one hand, surely? Maggie, please come and sit here, next to me.'

As soon as he spoke, the man on his right rose and offered her his seat. Maggie glanced nervously at Alexander, but he was looking at the man and gave no sign whether he approved or otherwise.

There was something going on here, she thought uneasily as she walked round the table. The antipathy between Alexander and this man, Tourell, was like a living thing in the room. Everyone at the table seemed to be watching, waiting for Alexander to make a move. There was an audible, collective sigh of relief when he suddenly drew out a chair and sat down.

Tourell stood as Maggie reached him and gave a small, courteous bow before offering her his hand. She took it, reluctantly, and was unable to disguise the tremor which ran up her arm at the first touch of his strong fingers curling round hers. Her hand felt cold as he let it go and resumed his seat.

This close, Maggie could see he was older than she had first thought, in his late forties, or possible even his early fifties. Studying him surreptitiously from the corner of her eye, Maggie ran her eyes over his face. The skin was tanned and smooth, his square jaw clean shaven. Deep grooves ran from his nose to the corners of his mouth and his eyes crinkled when he narrowed them. A deep frown line was etched between his eyebrows and Maggie found herself wondering what kind of life he had led which had drawn it there.

It was an interesting face, enhanced, not diminished by the ravages of time. It reflected the self-confidence which radiated from his every pore, the unmistakable air of a man who had nothing to prove, who was at ease within his own skin.

A man who was well accustomed to his own desires and needs. Maggie felt a sharp, piquant dart of lust shoot from her belly down to her toes and she clenched her teeth to cage the wholly inappropriate sigh which fought to escape from her lips.

Across the table from them Carla had draped herself over Alexander's shoulder. Antony took the other vacant seat and both men laid money on the table.

'You will play?' Tourell asked Maggie, his voice low.

'I . . . no, I'll watch, if you don't mind.'

She hadn't a clue what they were playing and she had the feeling that the man beside her was aware of this fact. Trying to concentrate, she watched as the male croupier opened a new deck of cards and shuffled them with breath-taking speed. With professional nonchalance, he dealt each player a hand and a hush descended on the table.

Maggie's left side seemed to prickle with awareness of the man beside her. Glancing at his cards, he laid them face down on the table before lighting up a thin cigar. The orange tipped flame from his lighter cast one side of his face in a burnished glow, so that as he turned towards Maggie, he looked quite sinister, almost satanic.

For a moment she thought he was about to speak to her, but he merely passed her a small, sardonic smile before picking up his cards and turning his attention to the game.

Maggie had the feeling that he was aware of the curious effect his proximity was having on her. Her entire body felt light, her hands trembling as she folded them onto her lap. Trying to keep her eyes on the table in front of her, she was aware of his presence beside

41

her with such intensity that she felt quite bemused by it.

She could smell his aftershave, a heavy, musky perfume, not too strong, which failed to disguise the unique fragrance of his skin. It was a clean scent, yet distinctive, almost like burnt wood. Maggie imagined burying her face in his bare chest and inhaling it deeply, sure that it would intoxicate her.

She did not know this man, could not tell whether she would even like him, and yet he had a strong, animalistic sexuality about him that attracted her like the proverbial moth to a flame. And beneath this overpowering attraction, she had a certain, unequivocal feeling that he was far, far more dangerous to her than fire to the cobweb-thin wings of an insect.

Something made her glance up as these thoughts raced in a jumble through her head. Her eyes clashed with Alexander's across the table and she quailed at the expression in his. She had to neutralise her reaction to this man, Tourell, she was being too obvious. Concentrating on breathing slowly and evenly, Maggie sought to bring herself under control.

Somehow, she managed to sit through the game. Who won, or lost, she couldn't say, but it was obvious that Alexander had decided that it was time for them to go. She rose as he signalled to her.

'You could stay.'

Tourell spoke softly so that only she could hear. Glancing down at him, she saw that he was not looking at her, he was merely gathering in his winnings and sorting them into neat numerial piles.

'No,' she murmured, her voice made husky by the dry atmosphere, 'I must leave.'

He looked up at her then she trembled at the expression in his eyes. They seemed to mock her, whilst at the same time they promised such a wealth of sensual delight . . .

'Come tomorrow evening, alone this time.'

'No, really, it . . . it's very kind of you, but . . .'

She could feel Alexander's eyes on her and she was unable to control the deep blush of colour which rose up into her cheeks. Tourell noticed it and his eyes darkened, whether in desire or anger she could not tell.

'As you wish. I'll be here tomorrow evening. Tell the doorman you are Tourell's guest and someone will show you through.'

'But—' Maggie bit her lip.

She had said she would not come. His attention was back on the game now and suddenly she felt foolish, standing at his shoulder.

'Goodbye, then,' she said awkwardly.

Tourell did not look up and she could not be sure if he had heard her.

The silence in the taxi on the way home was oppressive. Even Carla, having had her attempts to chatter rebuffed, was subdued. Maggie was unsurprised when she was left to wend her lonely way to bed in the flat below. In a way, she was glad. All she wanted was to soak in a warm bath, then crawl between her sheets and think about Tourell.

Antony hid a smile of triumph as Carla was afforded the same treatment as Maggie. Unlike Maggie, though, Carla protested at her banishment, pleading and sulking by turns until even she could see that Alexander's patience was wearing thin.

The flat was quiet once she had left. Antony watched from the door as Alex shrugged off his jacket and pulled his tie loose. He looked tired, uncharacteristically dejected and Antony felt a surge of tenderness for him.

'Can I get you anything?' he asked him.

Alexander kicked off his shoes and leaned back on the white leather sofa.

'Tea would be nice,' he said, throwing Antony a smile of such piercing sweetness he knew that if he'd asked for fried field mushrooms Antony would have driven out to the country there and then to look for some.

'What was all that about, back at the casino?' Antony asked when they had drained the pot.

Alexander passed a hand over his eyes and shook his head.

'Nothing, Tony. Hey!' he grinned as he caught Antony's hurt expression, 'I'm not hiding anything from you. Any chance of a shoulder rub?'

Antony did not believe him for a minute. Alexander would lie to him about the state of the weather, if it suited him. It didn't matter, he knew he'd find out in the end, eventually Alexander always told him everything. Smiling, Antony walked round to the back of the settee.

'Hmm, that's good!' Alex murmured as Antony began to knead the tense muscles in his shoulders.

Antony passed his lips lightly across the sensitive spot just behind his ear.

'Why don't we go through to the bedroom – you'll be able to relax more there,' he murmured.

Alexander smiled and pulled away.

'No, why don't you come and join me on the sofa?'

Antony didn't need a second invitation. From the moment when Alexander had entwined his fingers with his at the roulette table, he had longed to ditch the two women and show him just how much he loved him.

Moving around the sofa again, he sank into Alexander's welcoming embrace. They kissed, their tongues parrying in tender competition as Antony's hands worked on the fastening to Alexander's trousers. First the belt, pulled slowly through the loops and discarded

44

on the rug. Then the hooks, slipping eagerly from their anchors. Finally the zip, easing down noiselessly and giving access to the warm strength within.

Alexander dispensed with Antony's fastenings more quickly so that when Antony's hand closed on Alexander's heated, swollen penis constrained still by his boxer shorts, he too could feel Antony's member pressing through the thin fabric of his briefs.

Antony groaned, the sound captured deep in Alexander's throat as Alex released his cock from the prison of his underwear. Freed from its unnatural constraint, it swelled proudly until it filled Alexander's hand and he carressed its warm, velvet-skinned tip lovingly.

Fumbling with the button of Alexander's shorts, Antony grasped his long, slender cock and ran his fingertips from tip to root in an act which verged on reverence. Cupping his lightly hair-roughened testicles in the palm of his hand, he rejoiced in the heated weight of them, sure that it would take very little to ease their burden.

Alexander planted dozens of little kisses over his forehead, his cheeks and his closed eyelids as they began to match each other stroke for stroke. Desire turned inexorably into a more urgent, basic need as the familiar tingling grew in Antony's balls.

Both men were breathing heavily as they masturbated each other, faster and faster. Antony cried out as he came, flinging back his head and laughing for joy as the semen immediately began spurting from Alexander, pumping from him in hot, powerful bursts.

Alex pressed his lips fervently against Antony's arched throat, then Antony sagged against him.

'Hush, hush,' Alexander crooned as Antony gasped for breath.

Drawing him into the loving circle of his arms, Alexander allowed him to lay his head against his chest.

Antony lay quietly, listening to the steady, reassuring thud of Alexander's heartbeat as their heated skin cooled and the semen dried to a sticky film on their intertwined legs.

Lying between the white satin sheets, Maggie felt hot and uncomfortable. Already she had thrown off the bedspread, now she tore at her night-dress and flung that aside too. The sheets felt slippery and cool against her naked skin and she undulated against them, enjoying their slippery caress.

She could not get thoughts of Tourell out of her mind. What was it about him? He was handsome, certainly, but Maggie spent her life surrounded by good-looking men. The way in which the formal suit had clung to his shoulders and moulded the muscles of his thighs had hinted at a powerful physique.

It was a magnetism, a once in a lifetime animal attraction that had drawn her to him, she was sure of it. Antony and Alexander had both noticed it, she was sure. But had Tourell felt it too?

He was cool, she had to give him that. But her instincts told her that beneath that passionless exterior, there was an animal, an unleashed tiger pulling at its chain. Maggie shivered.

Those hands, broad hands but with those long, tapering fingers – those were the hands of a sensualist. How would they feel moving over the polished silk of her naked skin? She sighed as she ran the palms of her own hands down the sides of her breasts, dipping into the gentle indentation of her waist and moulding the perfect flare of her hips.

Feeling hot again she flung back the sheet, stretching her arms up above her head and twisting this way and that to feel the cool air on the skin. Tourell had asked her to return to the casino tomorrow evening. She smiled. She couldn't go, of course. Not without Alexander's suggestion, and she was quite sure after tonight that that would not be forthcoming. He *did* want her, though, she was sure of it.

Pointing her toes she stretched her legs, revelling in the delicious pull on the delicate skin of her vulva. How would it be with Tourell? She imagined those jewel-bright blue eyes passing over her now, devouring her nakedness and she arched her back, preening in the sure knowlege that he would like what he saw.

Closing her eyes, she ran her hands through her hair, fanning it out on the pillow, imagining they were Tourell's hands, arranging her for his pleasure. Arching her neck, she traced a path across her face and down her throat, stroking the sensitive skin at the dip of her collar-bone until her entire body began to feel soft and weightless.

Slowly, very slowly, she stroked her palms downwards, rising up to the rose-tipped peaks of her breasts. Her nipples were like polished buttons, hard and tempting beneath her palms. What would Tourell do now, offered such tempting morsels?

Bringing her fingertips up to her mouth, she lathed them with her tongue, circling the hard little nubs until they were wet and shiny, the saliva drying on them in the cool night air. Maggie moaned softly as she imagined Tourell's harsh mouth closing over first one, then the other quivering peak. Her breasts ached as she imagined the pull of his hot mouth on them, the dangerous proximity of his teeth as they grazed the tips.

Taking both nipples between her forefingers and thumbs, she squeezed them gently, until the dart of pleasure bordered on pain. How far would Tourell go, would he want to turn pain into pleasure, or would he be content to merely love her? Her breath quickened as she pulled gently, teasing her nipples into needy cones, little waves of pleasure running from her breasts to her belly in ever quickening ripples.

She could have come just from playing with her nipples, but she guessed that Tourell would not be content to stop there. *His* hands would travel downward, circling her navel, brushing across the hairless mound at the apex of the thighs and travelling down the length of her legs.

Maggie could only reach as far as mid thigh and she imagined Tourell pausing there, caressing the soft, white flesh of her inner thighs in little ticklish circles until they slackened and parted of their own accord. Then he would push her legs, gently but insistently apart, exposing the innermost flower of her womanhood.

Her flesh-lips would be swollen and pink, glistening with the strength of her arousal. Seeing this, he would smile and dip his head to taste the honeyed flesh, opening her, entering her easily with his fingers so that he could control her movements . . .

Panting now, Maggie slipped her index finger into the moist warmth of her crevice and parted her labia with the first and second fingers of her other hand. In her mind's eye, it was Tourell who brought up the moisture welling in the lip of her vagina and smeared it along the tender ridge which led to the very centre of her pleasure.

It was Tourell who caressed her there, his touch tantalisingly light, rubbing rhythmically back and forth over that little bud which rose up to meet his teasing fingers. It swelled, quivering temptingly under his fingertips until he was compelled to tap it back down, chastening it, sending Maggie into a paroxysm of pleasure.

It was Tourell, not Maggie who beat that lewd and

greedy bud with the tip of his finger, so that it sent frenzied zigzags of delight through Maggie's body, racing through her arms and legs so that she thrashed her head from side to side in uncontrolled release.

It was Tourell who soothed her sated flesh and pulled the covers round her limp body. *Tourell*. And as Maggie's eyes closed she knew her fate had been sealed the first moment she set eyes on him.

And Alex or no Alex, tomorrow night, she would find a way to see him again.

Chapter Four

Carla dressed quickly the following morning, arriving on time, for once, at the florists where she worked. Her heart sank as she entered the shop. Most of her college friends worked in factories or as till girls and Carla knew that she was envied for her job. It was difficult now to remember a time when she had thought herself lucky to be working here, amongst all this colour and fragrance, but she knew that she had.

But that was before Alexander walked into her life and changed everything. She could remember it quite clearly. Bunching roses, as she was now, her hand had slipped and she had torn her finger on a thorn. The tall, blond man she had been surreptitiously watching as he browsed round the shop, had come over to help her. Only he didn't suggest she run it under a tap as old Mr Leavens, the florist, would have done. Slowly, so slowly, he had brought her hand up to his lips and, without taking his eyes from hers, he drew her bleeding finger into his mouth . . . it made her shudder just to think of it.

Slipping her green checked nylon tabard over her

50

sensible navy blue dress, she smiled to herself as she thought of the tight, heavily boned lace corset she wore underneath. Mr Leavens's eyes would be out on stalks if he knew!

There was no doubt about it, the weeks she had spent with Alexander had shown her what life had been missing so far. She was even prepared to share him with Antony rather than risk losing the exquisite pleasure he gave her. She had considered giving up her job and moving in permanently. Everything was perfect.

Except that now Maggie had come back. Carla's eyes narrowed and she jammed the roses viciously into a bucket of water. Damn Maggie! She had known about her, of course, realised that she had been the one before her. But she hadn't expected her to return.

'Carla – can you come and serve please.'

She jumped as Mr Leavens's voice reached her from the front of the shop. Dragging her mind away from Maggie with an effort, she turned her attention to her work.

It was early evening when she saw her. Clearing the front window display, Carla crouched behind a huge silver urn as Maggie crossed the road and walked right past the shop, heading towards the taxi rank further along the road. Where was *she* going? Carla wondered.

Pulling off her tabard, she decided, on impulse, to find out.

'I'm off now Mr Leavens,' she called as she slipped through the door so that he couldn't call her back, 'I'll come in earlier tomorrow to finish the window.'

Maggie was still standing at the taxi rank. Carla frowned. It was odd that she wasn't taking her car. Unless . . . she smiled as she guessed that wherever it was Maggie was going, she was doing her best to conceal it from Alexander.

She was dressed in a long, black coat which concealed her clothes. From the smooth, elegantly coiled hair, though, Carla assumed she was dressed for the evening. Even from the doorway several yards away from where Carla was hovering, she could see that Maggie's make-up was immaculate, as always. Her long, slim legs were shown to advantage by the tall, spindle-heeled sandals on which she walked so confidently.

Three taxis arrived together and Maggie climbed into the first. Without stopping to think, Carla waited until it had passed her before sprinting to the second one.

'I've just missed my friend,' she gasped as she sank into the seat, 'she was in the taxi that just left – do you think you could follow it for me?'

The driver raised an eyebrow at her in the mirror and she gave him her most winning smile. He shrugged and fired the engine, starting with such a jerk that Carla was thrown back in her seat. Irritation that he had interpreted her request as *carte blanche* to behave like a rally driver turned to relief as Maggie's taxi came into sight.

'Do you want me to overtake your mate, then?' the driver asked over his shoulder.

'Er . . . no, just drop me wherever she stops.'

'Don't you know where your supposed to be going?'

Carla frowned. She certainly didn't have to explain herself to a cabbie!

'We were meant to meet at the taxi rank,' she said grudgingly. 'I was held up at work. You can stop here.'

Maggie's cab had pulled up outside a wine bar. Carla watched as she climbed out and paid the driver before disappearing inside. Quickly following suit, Carla approached the bar.

If Maggie was meeting someone . . . Carla grinned. If there was one thing Alexander insisted upon, it was complete subservience to his will. From the way Maggie was behaving it seemed obvious to Carla that she was acting behind Alexander's back. What would he say to that?

The wine bar was brash and noisy, crowded with young executives lingering on their way home from work. It took Carla a few minutes to locate Maggie. She was sitting at a table to the back of the bar, a long stemmed glass of white wine in front of her. And she was completely alone.

Carla's spirits sank. Buying herself a drink, she concealed herself behind a pillar and waited to see who Maggie was about to meet.

She seemed troubled, twisting her wine glass in her fingers and staring into its depths. Several times she glanced at her watch, but no one came to join her. After half an hour, Carla began to get bored. Maggie was attracting a fair amount of attention from the men in the bar, but she seemed completely oblivious to it. As Carla watched, a young man in an Armani suite made a move on her.

The look Maggie gave him was so frosty, Carla fancied she could feel the icy blast from across the room. The young man slunk back to the bar and Maggie went back to contemplating her drink.

From the way she held herself it was obvious that she was nervous about something. Carla put down her drink as Maggie suddenly got up and, abandoning her glass on the table, walked quickly out of the wine bar. Hoping fervently that she wouldn't be hailing another taxi, Carla hurried after her.

To her relief, Maggie didn't take a cab. Instead she walked, too briskly for Carla's shorter legs to follow confortably, turning off the main street and into a side road. It was seven o'clock now and the light was beginning to fade. The street lamps had already come on, their light ineffectual against the rosy pink glow of the sunset.

Carla began to feel hot and breathless. Where on earth was Maggie going? Half running, she turned a corner and suddenly, she recognised where they were. Carla stopped at the corner of the street and watched as Maggie paused outside the Island Casino, as if she might change her mind and not go in.

Carla willed her not to turn back, to climb the steps and disappear through the doors. It all made sense now – the secrecy, the hesitation. Last night Maggie had met the man Alexander had called Tourell. Carla wasn't stupid, she knew sexual electricity when she saw it. But she had never dreamed that Maggie would come back.

Maggie half turned away, then, with a little shake of her head, she walked purposefully into the casino. Satisfied that she had found a way to get rid of Maggie once and for all, Carla went to find a taxi to take her back to the Black Orchid Club.

Maggie gave her name to the taciturn Italian on the reception desk inside and was immediately whisked through a side door and up some stairs. As she was shown through a door, she realised that this was the direct route to the inner sanctum, the room where the serious gambling took place.

If she had been uncertain before, there was no time for procrastination now, for there was Tourell, walking towards her in the gloom, both hands stretched towards her in greeting.

'Maggie,' his throaty voice caressed her, his blue eyes lit with genuine pleasure as he ran them over her long, halter-necked black dress, 'come, have a seat. Are you hungry?'

She shook her head, the sensation of his rough palms

brushing against the pampered softness of hers sending little shivers along her nervous sytem.

'Some coffee, then.'

He signalled to a waiter and led Maggie over to a deep, buttoned velour sofa, half hidden in shadow.

'You're not playing tonight?' she asked him as he sank down beside her.

'Perhaps later. Perhaps not.'

His eyes held hers for a moment, full of innuendo, then he turned away, a small smile of amusement playing around his lips. Maggie gulped at the coffee she was handed, giving a small cry as she burnt her mouth.

Tourell's eyes held concern as he surveyed the damage, running the pad of his thumb gently across the damaged skin of her lower lip. Then, unexpectedly, shockingly, he dipped his head and soothed the tender place with the tip of his warm, wet tongue.

Maggie had to fight hard to resist the urge to press herself closer against him, to inveigle him to kiss her properly. He tasted of a heady mixture of fresh tobacco and cinnamon, the curious, burnt wood fragrance of his skin curling in her nostrils. Need, primaeval, irresistible, tugged at her innards, turning her limbs to liquid and her femininity to heat. Then he withdrew and Maggie was left feeling bereft.

'Did you have much trouble getting away?' he asked conversationally, his eyes watchful over the rim of his coffee cup.

Maggie stared at him, wondering how much he knew about her relationship with Alexander. She frowned as she thought of him, pushing his image aside almost superstitiously.

'Of course not – why would you think that?'

Tourell smiled, a slow, enigmatic smile which made Maggie's toes curl.

'Why indeed?' he said softly.

His attention was caught by a croupier and he rose.

'Excuse me,' he said as he put down his coffee cup.

Maggie watched as he walked over to the table and spoke to the man. He moved easily in the formal black tuxedo, looking relaxed and self-confident. His long, heavily muscled legs filled the narrow trousers, drawing Maggie's eyes upward to where the edge of his jacket concealed the moulding of his buttocks.

Both tables were in operation this evening. As before, the atmosphere was thick with tobacco smoke, the lighting barely adequate except on the tables themselves. Casting her eyes around the players, Maggie recognised the tension, the suppressed excitement on their faces as the game progressed.

She smiled as Tourell returned to her side.

'I'm sorry. Later we'll go to my suite downstairs where I've arranged for dinner to be served.'

Maggie's eyes widened.

'Were you so sure I'd come?'

Their eyes locked and Maggie's breath caught in her throat. There was desire mirrored in his and something else, an acknowledgement, perhaps, or a recognition . . . her lips parted slightly and her mouth ran dry.

'It doesn't do to be sure of anything in this life, Maggie,' he said softly.

Then he smiled and Maggie knew that her enslavement was complete. It was such a sensual smile, a smile of such promise . . .

'Come,' he broke the spell, 'sit beside me while I play a hand.'

As the night before, Maggie was supremely aware of him sitting inches away from her at the table. Whilst he was playing his concentration was wholly on the game and she was able to observe him openly.

His was an interesting face, the kind of face she would have liked to explore with her fingertips. She would run her fingernails lightly across the tracery of lines around his eyes and tangle her fingers in the thickness of his hair over his ears.

Those ears were quite small for a man, though beautifully shaped. She would like to caress their folds with the tip of her tongue and whisper words of love and lust into his ear . . .

Tourell turned his head at that moment and caught her expression. His eyes instantly darkened so that they were almost navy blue and Maggie knew that her thoughts were written plainly on her face.

A heated blush stole into her cheeks, though she raised her chin, determined not to be unnerved. A flicker of his eyes told her that Tourell had recognised her challenge and was aroused by it. There was a new tension in him, a wholly masculine power that drew the strength from Maggie, leaving her feeling weak.

Someone spoke, reminding Tourell to move and Maggie was left trembling as he removed his gaze from hers. He lost the hand. His expression was grim as he turned back to Maggie and indicated that he wished to leave the table.

'Are you hungry yet?' he asked her, his voice low in her ear as he steered her lightly by the elbow away from the table.

Her hunger might have little to do with satisfying her need for food, but she nodded, unable to trust her voice. Without another word, Tourell urged her towards a door at the far side of the room that she had not noticed before.

The apartment was like nothing Maggie had ever seen before. The large, basement room was open plan, divided into living, eating and sleeping areas by a series of plant covered trellises. There were no windows, no natural light, though there were several strategically placed lamps which cast their diffused glow throughout the room.

'How do you manage without daylight?' she asked curiously.

Tourell laughed, going over to the dining area where he poured them both a glass of white wine.

'I'm a creature of the night, at least while I'm in town. I have a house in the country for when I crave daylight. Here I make do with simulation bulbs.'

He flicked a switch and the room filled with light. The effect was remarkably natural, though Maggie was glad when he switched it off and they were plunged once again into the moody glow of the lamps.

The table in the centre of the dining area had been set for two. Large, heat resistant place mats had been placed over the glass top which reflected the sparkling silver cutlery and fine crystal glasses. An overhead light had been pulled low over the table in parody of the spotlights used on the gaming tables above.

Handing Maggie a glass, Tourell pulled out her seat before going across to the telephone. Pressing a button, he issued instructions into it before going to switch on some music. Maggie was startled when the haunting strains of 'Pie Jesu' filled the room.

Catching her expression, Tourell smiled.

'I like beautiful things,' he said simply.

He sipped his wine, his jewel-bright eyes never leaving Maggie's face. The pure young voice swelled around them, resonant in the vast room. Putting down her glass, Maggie closed her eyes.

As the last strains of the music faded away, Maggie glanced at Tourell and saw that he too had been wrapped up in the music, his face mirroring her own pleasure. He smiled at her and rose to change the tape, this time selecting a gentle classical movement which would act as a background accompaniment rather than take over the room. As he did so, the door opened with a discreet swish and two uniformed waiters arrived bearing a large tray.

Maggie's nose twitched as the distinctive aroma of rich boeuf bourguignonne wafted from beneath the lid of a large silver tureen. Without looking at Maggie, one waiter deftly served up fluffy white rice on the two gold-rimmed plates set on the table. Quickly ladling a generous helping of beef on top, he presented them with a large mixed salad as an accompaniment and the two men left with the empty serving dishes, as silently as they had arrived.

'This looks wonderful,' Maggie said as Tourell sat down. 'I hadn't realised I was so hungry!'

And indeed, the sight and smell of the meal had triggered her appetite so that she savoured the first bite. The meat was so tender it virtually melted in her mouth, the sauce rich and redolent of fine red wine.

Tourell watched her for a few moments before he picked up his own fork. Conscious of his regard, Maggie glanced uncertainly at him. He smiled.

'I like a woman with appetite,' he said.

Maggie could feel the flush stealing into her cheeks, His words had been innocuous enough, but his tone was heavy with hidden meaning. The heat in Maggie's face was matched by a sudden rush of warmth in the secret folds of her sex and she fought the urge to squirm before Tourell's steady gaze.

She was grateful to wet her dry throat with the soft, ruby red wine he poured her and she watched him surreptitiously in her turn as he ate. It was Maggie's view that the way a man enjoyed his food was often a good indicator of his sexual style.

Tourell ate in leisurely fashion, as if enjoying every morsel, prepared to spend all the time in the world over it. Maggie shivered, imagining him taking a similar pleasure in her body.

'Do you like playing games, Maggie?' he asked her suddenly.

Maggie glanced at him uncertainly, unsure how to read his tone.

'Games?' she echoed. 'Like roulette, you mean?'

He smiled.

'Amongst others.'

Maggie frowned, not quite understanding what he meant. It should have been a straightforward question, he was looking at her as if it was, yet she had the stomach churning feeling that there was far more to it than it at first appeared. There were layers to his enquiry, each one more intriguing than the last. She smiled.

'It depends on my mood, I suppose.'

Tourell toyed with his fork, twirling it in the remains of his rice as if thinking. When he looked up, Maggie gained the distinct impression that he had made his mind up about something.

'Are you under contract to the Black Orchid?'

Maggie's eyes widened and she felt that irritating, shaming blush begin again. If she had deluded herself that Tourell did not know of her relationship with Alexander and Antony, she was sure now that she was wrong. Embarrassed, she dropped her eyes.

'I don't know what you mean.' she muttered, ridiculously.

Chancing a glance at Tourell from beneath her lashes, she saw that he was watching her intently, his head held slightly on one side in enquiry.

'I understood you act as a recruitment consultant for them?'

Maggie almost sagged with relief. Wondering fleetingly how he knew so much about her, she did not think to question him, merely nodding in reply.

'And are you?'

'Sorry?'

'Under contract?'

Maggie grimaced ruefully as she realised that, in her panic, she had almost completely lost track of what he was saying. Trying to concentrate, she shook her head slowly.

'No, my employment is more in the nature of a gentlemen's agreement,' she told him.

He did not need to know that her job at the Black Orchid was little more than a blind for her true position there. Which was . . . what? She frowned as she realised she didn't really know where she stood, especially not now that Carla had arrived on the scene.

'Would you consider working for me?'

Maggie's eyebrows rose as Tourell's voice broke into her introspection.

'Working for you? In what capacity?'

Tourell held up his hand as the doors opened and the two waiters appeared as soundlessly as before. They removed the empty dinner plates and replaced them with two small bowls of daintily arranged fresh fruit, bathed in cream.

Waiting until the waiters had left, Tourell bit into a slice of fresh pineapple. Selecting a smooth-skinned grape, Maggie dipped it in the cream and popped it into her mouth. The juice burst down her throat as she bit into it and she began to cough, unable to catch her breath.

Tourell was at her side in an instant, rubbing her back and holding his own glass of wine to her lips. Crouching by her chair, he was at eye-level with her. Maggie gazed at him over the rim of the glass as he tipped it and the fragrant liquid flowed down her throat.

'Thank you,' she whispered as he took it away.

His nearness was intoxicating, befuddling her senses so that she felt incapable of rational thought. Her lips parted slightly and she moistened them with the tip of her tongue. Tourell's eyes followed the movement and she sensed the sudden tension in his body which matched her own.

He was so close, so very close, all she had to do was lean slightly towards him and the rough grain of his jacket would brush against the bare skin of her arms . . . she shivered.

Tourell frowned, his eyes darkening as he noticed the movement.

'You're cold,' he murmured, his wine-rich breath caressing her skin.

Following his gaze, Maggie looked down and saw that the skin of her shoulders and arms was raised in tiny goose bumps. She bit down on a small, involuntary cry of distress as, instead of taking her into his arms as she longed for him to do, Tourell rose and disappeared behind one of the trellises.

Maggie wrapped her arms around herself, rubbing her palms down her inexplicably chilled skin. Her stomach felt tight with longing for the man who was proving so elusive. He reappeared carrying a large silk scarf which he folded into a shawl and placed around her shoulders, tying it into a knot at her breasts.

Resuming his seat he smiled at her.

'Those colours suit you.'

Looking down, Maggie saw that the scarf was patterned in vibrant swirls of scarlet and fuchsia pink, tempered with gold.

'Hot colours.'

Maggie's head shot up as he breathed the last and she was caught by the expression in his eyes. He smiled slightly and she knew that her desire was revealed on her face.

'Have you finished your fruit?' he asked softly.

Maggie glanced down at her half-full bowl in confusion.

'I . . . yes,' she whispered.

'Come.'

He held out his hand to her and she grasped it gladly, following where he led. The living area was light and spacious, entirely free from distracting clutter. Maggie expected him to take her to the soft, low sofa in the centre but he continued on to where two wing-backed chairs stood at right angles to each other.

Sinking down onto the hard, scarlet chintz-covered seat, Maggie watched as Tourell moved the second chair so that he was facing her, no more than a couple of feet away. The absence of windows created a curiously claustrophobic atmosphere, as if reality began and ended in this room. The music had ended long before and the silence enclosed them, increasing Maggie's sense of isolation.

Nervously crossing one leg over the other, she jumped as Tourell suddenly spoke.

'Don't do that.'

Responding to the uncompromising tone of command in his voice, Maggie immediately uncrossed her legs.

'That's better,' he smiled, his voice once again soft, hypnotic.

Maggie stared at him as he withdraw a gold cigarette case from the inside pocket of his jacket and placed a cigarette between his teeth. She shook her head as he offered her one and watched as he flicked a lighter into life. The small flame flickered and flared, lighting up his face for an instant before it was extinguished.

Narrowing his eyes against the long stream of smoke, he leaned back in his chair.

'You're a beautiful woman, Maggie,' he said softly, 'a sensual woman. A woman with needs and desires that must be met.'

His voice was so low, so husky, Maggie felt as if she were being drawn into a vortex where reality had no meaning. Nothing mattered but that he should continue to talk to her, that his rich, throaty voice should continue to caress her senses.

Her breath began to come in short, shallow bursts, her breasts rising and falling with increasing speed as Tourell continued to weave his spell over her.

'Let down your hair for me,' he whispered.

Maggie reached up slowly and withdrew the pins from her hair, letting each one drop soundlessly onto the carpet. Her hair tumbled about her silk-covered shoulders in a heavy curtain.

'Shake your head.'

Her hair flew about her face and settled in disarray about her shoulders.

'Good. Now, take off the shawl . . . yes. No – don't drop it, leave it on your lap. That's right. Hold it there while you unbutton your dress.'

Maggie hesitated for a moment, her finger hovering level with her breasts. The dress was button-through, clinging lovingly to her every curve. So as not to spoil the line she had eschewed underwear, her pure silk hold-ups and shoes were the only other garments she wore.

'Go on, Maggie,' Tourell urged, 'unbutton your dress for me.'

Maggie watched his face as she slowly slipped each button through its buttonhole and her nakedness was exposed. He showed no surprise, not even when her carefully shorn sex came into view. She had to lean forward from the waist to undo the final three buttons, then she straightened and waited patiently for further instructions, trying to control the butterflies dancing in her stomach.

'Fold it back, let me see your breasts.'

Her hands trembled as she complied with his softly voiced request, exposing first one, then the other rosy peak. The cool air kissed her skin, coaxing the tips to aching hardness.

Tourell's eyes passed lightly over her breasts and came back to rest on her face.

'Beautiful. Larger than one would expect, given your slenderness. Will you lift them for me?'

Maggie's cheeks flamed with the humiliation of his cool appraisal of her, yet she did as he asked, cupping the undersides of her breasts in her palms and raising them up so that the nipples pointed straight ahead. Tourell smiled, as if in approval.

'Let them drop.'

Maggie swallowed at the sudden dryness of her throat before taking her hands away. Without their support, her breasts dropped, the firm flesh bouncing against her rib cage.

Tourell's eyes narrowed, though otherwise he seemed unaffected.

'Again,' he whispered.

This time Maggie lifted them higher so that this time the bounce bordered on pain. A soft groan escaped from her lips and Tourell leaned forward slightly in his seat. For one breathless moment, Maggie thought that he would reach out and touch her breasts, but no, he straightened again and merely smiled.

'The scarf, Maggie. Run the silk across your breasts.'

Maggie lifted the scarf and let it fall, feather-soft, across her breasts. She shuddered at the contrast of the cool, soft silk against the heated skin of her breasts.

'Does that feel good?'

She nodded.

'Tell me, Maggie – how does it feel?'

Maggie felt as if she couldn't breathe, the force of her arousal was so strong. Forcing the words through her lips, she barely recognised the husky voice that emerged as her own.

'It feels . . . so good . . .'

'Run the silk down your body, Maggie, pass it over the places your lover's lips like best.'

Tourell's words barely impinged on Maggie's consciousness. Her arousal had gained a momentum of its own now so that the mere sound of his voice was enough to provide a symphony to accompany the sweet sensations rippling through her body.

'Open your legs, Maggie, spread them wide so I can see the jewel you wear so well . . . wider, open yourself to me . . .'

Maggie reached down and spread her moist sex-lips with her fingers, exposing her innermost flesh to Tourell's voyeuristic gaze. it seemed natural to let the silk scarf flutter softly down, between her legs where it whispered against sensitive skin.

'Ah, Maggie, let me see you ride the silken saddle.'

Twisting the silk scarf into a rope, she lifted her bottom from the chair and passed it beneath her, reaching round with her other hand to grasp the end. Beyond all shame now, Maggie moved the silken rope back and forth, playing it over her wet flesh-lips until the pressure began to mount in her loins.

'Bear down, Maggie, press yourself against the silk . . . let it go . . .'

Maggie opened her mouth as the first waves of orgasm began to wash over her. Oblivious now to Tourell watching her, she writhed in the seat, spreading her thighs wide and pushing out her clitoris so that it scraped against the now wet silk of the scarf.

A hot flush spread from her sex through her body so that she was consumed by heat. She cried out as she lost control, sagging against the hard back of the seat, spent.

It wasn't until then that Tourell touched her. His hands were gentle as he took the sodden scarf from her limp fingers and buttoned up her dress. He smoothed the damp tendrils of hair from her face and smiled into her still-glazed eyes.

Maggie leaned gratefully against him as he helped her to her feet.

'Given the circumstances, I think it best if I don't drive you home. I'll arrange a cab for you.'

She nodded against his shoulder, gazing up at him through limpid eyes as he tipped her face to his.

'Will you come again?'

She nodded and he smiled.

'Consider the offer I made.'

Maggie frowned, forgetting, for a moment, that he had offered her a job. Outside, Tourell waited with her until the taxi arrived. Just as she was about to get in, he unexpectedly turned her and his mouth came down on hers.

The kiss was hard, uncompromising and Maggie clung to him, wanting more, so much more. The hardness of his unsatisfied arousal pressed against her belly, a reminder of his self-control. Then he pushed her gently into the taxi.

As it sped away, Maggie turned in the seat. He was standing on the steps of the casino, watching her departure, the silk scarf wound around his hand. And it was only then that Maggie realised that he had made no attempt to join her in her climb to the peak. And she wondered at it.

Chapter Five

Carla was waiting for Maggie when she stepped out of the taxi.

'Alexander wants to see you,' she said, her pale eyes alight with malice.

Maggie frowned. She was exhausted, all she could face tonight was a long, warm soak and then she planned to fall into bed.

'Tell him I'll see him tomorrow, will you?'

Carla put her hand on Maggie's arm, stopping her from turning away.

'He wants to see you *now*.'

Maggie recognised the spite in the younger girl's eyes and her spirits sank. Resigned, she shrugged her shoulders and followed Carla to the lift.

'OK.'

The dislike was palpable between them in the close confines of the lift. Privately, Maggie wondered what on earth Alexander had ever seen in Carla. The girl was . . . ordinary, a plain girl dressed up like a doll and doused in cheap perfume. Ashamed at the bitchiness of her thoughts, Maggie attempted a friendly smile.

Carla stared coldly back at her and Maggie made a mental note not to waste her time on overtures of friendliness again.

The first person who Maggie saw when the lift door opened was Antony. He was standing in the doorway to the lounge, naked from the waist up, his arms and legs spread-eagled so that he touched all four corners of the door. His mouth had been covered by a clean, white handkerchief and as Maggie approached, she realised that he was tied, the tendons at his armpits stretched to the point of discomfort.

Her step faltering, Maggie turned to Carla for an explanation, just in time to see the lift doors slide noiselessly to a close. The soft whirr of the lift mechanism bore the other girl away, leaving Maggie and Antony alone.

As she turned uncertainly towards him, Maggie saw that Antony's cool grey eyes seemed to be pleading with her. There was a curious nobility about the way he held himself, an air of willing submission to the containment of his wholly masculine strength and Maggie felt strangely moved. Her brows drew together in concern as she saw that his face was taut, streaked with tears and, disgusted with herself, she shook her head.

'Antony,' she said softly, 'what is going on?'

Now that the initial shock had worn off, Maggie moved forward swiftly and unfastened the gag. Antony's tongue snaked out to moisten his dry lips as she bent to release his legs, reaching up to untie his arms. His shoulders sagged and he leaned against her willingly as Maggie offered him her arm.

She led him into the bedroom, glancing furtively round her to check that Alexander was not lying in wait for them both. Antony sank down onto the bed, face down, and for the first time, Maggie saw the marks on his back. Thin, red, raised weals criss-crossed Antony's sculpted back in perfect symmetry.

Maggie stood and stared for a moment, unable to think straight. She had not believed that Alexander could ever do anything to shock her, but he had succeeded. To do this to someone he loved, unless . . .

'Did Alexander do this?' she whispered.

Antony turned his head and looked at her, his eyes clear now, free of guile. Incredibly, a hint of a smile touched the corners of his mouth as he replied.

'Do you think I'd let anyone else?'

Maggie knelt down on the bed beside him. The pattern of the marks of his chastisement held a strange fascination for her and she traced one gently with the tip of her finger. Antony winced and she pulled back her hand abruptly.

'I'll get some soothing oil.'

Her thoughts were in turmoil as she half ran to the bathroom and found the flagon of oil Antony used on her sensitive skin when he shaved her pubis. Trying not to wonder, not to think, she concentrated on carrying the heavy glass bottle carefully into the bedroom.

Antony had not moved, he lay on his stomach, his head turned to one side, his eyes closed. A small groan whispered over his lips and Maggie guessed that his arms would be hurting as the blood flowed back into them.

How long had he been hanging there, waiting for her to return? For she was quite sure that he had been waiting for her, or why would Carla have been put in place to accost her the minute she walked through the door?

Slipping off her shoes, Maggie knelt on the bed and poured a small pool of oil into one hand. Warming it first between her palms, she then spread the slippery oil across Antony's broad shoulders. He moaned, a sound half-way between pain and pleasure as she began to smooth the oil across his back.

'Am I hurting you?' she paused as she saw the muscles in his shoulders bunch with tension.

His lips barely moved as he answered, his voice slurred.

'Don't stop.'

The only sound in the bedroom came from Antony's deep, uneven breathing and the gentle squelch of the oil as it was moved between the two layers of skin. Maggie's forearms began to ache as she rubbed it into Antony's abused flesh, warming it so that it glowed a deep red beneath her palms.

Gradually, Antony's breathing steadied and he relaxed under her gentling hands. Maggie began to enjoy the feel of his well-toned muscles beneath her hands, moulding and shaping them as the soreness of his flesh eased under the soothing properties of the oil.

'Better?'

She leaned forward and placed a gentle kiss at the corner of his eye. Antony smiled, bringing up one hand to cup her cheek in a gesture of tenderness which brought an inexplicable rush of tears to her eyes.

Maggie moved off the bed as Antony levered himself up, turning to face her.

'Thank you,' he whispered.

She smiled sadly at him and shook her head.

'Why, Antony? Why did he do this to you?'

Antony dropped his eyes for a moment, as if in shame. Yet when he raised his gaze to hers again, there was a kind of defiant pride in their cool grey depths.

'Why not?' he responded simply.

'Was it because of me?'

Antony held her eyes levelly for a few seconds, then he looked away and she knew that her hunch was right.

'Alexander beat you because he found out I went back to the casino, didn't he? Antony?'

Antony's full, sensual lower lip tightened into a stubborn line as he recognised the anger in her voice.

'You don't understand.'

Maggie made a sound of exasperation, deep in her throat.

'You're damn right I don't! Why couldn't he have saved his fury for me, if that's how he felt? Why take it out on you?'

'Perhaps because you wouldn't have taken as much pleasure in it as I.'

Maggie regarded Antony incredulously. He was right, of course, she wouldn't have revelled in acting as a cipher for Alexander's wrath and she could not believe that Antony had submitted to it so . . . so *joyously*. Yet his eyes were shining now with almost evangelical fervour and Maggie knew that he spoke the truth.

Impulsively, she put her arms around him and drew his head down to her breast. Stroking his hair, she murmured, 'Oh, Antony! My poor love.'

Antony laughed, a muffled sound against the fabric of her dress.

'Don't pity me,' he said, bringing himself up so that they were on a level. 'I'm not the one who should be pitied. Look at me, Maggie darling. I am happy.'

He smiled at her bewilderment and leaned forward to touch his lips against hers. Maggie kept her eyes open, staring into his as his mouth lingered on hers. Something melted and flowed through her, something more than compassion, yet not quite desire.

Antony's eyes darkened to slate grey and his arms came about her. The kiss changed from one of friendship to the beginnings of passion and Maggie responded, bringing her arms up, around his neck and pressing herself against the solid wall of his chest.

72

After his submission to Alexander, Maggie sensed that Antony felt the need to re-assert himself, and she willingly allowed him to bow her body backward as his lips broke away from hers and sought the soft, smooth length of her neck.

Her long, dark hair, swept the covers as Antony pressed his lips against her throat, eliciting a small sigh of pleasure from her. The tiny pulse at the side of her neck throbbed erratically as Antony's lips worked their way down to where the front of her dress dipped to reveal the tempting swell of her breasts.

She shivered, her breasts hardening to aching peaks as the kisses turned into little, pinching nips. Her flesh rose up in tiny goose bumps as her fingers tangled in the thickness of Antony's coarse blond hair. Dragging his head across, she urged him to take the burgeoning, fabric-covered nipple between his teeth.

He was too strong for her, and tonight he would not allow her to direct him. Raising his head, he pushed her gently back down on the bed and began to unfasten the buttons which ran down the front of her dress. He did it so slowly, caressing each button in turn before slipping it through the buttonhole, that Maggie longed to push his hands away and rip it off herself.

Her skin burned as Antony unknowily rekindled the desire Tourell had incited in her earlier. It took a supreme effort of will to respond to Antony's unspoken desire that she should lie still and be done to rather than participate. Waiting until he had unfastened every button, he peeled back the sides of her dress, laying them carefully either side of her, as if he were unwrapping a present.

He smiled as he saw that she was naked beneath, gazing down at the perfection of her body for several minutes without touching her. Maggie's skin quivered, desperate for the touch of his long, cool fingers.

'Please . . .' the word whispered over her lips in spite of her efforts to cage it.

Antony smiled. In the dim light of the bedroom, his face loomed in shadow above her and she could barely discern the lifting of his mouth. The moonlight which filtered through the bedroom curtains formed a nebula around his head, giving him a sepulchral air, like a dream-lover drawn from her imagination.

Aroused beyond reason, Maggie lifted her arms towards him in a gesture of unconscious pleading.

Antony gazed down at the woman on the bed with a lump in his throat. Her slender arms were stretched towards him, lifting her full breasts in offering. Her skin was silvered by the moonlight, white against the black of the fabric crumpled around her.

She gave herself so sweetly, offered up the delights of her body with such generous abandonment, he could not help but love her. And he knew, with sudden clarity, that Alexander had known that this would happen, that this was his gift to Antony to salve the hurt he had inflicted upon him. There would be no recrimination if he chose to accept the gift of love that Maggie was offering him tonight.

Licking the first two fingers of his right hand, he placed them gently against the tender hollow at her throat and traced a line from her neck to her navel. The dampened skin quivered as it cooled in the air, her nipples puckering even more in reaction.

Dipping his head, Antony retraced the path with the very tip of his tongue. Her skin tasted slightly salty with an undertone of sweetness, like popcorn. As he neared her pubis, he breathed in the scent of her and caught the lingering fragrance of her earlier arousal.

His lips curved in a smile as he realised that Alexander had been right to be jealous of Tourell. Yet there

74

was not trace of maleness as he ran his tongue lovingly along the groove of her vulva, and he was glad.

She opened up to him slowly, like a flower drinking in the sun. The petal-soft skin of her labia was dewed with her arousal and Antony lapped at it gently, savouring the sweet, feminine nectar. Maggie groaned and wrapped her long legs around his shoulders.

Burying his face in her fragrant womanhood, Antony teased the tip of the clitoral hood until it slipped back to reveal the wanton bud beneath. Lathing it gently with his tongue, he revelled in the way it hardened and quivered.

Slipping his hands under Maggie's bottom, he lifted her up, his fingertips easing into the crease of her parted buttocks and squeezing the firm globes of flesh. Maggie's head thrashed from side to side as her orgasm washed over her. Allowing her no respite, Antony pressed his tongue hard against her throbbing clitoris, parrying with it until she cried out, begging him to stop.

'Please, Antony, please . . . no more!' she gasped, tangling her fingers in his hair and trying to pull him away.

The tender flesh of her vulva was flushed a deep rose, the inviting entrance convulsing as her climax went on and on. She wanted him there, he knew, wanted him filling her with the engorged flesh which was pressing uncomfortably against the seam of his jeans.

Letting her go, he stood and unfastened them, pushing them impatiently down his legs and kicking them aside. His cock sprang up, strong and ready and Antony felt a stab of deeply masculine pride as he watched Maggie's eyes feasting on it.

Her luscious mouth formed a silent 'o' of desire and he was gripped by a sudden perversity as he mounted her. Even while her legs came about his waist, urging him to plunge into her, he knew that was not what he wanted. And, suddenly, what *he* desired became of paramount importance to him.

Impatiently pushing her legs down, he shifted up the bed and nudged her full, red lips with his moist cock-head. Maggie's brows came together in a frown of anguish as she realised that he intended to deny her the fulfilment she craved. Yet her mouth opened and she enclosed him, sucking him in greedily.

Antony's breath caught in his chest as the skin of his scrotum grew tight and the familiar tremors began along his cock-shaft. Resting his buttocks on the soft cushion of Maggie's breasts, he fought against the urge to thrust into her mouth. To do so would have dulled the incredible sensations which now feathered along the length of him.

Maggie's eyes were closed in intense concentration, a frown etched between them as she drew on him. She was beautiful, her dark hair spread across the pillows in a fragrant cloud, her generous mouth stuffed full of cock. Antony closed his own eyes, blocking out all other stimuli so that all he was aware of was the exquisite pleasure of Maggie's hot mouth and her clever, knowing, lips and tongue.

His consciousness seemed focused on that one place, the tingling, engorged shaft that was his penis. It was as if his entire nervous system began and ended there in a mass of quivering endings.

Suddenly, there was a climactic shiver at the tip of his cock, followed by a great surge from the base of his scrotal sac. It flowed in spasmodic rhythm along his shaft until, at last, the semen pumped from him and into Maggie's hot mouth.

'Oh, oh, oh yes!' Antony gasped, cupping her cheeks

between his palms as she struggled to swallow the viscous flow of seed. 'Maggie . . . ah, Maggie . . .!'

Maggie gasped as Antony finally withdrew from her. Her jaw felt cramped, stiff with effort and her throat burned with the force of his emission. Between her legs the passage to her womb throbbed with disappointment and need. In desperation, she reached down and, licking lovingly at Antony's rapidly deflating member, she slipped the first two fingers of one hand inside herself. Frantically, she moved them back and forth, imitating a male member. Without finesse, she failed to find the elusive spot she sought and she groaned in frustration.

'Well well well, what a touching sight.'

Antony and Maggie were pulled rudely from their self-absorption as Alexander's mocking voice sounded from the doorway. Maggie gave up on her clumsy attempt to find satisfaction and Antony rolled off her, regarding Alexander warily through guarded eyes.

Alexander was wearing the uniform of the club; black trousers and a white cotton singlet, cut away at the shoulders in such a way as to emphasise the power of his upper arms. Fleetingly, Maggie recalled the first time she had seen him when she had believed him to be a mere employee. He had looked harmless then, a beautiful boy with an unusual knowledge of a woman's needs . . .

Now he looked anything but harmless, advancing like a sleek, golden panther, a sense of barely leashed violence palpable in the air around him. Maggie sat up, drawing the bedcovers around her, more in self-defence than out of modesty. She could feel Antony's tension as, slipping off his shoes, Alexander sat down on his side of the bed and the mattress dipped slightly under his weight.

The urgency of Maggie's desire receded slightly as

Alexander reached out a hand and smoothed the hair from Antony's eyes. The two men smiled at each other, such a loving, exclusive sort of smile that Maggie was struck by a bolt of sheer, naked jealousy.

As if sensing her sidelong glance, Alexander leaned across the bed and, without taking his eyes from Antony's, slipped his hand beneath the covers. His long, sensitive fingers were cool and dry against the heated skin of Maggie's outer thigh. She tensed at the casual contact, bristling with indignation as Alexander carelessly stroked his finger upwards to the apex of her thighs.

He and Antony were kissing now, a long, lingering kiss which excluded her. Closing her eyes, Maggie squeezed her thighs together against the invasion of Alexander's fingers. But he was insistent and she had been so close to release before he had arrived that Maggie could feel her secret flesh swell, glorying at his touch.

Closing her eyes against the shame of her arousal in the face of such indifference, Maggie lay back against the pillows and allowed the inevitable to happen. Her thighs fell open, exposing her moisture-slick flesh to the cool air and the skilful manipulation of Alexander's hand.

Rimming the entrance to her womb with his fore-finger, he, like Tourell and Antony before him, denied her the intrusion she craved, choosing instead to stroke and caress the slippery folds of flesh which shielded the centre of her arousal.

Maggie could hear the creak of the bedsprings as Alexander climbed over Antony, shifting his weight so that he was between them and could continue to stroke Maggie whilst his other hand was free to pleasure Antony. Maggie did not open her eyes, did not want to know what the two men were doing. Her entire consciousness was focused on that small, hidden button which even now was swelling and hardening so that it assumed an importance far beyond its size.

As always, Alexander knew with unerring accuracy when to be gentle and when to be firm. Maggie squirmed against the rumpled sheets as a warmth spread from that tiny core of her throughout her body. Mindlessly, she turned her face towards Antony's animal warmth.

Opening her eyes, she saw that he was lying on his belly, his face turned towards hers. His normally cool grey eyes were glazed and there was a sheen of perspiration on his forehead which glimmered in the moonlight. Of one accord, their lips fastened together. He tasted of sweat and the sharp, salty tang of tears.

Alexander pinched Maggie's pulsing clitoris between his thumb and forefinger and rolled it rhythmically. Antony swallowed the sound of Maggie's gasp as she came, licking at her upper lip as she cried out, her body thrashing about, out of control.

Satisfied that she was spent, Alexander withdrew his hand from between Maggie's legs. Maggie felt tears of shame burn her eyelids, hot, fat, salty droplets squeezing through her closed lids to roll down her cheeks. That she could respond so eagerly to such a careless caress . . .

Alexander was using the intimate moisture from Maggie's body to lubricate between Antony's buttocks. Maggie watched as he rolled a condom expertly over himself with one hand before mounting Antony to thrust slowly in and out of his raised cleft. Antony's eyes were closed now and there was on his face an expression of such beatific ecstasy that she knew he was being transported to his own, personal heaven where no one but Alexander could follow.

Raising her eyes to Alexander, Maggie saw that he

was frowning with intense concentration. Somewhere along the line he had stripped and his smooth, golden skin glowed in the moonlight.

Their eyes met and a question passed across his as he saw Maggie's anguish. Then he smiled and held her eye as the moment of his own release approached.

As he came, Alexander's mouth opened on a shuddering sigh. Acting on impluse, Maggie levered herself up and, cupping his face between her palms, she fastened her mouth over his.

He kissed her back, taking her with him as he collapsed across Antony's back. Groaning as the connection between him and Alexander was broken, Antony rolled over. Maggie and Alexander were still kissing, and Maggie's hands were roaming feverishly across Alexander's chest and shoulders.

Antony smiled, glad that harmony was restored. Folding his hands behind his head, he waited patiently to be included in the exhausted tangle of limbs.

Later, Maggie woke to find her cheek pillowed by the hard cushion of Alexander's chest. His arm was about her shoulders and he was playing with her hair, twirling it repeatedly around his fingers so that it lay in damp corkscrew curls across her face. Antony, lying with his back towards them both, was breathing in the soft, even rhythm of deep sleep.

Levering herself up with difficulty, Maggie gazed down at Alexander and saw that, far from being asleep, he was staring up at the darkened ceiling, deep in thought.

'Alex?'

He jumped visibly as she whispered his name, a deep frown appearing between his eyes. The cold light of dawn was beginning to filter between the gap in the curtains so that Maggie could see his face clearly.

Moving slightly so that her own features were no longer in shadow, she smiled tentatively at him.

To her relief, the forbidding expression slid from Alexander's face and he smiled at her. It was such an unthreatening, friendly smile that she was unprepared for the question that she knew he would eventually ask.

'Why were you planning to leave us, Maggie?'

Maggie could feel the heat steal into her cheeks and she dropped her eyes as she lied,

'I wasn't planning to leave, Alex.'

His lips curved in a small, sardonic smile.

'Don't lie to me, darling. You've been with Tourell.'

There seemed little point in trying to conceal it further. Not knowing what to say, Maggie waited for some sign of anger. When none came, she raised her eyes curiously to Alexander's.

He was watching her through half closed eyelids, his expression unclear in the murky dawn light. A chorus of bird-song suddenly erupted outside, shattering the tension of the moment.

'You don't mind?' Maggie asked, emboldened by the exuberant music beyond the confines of the bedroom.

A small pulse ticked in Alexander's jaw, though when he spoke, he sounded calm and in control, as always.

'Mind? Dear Maggie – what do you take me for? Will you go to the casino again?'

Now, now was the time to tell him of Tourell's offer, to brave his inevitable reaction. Maggie was horrified to hear her voice shake as she ventured,

'Tourell offered me a job.'

Still, the expected explosion did not come. Alexander merely raised one eyebrow at her and smiled. Trembling inside, Maggie knew she should not be fooled by his inscrutable expression.

'That's good.'

She gaped at him and he chuckled softly.

'Don't look so surprised, Maggie. I take it you're considering Tourell's offer?'

'Well, I . . . no, not really. I told him I already have a job, working for you . . .' Maggie trailed off as she saw that, far from being satisfied by her loyalty, Alexander was not pleased.

'It would be useful to me to have someone inside Tourell's organisation. Won't you reconsider?'

Maggie shook her head slightly as the implication of his words sank in.

'You mean . . . you want me to *spy* on Tourell for you?'

'That's not quite the word I'd use.'

'Oh? What word would you use then, Alexander?'

'You'd be an observer rather than a spy.'

'Who's a spy?' said Antony regarding them both through sleep hazed eyes.

'Go back to sleep, Tony,' Alexander said indulgently, as if to an eavesdropping child, 'this doesn't concern you.'

Antony's eyes flickered from Maggie to Alexander and back again. Maggie inclined her head slightly and, satisfied that she didn't need any input from him, Antony lay down and closed his eyes. Within seconds he was asleep again.

Alexander waited until he was sure Antony was asleep before speaking again.

'Phone Tourell in the morning and tell him you'll take the job. It shouldn't be too difficult to arrange to report back to me once a week.'

With that he smiled and rolled over so that he was curled against Antony's slumberous back. Maggie watched him for a few moments as he settled and swiftly joined Antony in sleep.

When Tourell had offered her the job at the casino she had at first thought it might be a means of escape, a way to wean herself out from Alexander's hypnotic spell. Now he had brought it into his own sphere of influence and Maggie felt trapped.

It was a case of being damned if she didn't take the job, and damned if she did. Yet she wanted to see Tourell again. Burned for the feel of his cool, restrained lips against hers. And she knew that, whether or not she would eventually play along with Alexander's latest scheme, she would make that call in the morning. Purely because she desired Tourell.

Chapter Six

The Island Casino looked quite nondescript in the harsh light of day. Without the lure of the neon sign above the door, the black and gold striped canopy could have concealed a restaurant, or a high-class hotel as easily as a gamblers' paradise.

When she telephoned, Maggie was told she would be met at the door. Raising her hand to knock, she let it fall to her side as it was opened on her approach and she was shown inside.

'This way, please miss.'

Maggie smiled as she recognised the Italian who manned the desk in the evenings. Divested of his smart, impersonal tuxedo, he looked different somehow. In open-necked white shirt and neatly pressed jeans he emanated a friendliness which he had never shown whilst on duty.

Taking her along a corridor she had never seen before, the man showed her into what looked like an office suite. A wide expanse of soft dove-grey carpeting rolled to the double doorway opposite. Two black Chesterfields were placed, facing each other, by the window, a glass-topped chrome table between them. There were several small dishes on the table, filled with prawn crackers, peanuts and more exotic canapés.

The opposite wall was covered by glass-fronted units which held, in their various sections, ornaments, spirits and books. A grey wood desk with chrome furnishings stood in the opposite corner of the room with a large, black leather seat behind it, unoccupied.

Maggie spun on her heel as the door clicked softly shut behind her. It was so quiet in the room, it was unnerving. Not a whisper from the central heating, nor the soft whirr of a typewriter came from the doorway opposite.

Maggie strained her ears, expecting to hear a distant ring of a telephone, footsteps, *anything* to reassure her that there was normal office activity going on in the room beyond, that she was not alone. She could have walked over and opened the door, taken a look for herself. She took one step, two, but something made her hesitate. There was no logical explanation for her reluctance to look beyond the room into which she had been shown, but the feeling that she must restrain her curiosity was strong.

Instead, she wandered over to the bookcase and read the spines of the books, opening the glass door so that she could run her black-gloved forefinger over them. Whatever she had expected; novels, reference books, she had not expected this. Pauline Reage, The Marquis de Sade, Anais Nin – Tourell was quite a connoisseur of erotic literature.

Taking out an erotic adventure by Anais Nin, Maggie closed the glass door quietly. She helped herself to a dry martini, mixing it with a glass stick placed conveniently in a glass and took it and the book over to one of the low sofas.

The one small window which overlooked the buildings opposite the casino allowed in such inadequate daylight that the room was lit by several low wattage uplighters which cast parts of the room in shadow. Reading was wearing on the eyes, but Maggie was soon absorbed in the book, sipping frequently at her glass and helping herself to the tasty morsels which she presumed had been set out for her.

It was warm in the room and after a while, Maggie slipped off the tailored black jacket she was wearing over a short, black, rib-knit dress. Kicking off her shoes absently, she curled her legs beneath her and turned page after page, fascinated by the trials of the heroine in the book.

Time passed, though she was barely aware of its passage. She rose once to refill her glass, but she did not stop to wonder why no one had come for her. It was curiously intimate, sitting alone, isolated apart from the powerfully erotic prose she held on her lap.

It was arousing and Maggie was sure that, had she been at home, alone, she would have taken the book to bed with her. The ultimate in safe sex. She smiled, running the flat of her hand in a light caress across her thighs and between them.

The strange silence was restful once the ear became attuned to it, and Maggie was reluctant to move. Her eyes became heavy and began to droop, and the words blurred on the page before her.

It wouldn't hurt to rest her head on the back of the sofa, just for a little while. She would be sure to hear if anyone came through either door . . .

When Maggie awoke, it was dark outside. The dim lighting was even more inadequate without the back up of daylight and Maggie was seized by an unaccountable sense of unease. There was something . . . different about the room, something she couldn't quite put her finger on.

It came to her in a flash. The quality of the silence had changed. There was a sound in the room now, a soft, but unmistakable disruption of air. Maggie pressed herself instinctively against the cool leather cushions as she realised that it was the sound of someone breathing.

Convinced now that she was not alone, she cast her eyes around the room, her searching gaze settling on the desk in the corner which was hidden by shadows. As her eyes became accustomed to the gloom, she felt certain that there was someone sitting in the chair.

'Who's there?'

Her voice sounded high and nervous in the darkness and Maggie cleared her throat uncertainly. She was embarrassed to have been caught sleeping on the sofa. Her hair was escaping from the neat roll she had pinned at her nape and her clothes were twisted and uncomfortable.

Tugging self-consciously at the hemline of her dress, she peered into the gloom. A soft chuckle came from the corner.

'I'm sorry, Toots, I didn't mean to startle you. You were so peaceful, I didn't have the heart to waken you.'

The voice was low and husky, but definitely female and Maggie relaxed.

'Would you mind coming out into the light?'

The voice chuckled again.

'Of course. I'm Cynthia – Cyn for short.'

She laughed throatily and emerged into the dim light. Maggie saw that the woman was older than her, probably in her early forties, with the kind of face that obviously smiled a great deal. Her hair was short and dyed a cheerful shade of blonde which framed her rounded face in a frivolous bonnet.

Although she was of average height, Maggie gained

the impression that she was probably quite small framed. But she was generously covered, not seriously fat, but substantial in the way that many women of that age are without the benefit of regular exercise. Cyn gave the impression of pride in her body, an impression which was underlined by her clothes. Bright orange, wide-legged trousers in a silky material were matched with a canary yellow over-blouse with a handkerchief hemline which billowed exuberantly around her hips as she moved.

Realising she had been staring for longer than was polite, Maggie smiled awkwardly.

'I'm Maggie.'

Cyn nodded and held out her hand. Her grip was strong, the palm of her hand soft as it brushed against Maggie's. Close to, her blue-eyed gaze was direct and frankly appraising. There was an expression at the back of her eyes which Maggie intuitively recognised and she felt a shiver travel from the point of contact between their two hands through her body and down to her toes.

Breaking eye contact, Maggie went to fetch her bag from the sofa.

'I helped myself to a drink, I hope that was all right?'

Cyn shrugged, unperturbed by Maggie's withdrawal.

'Of course. I'm sorry you were kept waiting for so long. You found something to occupy you, I see?'

Maggie followed the direction of her gaze and saw the book she had been reading discarded on the coffee table. Thinking of its content, Maggie felt a blush steal into her cheeks. She had the uncomfortable feeling that this smiling woman was aware that her panties were still damp from the gentle arousal the book had provoked. Sweeping the book up, she bore it off to the bookcase.

'Did you enjoy it?'

Was she imagining that note of amusement in Cyn's voice? Maggie composed her features into a mask of cool politeness as she closed the glass door and turned back to the other woman.

'It was . . . interesting,' she said lightly.

This time there was no mistaking Cyn's amusement, for she laughed.

'Not shocking then?'

Maggie's surprise was genuine. 'Not at all . . .' she trailed off as she saw the light of challenge in the older woman's eyes.

Maggie smiled slowly.

. 'Do I start work this evening?'

'As it happens, we're short tonight, so you'll be thrown in at the deep end,' Cyn answered levelly, though her eyes still sparkled at Maggie. 'I'm the manager here – Tourell asked me to show you around.'

Maggie suppressed a dart of disappointment that Tourell had not thought it necessary to meet her himself. Perhaps she had misunderstood his interest in her? Cyn seemed to read her mind, for she gave a small smile as Maggie approached her.

'Tourell hopes you'll be free to join him for supper at the end of the day?'

Maggie smiled wryly, mildly embarrassed that she was so transparent.

'If I'm still standing by then!'

Cyn glanced pointedly at her spindle heeled sandals.

'We provide you with a uniform, but your shoes are your own affair. Obviously we don't want you clomping around in your Doc Marten's, but take it from me, you'll cripple yourself in those.'

Maggie felt foolish. She should have thought. It was too late to do anything about it now though, so she shrugged philosophically and preceded Cyn through the door.

The corridor which lay beyond it was carpeted in the same dove grey as the outer room. Their footsteps were muffled as they walked towards the double doors at the end. These opened out into a more workmanlike room, filled with filing cabinets and computer hardware. Maggie's eyes were drawn to one corner where a large, well secured safe stood in full view.

'Don't ever cross the red line around the safe,' Cyn warned her as she caught the direction of her gaze. 'That line marks the beginning of an infra-red force field. We have a very sophisticated security system here.'

Maggie noticed the red line marked on the grey carpet for the first time and made a mental note to give it a wide berth. Thank goodness Alexander had merely asked her to observe Tourell's operation and not to actually rob him!

The very idea brought her up short. Surely she would have refused had Alexander tried to get her to go that far? Wouldn't she?

'This way, Maggie.'

The sound of Cyn's voice made Maggie realise that the thought had literally made her stop in her tracks. Feeling foolish, she smiled vacuously and followed the other woman through a side door. The idea had shaken her, though, and she barely noticed her surroundings as they went downstairs to the croupiers' changing room.

'The shift change has already taken place, ' Cyn told her, indicating the clothing and make-up strewn untidily about the place with a sweep of her hand.

There was another woman waiting for them there, elderly, unsmiling, grey hair, grey eyes, grey complexion set against a nondescript black dress. Maggie was not introduced to her and she tensed as the woman whipped out a tape-measure and swiftly took Maggie's measurements without a word.

'This will be your locker,' Cyn told her, indicating a small metal cupboard at floor level and handing her a key.

Maggie realised then that she was expected to strip off her everyday clothes and change into her uniform. She felt strangely uncomfortable pulling her rib-knit dress over her head in fron of Cyn. She could feel the woman's eyes brush across her half naked body and her skin rose up in goose bumps.

Wishing she had worn something more concealing than the filmy black-lace bra and thong briefs with their matching garter belt holding up her sheer black stockings, Maggie folded her dress and placed it with her jacket and gloves in the locker, self-consciously bending at the knees.

Taking her hairbrush out of her bag, she turned her back on Cyn and unpinned her hair, brushing it smooth in the brightly lit mirror which ran in a horizontal strip around the changing room. Maggie could see the other woman's reflection in the mirror and she glanced frequently at her, unsure of her reactions.

Cyn's face was impassive, though Maggie noticed that her eyes roamed at will across Maggie's partially clothed body. Their eyes met once in the mirror and Cyn smiled faintly before Maggie hastily looked away. The atmosphere in the room seened to Maggie to be thick with tension as she reapplied a dark pink lipstick. She was relieved when the dour bearer of the tape-measure returned with a dress over one arm, wrapped in cellophane.

It was emerald green, peacock bright, made in a slippery, synthetic material which made Maggie cringe as she ran her fingers across it. It wasn't well made, the seams were skimpy and the zip at the back scratched slightly as she fastened it.

'Not what you're used to, Toots, I'd guess?'

'It's all right, ' Maggie demurred as Cyn stepped forward to help her do up the fiddly hook and eye fastening at the top of the zip.

Her reflection gazed back at her from the full-length mirror at the end of the room. The dress was a simple design with a cross-over bodice and slightly flared skirt. It was neither very long, nor very short, brushing against her calves in a shiny swirl.

'It makes you look very young.'

Maggie jumped as Cyn's voice sounded close to her ear. She was right; the casino uniform reminded Maggie of a party dress she had worn with pride on her sixteenth birthday. With her long, dark hair lying loose around her shoulders, softly framing her face, she looked vulnerable, ridiculously innocent.

She grimaced at her unfamiliar reflection and swiftly pinned her hair back up on top of her head, adding to her height and regaining some of her usual poise. Cynthia smiled knowingly at her.

'Ready?'

Maggie nodded.

'As ready as I'll ever be!'

The smoke and the low murmur of voices hit Maggie as she stepped through the double doors leading into the casino. The main body of the building must be sound-proofed, Maggie realised, which would explain the curious sense of isolation she had experienced whilst waiting in the outer office.

She could feel the casual brush of curious eyes over her as she followed Cyn to the roulette tables on one side of the room. Just before they reached them, they were waylaid by a large man, sweating in his lounge suit. He spoke to Cyn, though his eyes were fixed on Maggie's tightly covered breasts.

'I feel lucky tonight, Cyn,' he said heartily.

'On the table, you mean, Sam?'

The man gave a dirty laugh which made Maggie's flesh creep.

'You know the rules, Sam. Enjoy yourself on the tables, but don't upset my girls.'

Cyn smiled at him as she moved Maggie smartly on.

'You ought to know it's against the rules to fraternise with the members,' she said in an aside. She chortled as she saw the shudder Maggie was unable to hide. 'At least in theory.'

Maggie wanted to ask her what she meant, but was prevented by their arrival at the farthest table. It was manned by a young girl with a fresh-faced complexion with short blonde hair and limpid blue eyes which were glazed with boredom.

'Gina – this is Maggie who's just joined us. I'd like her to watch you for an hour or two. Maggie – stand here beside Gina and you'll soon get a feel for the game.'

Cyn unexpectedly squeezed Maggie's hand before marching briskly away. Maggie smiled at Gina and the girl nodded impassively.

'Place your bets, please.' She smothered a yawn with the back of her hand.

There was a last minute rush to place the piles of chips across the board. A middle-aged woman in a red suit placed her entire store on red thirty-six on the bottom right-hand corner of the table, while a bespectacled oriental gentleman scattered small piles of chips across the table so that it seemed to Maggie that he couldn't fail to win.

From the information board strung above them, Maggie saw that there were minimum and maximum bets allowed and that these limits varied from table to table. Gina activated the wheel and everyone concentrated on the spin of the small, gold coloured ball.

It settled on red twenty-one and the Chinaman cleaned up. The middle-aged woman turned away and an elderly gent in a pork-pie hat took her place. Maggie noticed that he placed his money for chips on the table

93

rather than the croupier's hand and soon learned that this was correct procedure.

'Does each table have its own chips?' she asked Gina.

Gina nodded and spun the wheel. She seemed disinclined to talk and Maggie concentrated on trying to understand the mechanics of the game. It wasn't long before she grew bored and she shifted her weight from one foot to the other.

A new client joined the table, replacing a small group of businessmen who had taken their winnings to the blackjack tables. Maggie wouldn't have noticed the new arrival but for the effect he had on Gina. Her back straightened, a sparkle came into her eyes and her demeanour seemed to undergo a complete transformation.

Maggie watched the man as he placed his chips. He was probably in his early sixties, though still handsome in an erect, English gentleman style. His dark hair was shot through with grey and his eyes were slightly faded as they rested on Gina. There was a definite crackle of electricity between the older man and the young croupier and Maggie was intrigued.

'How are you getting on, darlin'?'

She jumped as the fat man she had met earlier came up behind her and put his arm around her waist.

'Fine, thank you,' she replied tightly, moving easily out of his clumsy embrace. He immediately followed her, his fat, sweaty hands exploring the rounded globes of her bottom.

'I'm on a lucky streak tonight,' he told her.

His thick, bushy eyebrows waggled up and down suggestively and Maggie resisted the urge to laugh.

'Really? Well your lucky streak ends right here.'

She smiled sweetly and ground her spiked heel into the top of his foot.

His yell of pain and surprise brought Cynthia running. Taking in the situation with one practised glance, Cyn took the fat man by the elbow.

'Take Maggie for coffee, Gina, and tell Julie to take over your table. I'll be along in a minute. You come with me Sam and have a drink. Hush now, we don't want that kind of language in here. It's on the house . . .' Cynthia's voice faded as she steered the protesting member through the crowds towards the bar.

Gina didn't seem too happy to have to go to tea early. Maggie noticed the look that passed between her and the distinguished looking gentleman and realised that, by her actions, she had inadvertently upset the croupier.

'You sit there and wait for Cyn,' Gina told her curtly as she showed her into the Rest Lounge.

'But . . . where are you going?'

The look the younger girl shot at her was pure ice.

'Mind you own bloody business!'

Maggie shrugged and went to help herself to a cup of coffee from the jug percolating in the corner. It was sheer bliss to sit down. Already the soles of her feet were sore and the tendons in her ankles were aching. She had just stretched her legs under the table and closed here eyes when Cyn bustled into the room.

'Be a bit more subtle next time, Maggie, there's a good girl.'

Maggie opened one eye.

'Sorry,' she said meekly.

Cyn fetched herself a coffee and came to join her.

'Not that I blame you. If ever there was an argument to keep men in quarantine, Sam Weatherall is it.'

Maggie laughed, regarding Cyn shrewdly over the rim of her coffee cup.

'Can I ask you something?'

'Sure. Fire away.'

'Why is there a non fraternisation rule?'

Cynthia's overplucked blonde eyebrows shot up.

'Don't tell me you're having second thoughts about Sam?'

'Ugh, certainly not! I just wondered, that's all. I mean, I would have thought that this job would attract the type of girl who was looking for a rich boyfriend.'

Cyn shrugged her broad shoulders.

'Maybe. We have to be so careful – any hint that the casino was fronting for any kind of irregular activity and our licence would disappear quicker than a prostitute's knickers.'

Maggie smiled.

'I see.'

'So don't go getting any ideas, Maggie.'

Maggie shook her head.

'It's all right, Cyn, you don't need to worry about me.'

Cynthia looked at her hard. Her lips twisted in a wry smile.

'I'm glad to hear it. Well, I'd best be getting back on the floor. You take another ten minutes, Maggie, then take yourself off to the blackjack tables. All right?'

Maggie nodded. After Cyn had gone and Maggie had finished her coffee, she decided to go down to the cloakroom to renew her lipstick. Something made her pause just outside the door. Pressing her ear up against it, Maggie realised there was a muffled sound coming from inside.

She pushed the door ajar very, very slowly until she could see into the room. The entire room was telescoped into the full-length mirror at the end. Maggie's hand flew up to her mouth to stifle a gasp of surprise as she recognised the girl who was on all fours in the corner.

Gina's dress had been pulled down to the waist and her little, pink-tipped breasts hung down like two small, ripe fruits. Her eyes were closed as she rocked rhythmically back and forth on her hands and knees. Her skirt was gathered up about her waist and her bare bottom shone white under the harsh fluorescent strip lights.

The man with the grey streaked hair was driving into her from behind, his long, thin white penis pumping in and out of Gina's tight behind with gathering speed.

Neither party noticed Maggie watching their reflection from the doorway.

'Bark for me,' the man gasped, 'bark like a dog!'

Maggie's eyebrows rose as Gina began to yip softly, opening her mouth and panting heavily. She could see the perspiration break out on the man's brow as his body began to convulse and at that moment, Gina's eyes opened and locked with Maggie's in the mirror.

Shock chased away the glazed expression and she narrowed her eyes viciously. Maggie smiled at her and put her forefinger to her lips to indicate that she wasn't going to give her away. Then she stepped back and closed the door softly behind her.

Gina's eyes sought hers across the gaming room as Maggie took up her new position next to Andrew, the croupier on the blackjack table to which Cyn had assigned her. Maggie passed her a conspiratorial smile and confusion chased across Gina's features.

No doubt the other girl was afraid that Maggie would use her knowledge of what she had seen to have Gina fired from the casino. Maggie smiled to herself. It might be useful to let her go on thinking that for a while, she might need Gina as she settled in.

Gina couldn't know that her job did not hold the slightest interest for Maggie. It was the proof that at least one of the girls used their position at the casino for their own ends that was valuable to her. For it gave her something tangible to report back to Alexander.

Chapter Seven

M aggie enjoyed watching the blackjack far more than she had the roulette. Here, an element of skill was involved and it was fascinating to watch as each player, all male at this particular table, worked their own system.

Some relied completely on chance, some appeared to be sticking to a rigid pattern of bets, whilst others earnestly studied the cards overturned in an attempt to work out the probabilities involved. The atmosphere, despite the not inconsiderable amounts of money being gambled, was relatively relaxed and Andrew, the croupier, appeared to know most of the players by name. In between dealing the cards he indulged in a light and easy banter which made Maggie smile.

He was a personable young man, skinny in a gawky, boyish sort of way. Maggie could see that he would likely fill out nicely as the years passed, especially if he took the trouble to work out and eat properly. His skin was clear, his jaw smooth and slightly pink looking, as if he had recently, and unnecessarily, shaved.

Catching her eye, he grinned and made way for her

to deal the next hand. For all her self-assurance, Maggie found her hands trembling as she slid each card out of the shoe. Glancing at Andrew for reassurance, she offered a further card to the first player.

To her surprise, the hand was played within minutes and she made no mistakes when she gathered in the losing chips. Pleased with herself, she felt quite sorrry when Andrew resumed his position.

Apart from that short foray into dealership, Maggie's first night at the casino consisted of watching the play and observing how the other croupiers worked. If it hadn't been for the task set for her by Alexander, she would have walked out before closing time, she was not used to such inactivity.

The banal, continuous music grated on her nerves as the night progressed. The aching in her feet grew steadily worse until sharp, needle-like pains were shooting intermittently up her calves and even her knees began to feel the strain.

She was used to late nights, often slept through the day to compensate for her nocturnal hours, but there was a whole world of difference between partying all night and working. Or rather, watching other people work. Thinking of supper with Tourell was like a reward for her fortitude.

She saw Tourell only once during the evening. It was soon after her brief foray into the role of a dealer. Standing, marvelling at the speed at which Andrew dealt the cards, she felt the small hairs on the back of her neck stand up and bristle.

Turning her head slowly, Maggie was unsurprised to see Tourell standing by the carefully guarded entrance to the private room. Dressed as always in a well-cut, black tuxedo, he looked no different from the rest of the largely male management team. Yet it was easy to see that Tourell was no mere employee.

Perhaps it was something in the way he held himself, a self-assurance about his posture which signalled he was no ordinary man. Maggie was aware that she was not the only woman in the room looking at him. Yet he seemed to have eyes only for her.

Her mouth and throat dried under his intense scrutiny. Even from across the room she could sense that his eyes were travelling slowly down the length of her body and she unconsciously straightened her back. Her skin tingled, a tight knot of sexual tension forming in the pit of her stomach. Warm tendrils of anticipation curled through her limbs, making her tremble.

If he could have this effect on her, from this distance . . . Maggie shivered involuntarily, aware that her nipples had grown hard in response to her thoughts. Without looking, she knew their outline would be clearly visible through the cheap fabric of her dress and she wondered if Tourell was aware of her arousal from across the room.

Suddenly, unexpectedly, he turned away, and, without acknowledging her, he disappeared into the private room. A cold wave of disappointment swept through her body and Maggie realised that she had been longing for him to come over to her, to speak to her. To take her away.

The long night passed without further incident and Maggie sagged with relief as the casino doors were finally closed behind the last customer at four. Filing into the changing room with the rest of the croupiers, she only half listened to their bright chatter.

It was a relief to exchange the cheap, shiny green dress for the luxurious softness of her own. Letting down her hair, she bent from the waist and brushed it vigorously, allowing the blood to rush to her head.

As she straightened, she was aware of Gina standing

close by, watching her. Their eyes met in the mirror and Maggie smiled.

'Do you have far to go home?'

She noted the look of confusion that passed across the other girl's features and smiled to herself.

'Are you going to say anything?' Gina blurted, her face a sullen mask.

'To whom?'

'To Cyn, of course. Or Tourell.'

It was curious, the way everyone referred to Tourell by that name, never 'mister', or by a first name, just 'Tourell'.

'I shouldn't think so,' she replied truthfully, leaning forward towards the mirror to reapply her lipstick.

'Why not?'

Maggie shrugged. 'No reason to. Does that old gent pay you well?'

Gina's cheeks flushed and she shrugged. 'Enough.'

'Good.' Maggie put her lipstick in her bag and turned to face Gina. 'Is there anyone elsc?'

'Mind your own bloody business!'

'Maybe it could be my business,' Maggie replied lightly.

Gina's eyes narrowed.

'I doubt it – most of the men here like their girls really young.'

It was a calculated insult and Maggie almost laughed aloud. Instead, she merely picked up her bag and brushed past the girl on her way out of the changing room. 'Miaow!' she commented pleasantly. 'Or should I say *woof*?'

She could feel Gina's eyes boring resentfully into her back as she stepped smartly through the door.

Gina was quickly forgotten as Maggie tried to find her way to Tourell's basement apartment. The main floor of the casino was in darkness as she let herself back in. Everything had been cleared away by the catering staff and an eerie silence had settled over the empty gaming tables.

Maggie felt as if she should tiptoe across to the doors on the far side of the room, but her aching feet would not let her. Glancing from side to side, she had the distinct sensation that the deep shadows held danger, that the room was not as empty as it appeared.

Spooked, she half ran across the floor, dodging between the tables and wrenching open the door on the far side. The Private Room was still and dark, the air thick with the evening's smoke which added to the previous evening's, and the one before that. Maggie wondered, inconsequentially, whether the room was ever aired. There were several doors leading off it and Maggie stood for a moment, trying to remember which one led down to Tourell's apartment.

A sound from the larger room behind her made her jump. Sure that everyone had left in the armada of taxis which arrived each evening, Maggie instinctively pressed herself back into the shadows. Holding her breath, she watched with increasing horror as the door handle moved slowly down and the door began to open.

Visions of Sam Weatherall or Gina's beau raced through her head. Both had reason to dislike her after this evening and the entire atmosphere of the deserted casino had made her uneasy. Besides, no one had any right to be creeping about the place like that at this time of night.

Imagination running riot, Maggie cast desperately about for something to use as a weapon should her worst fears come to light. There was only the dealer's wooden card-shoe on one of the tables. Snatching it up, Maggie felt the heavily embossed brass rim under her fingers and was marginally reassured.

As the door opened fully and the shape of a man presented itself, Maggie raised the shoe up in the air, bringing it down with a grunt. She cried out in alarm as her arm was caught mid descent and she was thrown bodily onto her back across the card table. The air was driven out of her with a whoosh as the man's heavier frame came down on top of her, pinioning her to the table.

All Maggie's worst nightmares seemed to be about to come true. Somewhere in the back of her mind she was aware that he was speaking to her, but in her panic his voice seemed to be coming from a long way off and she could not make out what he was saying.

The man was frighteningly strong. She felt puny in comparison, and totally helpless. His face was so close to hers she could feel his warm breath on her cheek, yet his features were indistinguishable in the darkness.

Maggie was incapable of reason, all she could think was that if she screamed loudly enough, for long enough, Tourell would hear her and come to her rescue. The sound tore from her throat and she felt the man wince. He shook her by the shoulders and she was aware again that he was saying something to her, trying to make her quieten.

Maggie merely screamed harder, remembering now that the whole building was sound-proofed. The man cursed, loudly, before covering her mouth with his. Maggie's scream vibrated in his throat as he held her head immobile. It was not a punishing kiss, but it was a determined one and it had the desired effect of stopping her from screaming.

Gradually, Maggie's hysteria subsided as she realised that she recognised the scent of the man's skin, musk and woodsmoke. And at once she knew who it was.

'Tourell . . .' she whispered against his roving lips.

Slowly, he lifted his face from hers and allowed her

103

to raise her arms. The darkness was still too thick for her to see him clearly, but as she ran the pads of her fingers over his face, she could feel the deep line between his eyebrows, the defiant cleft of his chin and the grooves which ran from nose to mouth and she knew without doubt that it was him.

'Oh Tourell, you gave me such a fright!'

She saw the glint of white teeth as he smiled.

'I'm a little shaken myself,' he said wryly, removing the dealer's shoe which was still clutched firmly in her fist.

Maggie felt her skin grow warm and was glad for the cover of darkness.

'I . . . I'm sorry, I thought . . .'

'Did you?'

He didn't seem to be in a hurry to let her up from the table and for the first time Maggie was aware of the hard length of his body pressing into her. Her heart-rate quickened and she put out her tongue to moisten her dry lips.

'I couldn't find the way . . .'

Tourell rose slowly, as if he were as reluctant as she to break the contact between them. Maggie shivered as his weight was removed and he put out a hand to help her up.

'There's a corridor which leads off from the rest room,' he told her as he led her back through the main body of the casino to the reception area. 'I sent Cyn for you. When you were nowhere to be found, I came to look for you myself.'

Feeling foolish, Maggie protested.

'But why didn't you put on the lights?'

'They're on a timer mechanism. To override it would have caused no end of problems. Besides, I hadn't anticipated quite such a heated welcome!'

They were moving downwards now and Maggie fancied she recognised this corridor.

'This place is like a rabbit warren,' she complained mildly.

Tourell laughed, a rich, gravelly chuckle which scraped deliciously over her skin. 'It keeps unwanted visitors at bay.'

They were still holding hands and he pulled her up short before they reached the door at the end. Maggie caught her breath as he put one hand behind her head and drew her closer to him. His eyes were like mirrors, reflecting the maelstrom of emotion which was tumbling in her breast.

'The only trouble is, they keep some visitors who *are* wanted out too.'

His voice was so low, so hypnotic. Maggie's legs felt weightless as she swayed imperceptibly towards him. She jumped as his mood inexplicably changed.

'Come on – there's time for you to shower before dinner if you'd like to freshen up. You're not tired yet, are you Maggie?'

Confused, yes, tired . . . she wasn't so sure as he opened the door to the apartment and they were once more enclosed in its curiously cloistered atmosphere.

'That . . . would be lovely,' she agreed.

Tourell showed her into the shower cubicle and closed the door behind them. Maggie's eyebrows shot up in surprise as he casually sat down on the small stool in the corner of the room, as if it was the most natural thing in the world for him to watch her shower. As if he had the right.

There were two ways she could play this, she thought to herself as she turned her back on him and slipped off her shoes. Either she could act with a primness which was entirely out of keeping with her character and insist that he leave. Or she could make the most of the opportunity and see what transpired.

Knowing that there was no contest between the two options, Maggie smiled to herself as she began to take off her clothes. Tourell watched her impassively as she turned slowly to face him. Hooking her fingers under the hem of her short dress, she eased it up and over her head, turning it inside out on the way.

Her nipples hardened under their filmy, black lace covering as the warm air caressed her skin. Tourell's eyes brushed over them as they travelled down to where her garter belt clung to the slender dip of her waist. Seeing his gaze linger on the small keyhole of light between her thighs, Maggie turned round slowly. Bending forward to unfasten her stockings, she treated him to an uninterrupted view of the perfect white globes of her buttocks, neatly dissected by the thong of her briefs.

Silence hung around them like an itchy blanket. Maggie longed for him to say something, *anything*, but when she turned back towards him, Tourell merely watched her, unsmiling, his expression unreadable.

Turning on the shower, Maggie stripped off her underwear without ceremony and stepped into the cubicle. The water temperature was just right, neither too hot, nor too cold and Maggie simply stood beneath the spray for several minutes, enjoying the sensation of the water cascading over her naked skin.

She could feel Tourell's steady gaze on her through the frosted glass of the shower cubicle. Knowing he was watching her made her skin tingle with awareness, a heavy, honeyed heat making her limbs feel heavy.

Suddenly, her awkwardness fled and she began to enjoy herself. Ever conscious of Tourell's presence, she played to her audience, linking her hands behind her head to lift her wet hair away from her neck and thrusting her chest out in deliberate provocation. Aware that he would be able to see the water streaming down the valley between her breasts through the misted glass, she let him look his fill.

There were two bars of soap by the shower-head; one smelled of musk, the other of roses in the early morning. Maggie rubbed her hands together to work up the rose fragranced lather and spread the creamy result down her neck and across her breasts. Her nipples were two hard buttons under her palms as she circled her hands slowly over them and Maggie closed her eyes.

Her hands slipped lower, over the gentle swell of her belly and down to the tender pink flesh of her hair-free mons. Forgetting, for the moment, that she was not alone, she allowed her fingers to play gently over the smooth mound, teasing herself until she felt the delicate flesh within swell and become slick with desire.

Her breath caught in her chest as she remembered the man watching her. Why didn't Tourell get up, strip off his own clothes and join her? She ached for the feel of his strong arms coming round her, his naked flesh pressing against hers. What was stopping him?

Opening her eyes, she turned her face towards the stool where he sat, an invitation ready on her tongue, her arms reaching out in welcome. She blinked, her hands falling loosely by her side as she saw that the stool was empty, her eyes skittering towards the door. It was just closing gently, a cool draught of air heralding his departure.

Maggie's desire fled rapidly, to be replaced by a cold knot of disappointment which lay heavily in the pit of her stomach. She wasn't used to rejection, and it left an unpleasant taste in her mouth. She felt foolish. Presumptuous. And yet, she had been sure that Tourell had expected . . . something.

Turning off the water, she saw that he had hung an

enormous, fluffy white towel on the ring beside the shower cubicle. Rubbing herself vigorously all over, Maggie reflected that Tourell had been right about one thing; the shower had refreshed her. She didn't feel tired any more, if she discounted her still aching feet.

There was a soft, white, terry towelling robe hanging on the door. Assuming that was for her use too, and unable to bear the prospect of putting her tight clothes and high-heeled shoes on again just yet, Maggie snuggled into it, belting it tightly round her narrow waist. Leaving her damp hair lying loose on her shoulders, she emerged, glowing pinkly from the shower.

Tourell was lounging comfortably on a sofa, a book open on his knee, looking for all the world as though he had never followed her into the shower. He looked up as she closed the bathroom door and smiled enquiringly.

'The mirror in there is all steamed up – do you have another where I can renew my make-up?'

'You look lovely, Maggie, like a fresh summer flower. Please don't bother to gild the lily on my account. Come – sit down. I thought we'd have a simple supper here on the sofa.'

Maggie shrugged her shoulders slightly and went to sit next to him. Her eyes moved restlessly to the hard, brocade-covered wing-backed chair where she had sat the last time she had been here. A pulse beat dully between her legs as she remembered.

Such total abandonment . . . Glancing at Tourell from beneath her lashes, Maggie saw that he had noticed the direction of her gaze and knew what she was thinking. His eyes rested thoughtfully on her, though his mouth smiled, as if his memory of her last visit brought him pleasure. Feeling the heat seeping into her cheeks, Maggie averted her eyes from his, looking at her hands, folded nervously in her lap. At that moment it seemed the only safe place to look.

The sofa was very low, but with a high back for comfort. The softness of the deep red velvet caressed the bare skin at the back of her knees. As before, the open plan apartment was lit by numerous lamps which bathed them in their suffused, golden glow.

'Are you hungry?' Tourell asked her politely.

Maggie was surprised to realise that she was and her attention turned to the low, glass-topped coffee table in front of them. It had been laid with a selection of dishes, oysters arranged in their shells, fat, succulent looking grapes and tiny, bite-size portions of cheese, skewered with fresh pineapple. Asparagus tips and fresh caviar heaped high glistened temptingly. Maggie's mouth began to water.

Tourell picked up a plate and filled it with a selection before handing it to Maggie.

'Here. I like to see you eat.'

His eyes twinkled at her as her appetite suddenly receded. Then he turned his attention to his own plate and Maggie began to pick at the food. It was delicious. Everything seemed designed to slip effortlessly down her throat with the barest effort from her. Sipping at the glass of crisp Sancerre he poured for her, she watched as Tourell ate with obvious enjoyment, his eyes never far from hers.

'How did you like your first night in the casino?' he asked her when they had both eaten their fill.

They were lounging comfortably on the sofa, a moody classical piece on the stereo. Maggie felt replete from the delicious food and wine which had combined to dull slightly the excitement which ran through her in Tourell's presence and she felt relaxed and happy. She grimaced at his question.

'My feet hurt!' she told him with feeling.

Tourell laughed.

'Let me see.'

Maggie did not resist as he lifted one of her bare feet and placed it on his lap. She shifted slightly on the sofa so that she was in a more comfortable position, her back against the side of the settee, and he lifted the other foot so that she was virtually lying on the sofa, at right angles to him.

Maggie's tension returned with a vengeance. Tourell's hands were large with long, sensitive fingers tapering from broad palms. Cradling the sole of one foot in his hand, he began to massage her toes with his other hand. Maggie moaned softly as he manipulated each toe, sending countless messages of bliss along each little nerve ending.

Next he stroked the sensitive skin on the top of her foot from ankle to toes before rubbing the sole of her foot with firm, circular motions. He began to massage her sole in earnest with a firm, knowing touch and Maggie relaxed against the moiré silk of the sofa cushions.

Closing her eyes, she revelled in his attention as he gave the other foot the same treatment as the first. By the time he progressed to her calves, she felt as if she could purr. Little vibrations of pleasure travelled up her legs in ever-increasing waves in response to his expert touch.

Maggie squeezed her thighs together tightly, conscious of the gathering moisture there. It amused, yet embarrassed her that she should become so aroused when his hands had roamed no further than her knees!

He was caressing her knees now and gradually Maggie became aware that there was a difference in the way he was touching her. Before his touch had been almost impersonal, similar to a professional masseur. Gradually, though, he was stroking her more as a lover would, lingering over the delicacy of her ankle-bone, seeking out the soft skin in that tender place behind her knee.

Maggie shivered as his fingers roamed again to her feet and he lifted one a little higher, off his lap. His lips were warm as he kissed the tip of each toe, little, butterfly kisses which sent flutters of delight from her toes to her stomach.

Need, urgent and basic, pulled at her insides as he drew her big toe into the warm, moist cavern of his mouth. Maggie had never thought of her toes as being part of an erogenous zone before, but she knew that she would never take them for granted again. She almost groaned aloud in protest as he withdrew her toe and brushed his lips acros the inner arch of her foot and up to her ankle.

Opening her eyes slowly, she saw that he was watching her face with a curious intensity, almost as if he were gauging her reaction to his touch. Seeing her looking at him, he smiled gently.

'You have such beautiful skin, so white and soft,' he murmured as he stroked the back of her knee with the very tips of his fingers.

Maggie could have told him that the perfection of her skin was due to the amount of time and care Alexander and Antony lavished on it, but she did not. Instead, she smiled seductively at him and moved slightly so that he was encouraged to move his fingers further up her legs.

He did not disappoint her. Little thrills travelled along her nerve-endings as he began to describe small, ticklish circles across the sensitive skin of her inner thigh. As he neared his ultimate destination, Maggie's thighs relaxed, parting slightly in anticipation of his touch.

He smiled slightly at her small, unconscious moue of disappointment as his fingers lifted slowly, almost regretfully, from her skin. Dispensing swiftly with the

111

tie belt of her robe, Tourell peeled back the sides of it, exposing Maggie's nakedness beneath.

She caught her breath as his eyes dropped from hers and feasted openly on her body. She arched her back, knowing without conceit that he could not fail to be satisfied with what he saw. Maggie knew without looking down that her nipples had grown taut, pointing rosily towards him in blatant invitation. Longing to feel his fingers pressing on them, his hot mouth suckling their sweetness, Maggie sighed, so deeply that it vibrated through her body to her toes and fingertips.

Tourell, though, seemed content to look for now, one hand reaching out for the dish of caviar on the coffee table. Maggie could not keep her eyes off his hands, the long, sensitive fingers curling round the small dish whilst with the other hand he hooked the first two fingers into the plate of caviar and offered it to her.

Without thinking, she opened her mouth and sucked it from his fingers, drawing them into her mouth and licking them clean with her tongue.

'Taste good?' he murmured, his face close to hers.

She nodded, her eyes closing momentarily as she swallowed. Tourell reached for her glass and held it against her lips, tipping it slightly so that the cool, crisp white wine chased the caviar down her throat.

As he removed the glass from her lips, he tipped it slightly, and cold wine splashed across Maggie's breasts, making her gasp aloud. The heat of his mouth was in erotic counterpoint to the chill of the wine as he took one nipple into it and sucked gently on it.

Maggie groaned, allowing herself to relax into his arms as he raised his head and pulled her against him. Limp as a rag doll, she felt him turn her so that her still towelling covered back was leaning against him. He was still fully clothed and Maggie found the thought of her nakedness against his clothes powerfully erotic.

112

She gasped as his hands roamed over her belly and parted her thighs. Lifting one arm up, behind her head, she encircled his neck, tucking her legs beneath her and rising up on her knees, her head twisting so that she could press her lips against the warm skin of his throat.

Vaguely, she was aware that he had again reached across to the table. This time, she saw through heavy-lidded eyes, he picked up a small, lacquered box which had escaped her notice before. Her eyes closed as, with his other hand, he began to stroke gently along the crease between her legs.

Her most intimate flesh opened eagerly to him, inviting him to probe deeper, to caress the silky pink folds which surrounded the core of her femininity. He had partially aroused her more than once already this evening, leaving her hanging on, unfulfilled. Now Maggie knew it would not take much to tip her over the edge into a vortex of ecstasy.

She was barely aware of what he was doing with his other hand. Welcoming the invasion of his first and second fingers into the moist crevices of her labia, she was only vaguely aware that he had opened her, was holding her apart as, with his other hand, he touched something rounded, cold and smooth against her entrance.

Whatever it was, it was hard, unyielding. Maggie's eyes flew open in shocked surprise as he suddenly, deftly, slipped it inside her. Tourell cupped one hand beneath her as she tensed and tried to expel the object.

'Ssh! Relax, there's nothing to worry about.'

His voice was hypnotically reassuring, but still Maggie tried to wriggle away from his hand. It wasn't that what he was doing to her was unpleasant, in fact she could already feel little tremors of sensation radiating out from the centre of her, but she had been taken by surprise.

'What—'

'There's another . . . ready?'

He inserted a second object gently inside her and Maggie relaxed as she heard the familar clack of the Chinese love balls as they rolled together inside her. Oh God, how did he know this was guaranteed to send her wild?

Maggie stretched her back as Tourell gently impelled her to lean forward, opening herself even wider to him as he manipulated the small chain which connected the two metal balls. At first, he merely held it steady, allowing Maggie to get used to the intensity of feeling they had invoked.

The balls rolled inside her with a momentum of their own, like a metronome, and she clenched her most intimate muscles in a desperate attempt to keep them in place. They felt so large, filling her almost to the point of discomfort.

Maggie felt a fine sheen of perspiration break out over her skin as Tourell put one arm around her waist to support her, the fingers of his other hand still looped around the chain of the love balls.

Leaning across her, he pressed his lips against the tender skin below her ear. Maggie could feel the shape of his erection against the smooth curve of her hip and she was glad of this evidence that he was not as unmoved as he appeared. Beginning to rock her gently back and forth, he set up a rhythm in the balls that made Maggie gasp.

His breath was warm in her ear as he whispered,

'Let it come, Maggie, show me how you enjoy it.'

His voice mesmerised her as she concentrated on keeping hold of the balls. Her body seemed to be fighting against their cold, metallic intrusion even while their presence drove her on to new heights of awareness.

'How did Alexander take the news that you were coming to work for me?'

Maggie frowned as she tried to make sense of his words. The question, put with such seductive, deadly calm, seemed to be coming from far away, like hearing music coming from a neighbour's room, it had so little to do with what was happening between them.

Tourell bit gently on her earlobe and tugged very slightly on the chain. Maggie squeezed her pelvic floor hard as the balls threatened to slip out of her. She couldn't let them go now, not when she was so close . . .

'Tell me, Maggie, tell me about Alexander.'

Maggie's tongue felt swollen in her mouth, as if it had been coated in honey. As Tourell stopped rocking her, she realised that he was determined that she should reply. Struggling to grasp her thoughts through the mist of lust clouding her mind, Maggie tried to form the words.

'What . . . do you want?' she slurred.

'You, Maggie. I want you.'

She tried to wriggle her bottom, to start the love balls moving again, for they had stilled and lay heavily inside her. Tourell, though, held her fast and she realised that he had taken total control of her body and its reactions. Only Tourell could grant her the release she so craved.

'Yes,' she whispered.

He rocked her very slightly again. Maggie tasted salt as she ran the tip of her tongue along her upper lip. Tourell was speaking again, his voice almost musical in her ear.

'Why did you change your mind?'

'Change . . .?'

He tweaked the chain and the balls rolled inside her, making her cry out in delight.

'Did Alexander send you to spy on me?'

Alarm bells began to ring in her mind, but they were drowned out by the roaring of the blood in her ears as she neared her climax.

'Nooo . . .' she sighed. 'Oh please!'

Tourell was holding her still again and, once more, she could feel the delicious sensations begin to ebb away, so that they were just beyond her reach. Tears of frustration started in her eyes.

'Tell me.'

The words whispered over her ear, like voices in the wind. *Tell me*. She tried to think why she shouldn't tell him about Alexander, but her brain would not function properly. All she cared about was that he should resume the rocking, allow her to follow the sweet torture of the love balls to its inevitable conclusion.

'Yes,' she sighed, 'please . . .'

She felt, rather than heard him chuckle.

'Please what?'

He kissed her cheek; little, licking kisses which made her shiver. She didn't want to plead any more, didn't want to debase herself when she didn't know what it was he wanted from her. She wished she could see his face, read his expression.

'Please . . .' she murmured again.

Her belly sagged with relief as he began the rocking again, though his voice continued, relentless, in her ear.

'Please rock me? Please let me come?'

'Yes!'

It was building again now, small waves rippling from her belly out to her limbs, bathing her with heat, making her hair stick damply to her brow.

'Please forgive me? Please don't let me go? Please fuck me?'

'Yes, oh yes!'

Maggie was fast reaching the point beyond control now. Grinding her bottom against his thighs, she tried

116

to bear down without losing the precious balls. Her head moved from side to side in frustration as she reached for that elusive release, the final thrust of which kept escaping her.

Tourell seemed aware of her predicament, for he licked the whorls of her ear, flooding her mind with words that she did not understand, though the sound of his voice inflamed her. Until, gradually, the sense of his words filtered through the fog of desire which had enshrouded her reason.

'I'll rock you, I'll let you come, in a moment. I'll forgive you – sweet, sweet Maggie, I'll even fuck you. But you have to do something to me in return.'

Even though her body continued to race towards the ultimate abandonment, Maggie was able to gather sufficient wit to gasp, 'What?'

'I want you to report back to me on Alex.'

Somewhere in the back of her mind, Maggie was aware that his last words should have had the effect of a dousing of cold water.

'You . . . you want me to *spy* for you?' she panted, her breath coming in short, almost painful gasps.

'That's right.'

'But . . . Tourell, why on earth would I do that?'

She twisted her head awkwardly and collided with the glitter of his eyes. Tourell held her gaze for an interminable moment. He seemed to be able to see into her very mind, so intense was his scrutiny.

He smiled slowly then and began to pull on the chain which dangled from her vagina. Maggie cried out in dismay as the balls began to slip inexorably from her body. Her senses reeled as the bearing down sensation intensified and one metal ball was expelled from within her with excruciating slowness. She knew, without a doubt, that when the other followed, *then* she would come.

Her brows knitted together in a frown as Tourell stopped pulling. He held her eyes, smiling as he saw her frustration.

'Please?' she whispered.

The beginning of her orgasm was already feathering along her spine. She could not bear it if she was to be denied after all this time, when she was so close. She would do anything to make him finish what he had started.

Signalling this to him with her eyes, she implored him to continue. Tourell searched her eyes, smiling as he found the capitulation which he sought. He held her gaze as he gently pulled on the chain and the second ball slipped slowly out of her body.

His face blurred before Maggie's eyes as the sliding sensation tipped her over the edge. Her entire body shuddered, convulsing around the empty space left by the expulsion of the love balls. Lights exploded before her eyes, like fireworks and she shook her head from side to side in passionate denial as she realised how completely she had given herself to Tourell.

And when, finally, her climax began to ebb away, leaving her exhausted, wrung out, she found that he was still watching her with that calm, knowing expression. His eyes seemed to ask a question of her as she stared at him. To Maggie's dismay, a sob escaped her lips.

Tourell smiled. Then, and only then did he lower his head and cover her mouth with his.

Chapter Eight

*H*is lips were firm, his mouth warm and inviting. Maggie's limbs turned to liquid heat as he teased and tasted her lips, tracing the tender skin within her lower lip with the very tip of his tongue.

She clung to him, her fingers with their long, red-painted fingernails digging into his shoulders, relying on him to keep her balanced. Without his strength she would have collapsed in a crumpled heap on the sofa, so weak was she with longing.

Tourell spent a long time kissing her, waiting for her to recover. Maggie was content to let him make the pace. Somewhere in the back of her mind, she knew she was being manipulated, but she could not gather sufficient energy to care.

At this moment the fact that Tourell had persuaded her to report Alexander's activities to him mattered not one jot. All that she cared about was that he should go on kissing her, that he should not withdraw and send her home as he had before.

She wanted this man, wanted him with a need that went beyond pure lust. Even now, when her innermost flesh was aching and spent she could feel the honeyed moisture lying slick across the sensitive folds of skin.

Tourell's fingers touched her gently there and she felt his lips curve in a smile of satisfaction as he felt her readiness. Bending his dark head he lathed one tumescent nipple with his tongue, drawing the entire aureole into his mouth and suckling on it.

Maggie could feel an answering pull deep in her gut. Tangling her fingers in the crisp hair at the side of his head, she held him to her, throwing back her head so that her long hair fell like a soft curtain down her back. The towelling robe had slipped off her shoulders now and, releasing Tourell, she shrugged it off so that she could put her arms around him.

His eyes were over-bright as he watched her, his fingers straying to the buttons of his shirt. Maggie lay back against the cushions and watched as he removed his shirt. He had a powerful, well-sculpted chest, lightly dusted with coarse, dark hair, sprinkled with grey. Holding her gaze, he unbuckled his belt and stood to remove his trousers, revealing crisp white cotton boxer-shorts.

Maggie's eyes were drawn irresistibly towards the tumescence straining against the button placket and she reached forward to release it. He had a beautiful cock, long and straight with a smooth, bulbous head already standing clear of its foreskin.

It twitched slightly in response to the coolness of her hand as she enclosed him. Drawing him down towards her again, Maggie relished the opportunity to kiss him while she slowly ran her hand back and forth over his penis.

Tourell sighed against her lips as she traced the tiny, moist crease at the tip gently with her thumbnail. Cradling his testicles with her other hand, she found they were warm and heavy beneath their protective covering of hair.

She didn't want to wait any longer. Adjusting her body so that the tip of his penis nudged at the opening of her body, she ran her fingertips feverishly across his face, tracing the outline of his nose, his jaw, the delicate skin of his eyelids.

'Tour-*ell*,' she breathed, making the word sound like a plea.

Tourell paused only for long enough to slip on a condom. He balanced himself, poised to thrust into her, making her wait an excruciating second longer. Smiling wickedly, he eased himself in, slowly, inexorably filling her until at last the full length of him was sheathed in her hot, silky flesh.

Maggie's arms came about his shoulders and her eyes closed as he lay there on top of her, content for now merely to be resting inside her. Just as she thought she would cry out in frustration, he began to move, hardly at all at first, just enough to send little feathers of delight travelling along Maggie's nerve-endings. Her already oversensitised flesh caught the urgency transmitted by his and it began to tingle.

As the dry tinder of her desire caught fire and began to burn, Maggie moved her hips in rhythm with his, meeting each deepening thrust, welcoming him inside her body with joyous abandon. Tourell's face was tense above hers as he neared the point of no return.

A film of perspiration broke out on his forehead and his skin grew hot beneath Maggie's palms. Now when their bodies collided, their skins clung together, reluctant to part. Soon her sweat was mingling with his, his limbs tangling with hers. the thought of Tourell, this cool, oh so controlled man surrendering himself to her added piquancy; to Maggie's pleasure.

She watched him closely as he neared his climax,

revelling in the conflict she could see mirrored in his eyes as he fought the moment off. Suddenly gripped by a determination that *she* should be the one to decide the exact moment of his release, Maggie squeezed her muscles around his marauding cock, milking him with every ounce of skill she had learned.

He came then, as she had intended, but silently, his lips pressed tightly together, denying her the ultimate victory of seeing him lose control. To Maggie's disappointment, he withdrew from her almost immediately, dispensing neatly with the condom before lying alongside her on the sofa, unselfconscious in his nakedness.

Considering the narrowness of the seat, Maggie was amazed at the distance he managed to keep between them. Supporting his head on one hand, he perused her face with deep dark eyes, his expression infuriatingly enigmatic.

Without the heat of his body covering hers she could feel the perspiration cooling on her skin and she shivered.

'Would you like to take a bath?' he asked her, noticing the goose bumps rise on her flesh.

Maggie shook her head. 'I . . . I'd better not. I'm so late . . .'

Tourell's expression changed. She could read it now all right – pure, undisguised contempt.

'Does Alexander clock you in and out?'

Maggie stared at him, irritation swiftly replacing her earlier desire. Sitting up, she waited for him to rise so that she could retrieve her clothes from the bathroom.

'I think you have the wrong impression about Alexander and me,' she said as she pulled her dress over her head.

Coming out of the shower, she saw he had put on the white towelling robe she had previously discarded. He was half lying on the sofa, his strong, brown calves protruding from the stark whiteness of the robe, his feet bare. The coarse black hair which grew in whorls over his legs invited her touch and, despite everything that had happened in the last hour or so, Maggie felt a residual wave of desire.

'I'm my own woman,' she said softly, 'I don't have to answer to Alexander.'

Tourell's eyebrows rose, though he didn't say anything. Instead he picked up the telephone and ordered coffee.

'Will you join me?' he asked her as she picked up her bag.

Maggie laughed and shook her head.

'Don't your staff ever sleep? No, thanks. Speaking of sleep, I must get some myself.'

Tourell shrugged and picked up the phone again. Contrarily disappointed that he hadn't tried harder to persuade her, Maggie listened while he organised a car to take her back to the Black Orchid. Then he rose and moved towards her, unexpectedly putting one hand at the nape of her neck and drawing her towards him.

Maggie's eyes closed as he kissed her, her whole body tingling at his now familiar touch.

'There's a staff flat here you can use if things get difficult for you,' he said, his eyes regarding her seriously.

'I'll be all right,' she murmured.

He shrugged almost imperceptibly, letting her go as there was a knock on the door. Striding across the apartment to open it, he took the tray of coffee from the waiter and nodded at something he said.

'The car's waiting for you,' he told Maggie, as coolly as if they'd just spent an evening playing gin rummy together. 'Liam here will show you the way.'

Realising she had just been dismissed, Maggie gathered her dignity about her and walked towards the door.

'I'll see you on Friday,' he said as she reached him.

Maggie looked squarely at him and raised her eyebrows. There was a challenge in his eyes, and an unmistakable hint of amusement.

'I'll be here,' she told him, unable to control the tiny, betraying tremor in her voice.

Tourell nodded before suddenly reaching out and passing his thumb along the trembling inner flesh of her bottom lip. Maggie swallowed a breath at the unexpected eroticism of his touch. Unable to help herself, she turned her face into his palm and pressed her lips against its centre.

'We'll talk again on Friday,' he said, his voice low and seductive. 'Agreed?'

Aware that she was agreeing to far more than seeing him on Friday, Maggie nevertheless nodded her head, aware that her cheeks were ablaze. Then she turned and followed the waiter out of the door.

Carla pressed herself further into the pillows and watched as Antony took Alexander into his arms. Relief, pure and sweet, flowed through her veins as she saw the ferocious animal Alex had been tonight recede to be replaced by the cool, self-possessed man she loved.

The tender flesh between her legs ached where he had taken her over and over again. She felt used, stretched in every orifice by Alexander's punishing hands and cock. Even Antony had seemed shocked by the almost frenzied manifestation of Alexander's lust. It was Antony who had held her in his arms and kissed the inevitable tenderness that his lover had caused.

She knew what had provoked him of course. Her lip twisted as she thought of Maggie, whoring at the casino. She could understand Alexander's anger. But she couldn't understand why he had to take it out on her. She didn't like things to get too rough, he knew that, and until now he had always respected the limits she preferred.

Damn Maggie and her influence in the club! She would make her pay for this. A lone tear trickled down Carla's cheek. She hadn't needed any clearer a demonstration of how little she actually meant to the two men whose limbs entwined beside her. She had been deluding herself if she had thought she could take Maggie's place. But she wasn't prepared to give up what little she had. And she wasn't about to let Maggie spoil things for her.

Silently, Carla slid off the bed and reached for a robe. With one last glance behind her, she left for the sanctuary of her bedroom. Antony and Alexander never even noticed her leave.

Antony lay wakeful in the big double bed and watched the pale pink fronds of light pierce the gap in the curtains. Seven o'clock in the morning and Maggie had only just got back. He hoped she'd had a good time.

The deep, even breathing beside him told him that Alexander was now asleep. Turning onto one side, he levered himself up onto his elbow so that he could study Alexander's face. Even in sleep, the frown was still there.

Antony reached out and ran his fingertips lightly over the puckered skin between Alexander's eyes, massaging gently until the muscles in his forehead began to relax. Tenderly smoothing back the thick, golden blond hair, he watched Alex sleep.

Antony wished Alexander hadn't pushed Maggie into getting involved with Tourell. He must know that Tourell was one man over whom he would never have any control? Antony frowned himself as he realised that even he wasn't sure what Alexander was playing at.

All this evening while Maggie had been at the casino he had been so jumpy that no one had had a moment's peace. Poor Carla, pushing for a night of passion had got far more than she'd bargained for. It had been a relief when she had gone.

Carla meant nothing to Alex, Antony was certain of that. He would have passed Carla on to Tourell without a second thought, had it suited him. But to coerce Maggie . . .

Maggie was different. Alexander loved Maggie, in his way. And yet, strangely enough, Antony never felt jealous of Alexander's relationship with Maggie. For he loved her too. And now here was Alex deliberately pushing Maggie away.

Antony lay back on the pillows and closed his eyes. He had a bad feeling about Maggie's involvement with Tourell. A quiet conviction that, for once, Alexander was going to get hurt.

Drawing Alexander's warm body towards him, he sighed. When it happened, he would be there to pick up the pieces. And maybe one day Alex would come to realise that the two of them was enough, they had no need for anyone else.

He felt a twinge of regret when he thought of losing Maggie. But he knew that nothing would make him happier than to have Alexander all to himself – heart, mind and body.

Maggie slept late so that when, finally, she surfaced and flung back the curtains, bright daylight streamed through. There was a note under her door from reception. It simply read: *'Delivery at the desk for you.'*

There was no indication of what the delivery might

be, so Maggie put the note on her desk and went to run herself a hot, bubbly bath.

Memories of the night before crowded behind her eyelids as she sank back in the water. One erotic picture after another; herself displayed before Tourell's enigmatic gaze, the strength and beauty of his naked body as he covered her, the joy of their coming together. And finally, the memory of the climb to that summit of sensation where nothing else existed outside her own skin . . . the echoes of that feeling zigzagged through her like little bolts of lightening.

She didn't have the energy to work out, so she dressed for comfort in a cornflower blue track-sweater, black sweat pants and Reeboks. Tying her hair in a loose braid, she applied a covering of tinted moisturiser to her face and made do with a hint of mascara and lipstick.

Remembering the note from reception, Maggie made that her first port of call.

'Do you have something for me, Trish?' she asked the languid red-head who was entering the latest batch of new members onto the computer.

'Hi, Maggie!'

The girl's smile lit up her face as she slipped off her stool and bent down to pick something up. Maggie tried not to notice the way Trish's fitted grey skirt moulded the perfect contours of her bottom as she bent over. After last night she was quite sure she wouldn't be able to summon the energy for Trish's enthusiastic love-making.

All such libidinous thoughts fled as Trish straightened, grinning, her arms full of the most enormous bouquet Maggie had ever seen.

'Aren't they gorgeous?' she laughed as she handed them over.

Maggie stared down at the enormous purplish-black

127

orchids which formed the centre of the bouquet and felt her cheeks suffuse with heat. It could only be Tourell. There was a box attached to the stems, behind the ubiquitous card.

'That box is really heavy – I've been dying to know what's inside!'

Maggie smiled sheepishly at Trish as the other girl urged her to open it. Some particle of self-preservation made her open the card first. The handwriting, in black felt-tip, sloped boldly to the right and Maggie knew instinctively that Tourell had written it himself.

'To a lady who is more rare than the black orchids she holds. It will give me pleasure to know you are wearing the enclosed on Friday night.'

Maggie's heartbeat quickened as she put the unsigned card aside. Oblivious, suddenly, to Trish's avid gaze, she opened the black box which had been attached to the bouquet.

She had known what would be inside, yet her mouth dried as she saw it. A dull pulse beat rhythmically between her legs as she remembered the night before. And anticipated the night to come on Friday.

'What is it?'

She glanced up at Trish with glazed eyes. Moistening her dry lips with the tip of her tongue, she looped her finger round the small chain and held up the pair of metallic Chinese love balls.

The other girl's mouth dropped. Maggie could see a dozen questions reflected in her eyes. She smiled and enclosed the balls in her fist, slipping them into her pocket, where she could feel them, smooth and cool against her palm.

Chapter Nine

Friday could not come soon enough. All week, Maggie had kept the love balls close to her, in her pocket, in her bag, under her pillow. Never where they were meant to be – she knew, somehow, that she should save that for Tourell. She also knew that he had probably intended his gift to make sure that he was never far from her thoughts. And he wasn't.

She was aware of a constant sense of arousal. The tender flesh between her thighs was continually swollen and moist, in perpetual readiness. Alexander noticed her distraction and took her to task about it when he found her in her office, a ledger lying open in front of her, unread.

'What's happened to your self-discipline, Maggie?' he asked, his voice dangerously soft.

Maggie was aware of her cheeks growing red and she turned away from him, knowing that it was too late, he had seen. Nothing ever escaped Alexander's eagle eye and she resolved to be more careful in the future.

'How did you enjoy your first night as a croupier?'

Alexander folded himself into the leather armchair

opposite her desk and watched her through half closed eyelids. Maggie felt rather as she would imagine an insect would feel when stuck on the end of a pin and subjected to intense scrutiny.

'It was hard on the feet,' she mumbled.

'Only on the feet?'

He smiled, infuriatingly, when Maggie glared at him.

'Darling Maggie, you are so transparent.' There was an edge to his voice which betrayed his anger at her liaison with Tourell, and Maggie quickly sought to reassure him.

'I thought you wanted Tourell to take me into his confidence? Obviously, he has to trust me enough to allow me to get close to him. I already have some information for you, by the way,' she added, a trifle desperately as she saw that he was unconvinced.

'Really? And how did you come by that? Pillow talk?'

Maggie frowned, puzzled by his attitude. If she didn't know him better she would almost have said he was jealous.

'As a matter of fact I merely kept my eyes and ears open. Did you know that the rules regarding fraternisation between staff and customers is being broken on a regular basis?'

Alexander stared levelly at her for such a long time, Maggie began to feel uncomfortable.

'Isn't that the sort of thing you wanted me to find out?'

She was annoyed that her voice suddenly sounded so small. Alexander's well-shaped lips curved slightly, acknowledging her discomfiture and Maggie could not help but think he was pleased by it.

'Why are you asking me to do this?' she burst out, unable to keep the words inside.

Alexander stood and walked slowly across the room.

At the doorway he turned, his face a mask of impassive perfection.

'It amuses me,' he said simply.

Maggie stared at the door as it swung closed behind him and fought the urge to throw something at it. Of all the infuriating, insufferable . . . Her anger cooled as she thought of Tourell's determination that she should report back on the Black Orchid Club in turn. None of it made any sense to her. The whole thing left her with a feeling of unease.

Feeling suddenly restless, she abandoned all pretence of examining the ledger and set off for the gym. Maybe a good, hard work-out would help her work off the unnaturally high state of tension engendered by Tourell's gift.

Her hand strayed into the pocket of her skirt and she felt the now familiar coolness of the love balls. And she shivered.

Maggie took great care with her preparations for work on Friday evening. After indulging in a deep, fragrant bath, she polished her skin until it shone, rubbing the heavy, perfumed oil carefully into her hairless pubic mound.

Standing naked in front of a full-length mirror in the fading light, Maggie ran the palms of her hands down her sides, from her breasts to the tops of her thighs. The light coating of oil made her skin shine, inviting a caress.

Moving her feet apart slightly, her eyes travelled down to the pink skin of her pubis where the darker pink outer labia peeked coyly out. Imagining Tourell's eyes on her body, she ran a finger lightly across the soft skin, sending delicious, ticklish sensations through her vulva.

The flesh began to protrude slightly more as it swelled

131

and opened under her tender touch. Soon the darker, more intimate lips were revealed, glistening invitingly around the opening to her body.

Maggie slipped the tip of her middle finger gently inside herself, then bore down on it, rotating her hips lewdly so that she screwed her body down on the rigid digit. Her long, fresh painted fingernail scraped lightly across the vulnerable inner flesh as she withdrew, then bore down again, bending her knees so that she could reach deeper inside.

Sweat broke out on her body as, with the first two fingers of her other hand, she exposed her burgeoning clitoris and compressed it between the pads of her fingers. It slipped out of her grasp, yet even whilst it sought escape, it quivered, pressing compulsively against her circling fingertip.

As she closed her eyes, Maggie wondered if there was anyone behind the two-way mirror which was set into the wall behind her bed. If so, she knew that they would be able to see her from all angles, her front reflected by the long, thin mirror, her back and out-thrust bottom cheeks open to view.

She didn't care. Driven by a need so insistent that she eschewed all rational thought, Maggie ground down on her own finger, tapping the hard, pulsing bud of her clitoris with the end of another finger.

It wasn't enough. Reaching blindly for the drawer in her dressing table, she pulled out a vibrator and pressed it against her clitoris. Switching it on, she gasped as the rhythmic vibrations pulsed through her in waves, triggering the climax that had been building steadily from the start.

The vibrator slipped from her fingers as she backed towards the bed and collapsed across it, on her back. She wished she had someone with her, someone with strong arms to hold her as the last vestiges of her

132

orgasm trickled away. But there was no one, and there had been a purpose to her self-abuse.

Maggie smiled at the old fashioned phrase. Self-*love* was a far more accurate term, she had always thought. Tourell's gift was under her pillow. She reached for it almost reverently, aware that her mouth and lips had dried and that excitement cramped in her belly.

The Chinese love balls rolled together in her palm with a satisfying 'click'. Maggie swallowed, holding them up by the connecting chain so that they dangled before her eyes. They caught the light, glinting silver at her, making her blink. Closing her hand over them, she lay back on the bed.

Still wet from her climax, Maggie's body opened easily at the first touch of her fingers against her skin. Dangling the balls by their chain, she touched them against the warm flesh of her vulva, shuddering at their coldness. With one hand she spread her labia, working the moisture in around the membranes of her vagina.

The first ball slipped inside her as if it had been made to fit the delicate contours of her body. Maggie closed her eyes as she felt it work its way higher, helped along by her well-tutored muscles. The second ball lay at the end of the chain, touching her tender skin. Taking a deep breath, Maggie pressed it against the entrance to her passage.

Her body resisted at first, protesting at the size and weight of its dual burden. Maggie persevered, spreading her thighs wider and forcing her muscles to relax until, at last, the membranes of her vulva gave and the second ball joined the first, deep inside her.

Afraid, for a moment, that she would not be able to retrieve the balls should she need to, Maggie felt for the chain, breathing a sigh of relief when she was able to pull the loop so that it lay outside her body, resting against her inner labia.

She lay like that for several minutes, accustoming herself to the sensation of holding the balls inside her. There was a hand mirror on the bedside table and she reached for it, then held it down, between her legs, so that she could see the chain emerging from her opening.

The skin of her vulva was very red, the labia distended, held open by the weight of the balls. It seemed to Maggie that the whole area bulged, forcing her spent clitoris to stand clear of its hood, exposed.

Gingerly, Maggie tried to sit up. It felt as though she were sitting on a bowl of apples and she realised that she would have to spend most of the evening on her feet. Not that she would have much choice in that anyway, she mused wryly as she stood up and went to dress.

Her hand strayed to the wispy fabric of a pair of crotchless knickers at the back of her drawer, but settled instead on a pair of generously proportioned briefs, made of extravagant black lace. She blushed as she thought with horror of the indignity of dropping the balls in front of everybody at the casino.

The soft cotton of the gusset brushed against her exposed bud, making it shudder. The love balls moved inside her and Maggie had to cling to the wardrobe for support. How was she going to get through the night? Act as if nothing was happening when she was to be stimulated constantly by the device she wore?

She bent cautiously from the waist to ease up her stockings and the balls moved with her, sending little arrows of sensation down the insides of her thighs. Every step she took in her high-heeled sandals made her hips roll from side to side, activating the balls.

Maggie felt hot, sure that she would soon come close to the edge of release again. Had this been Tourell's intention, to tease and torment her like this? Pulling a short skirt over her hips, Maggie buttoned a white silk blouse over her bare breasts. The expensive fabric caressed her nipples, already standing proud, awaiting attention.

Checking her appearance in the mirror once more, Maggie saw that her cheeks were unnaturally flushed, her eyes held a tell-tale brightness which hadn't been there before. Surely anyone would be able to tell she was aroused just by one glance in her direction?

She found the thought oddly exciting. Brushing her thick, dark hair into a smooth, loose curtain, she picked up her coat and bag and set off for the casino.

Thankfully, Tourell had sent a taxi for her. She doubted if she would be able to drive, she was barely able to sit in a respectable position. Shuffling her bottom on the cracked vinyl seat, the balls began to click alarmingly and she coughed to cover the noise as she saw the taxi driver glance at her in the rear-view mirror.

He looked at her strangely as she paid him and she got out hurriedly, her face aflame. How was she supposed to control the infernal things? Walking along the corridor towards the croupiers' changing room, Maggie tried to walk in numerous different ways in an attempt to find a motion that was comfortable. It seemed, though, that no matter what she did, an unexpected 'click' would eventually emerge from inside her pants.

Luckily, the changing room was full and noisy enough to cover any indiscreet sounds. Maggie forced her way through to her locker and changed quickly into the shiny green dress.

She had brought one of the black orchids from Tourell's bouquet with her, made into a corsage. Pinning it now onto the front of her dress, her fingers lingered, stroking the soft perfection of the petals. Gina caught her eye in the mirror as she refreshed her lipstick, looking away quickly as Maggie raised an eyebrow at her.

She's afraid of me, Maggie thought to herself. I wonder what she would think if she knew what secrets I'm hiding? She smiled, her usual confidence returning as she made her way up to the casino floor with the others.

She had been assigned to Andrew again, although tonight, he informed her with mock gravity, she was to operate alone when he took his breaks.

'Can you trust me?' she simpered ironically and Andrew laughed.

'To deal the cards, maybe.'

Maggie had no time to ponder the cryptic nature of his remark for the doors had opened and already the early members were streaming through.

Some time later, Maggie dealt her third hand to the semicircle of business men at her table and tried to stop her eyes from glazing over. She was quite sure that the customers would assume her glassy-eyed expression was due to boredom. She wondered what they would think if they knew it was because she had experienced at least three minor orgasms in the past half hour?

If she could only get away from the table without drawing attention to herself, she would make straight for the powder room and pull the balls out. It's not as if Tourell would even know – he hadn't so much as shown his face on the floor since she had arrived.

There was a game taking place in the Private Room, she knew from the number of members admitted through the heavily guarded door. But he could at least have come out to check she was there! It irked her that he was so sure of her, so confident about her obedience to his whims.

She felt exhausted. Constant stimulation, she was quickly finding out, very soon became uncomfortable if there was no respite. Her mouth felt dry, her unprotected nipples sore from the friction caused by the cheap fabric of her dress. And her legs were beginning to feel weak.

'Well, well, well, quite the little dealer, aren't we?'

Maggie's head shot up as she recognised Carla's sarcastic voice.

'What are you doing here?' she hissed under her breath.

Carla waited while Maggie finished the hand currently being played.

'You don't seem too pleased to see me,' she grinned, making no attempt to disguise her delight that she had the advantage over Maggie.

Realising that, while Carla could simply walk away from any confrontation between them she was bound to the blackjack table, Maggie bit down on her instinctive response.

'Here alone?' she asked with forced politeness.

Carla laughed.

'Of course not! Alex and Tony asked me along.'

Maggie tried to concentrate on the game as her thoughts whirled in her head. What the hell were they doing here tonight? She felt uncomfortable, guilty about her planned tryst with Tourell now that she knew she was being watched. For she was quite sure that was Alexander's intention.

The game ended and several of the players left their seats. Maggie's nerve endings tingled in awareness as Alexander and Antony replaced them.

'You're looking very lovely tonight, Maggie,' Alexander said softly.

Maggie blushed, not trusting herself to meet his eyes. Alexander knew her so very well, had schooled her sexual response to such a fine degree, she was quite sure that he had only had to take one look at her to know how highly she was aroused.

She dealt the next hand in silence. As dealer, she

held a jack and an eight. Alexander requested a third card instead of sticking on nineteen. Drawing a four for herself, Maggie dealt Alex an ace and pushed his winning chips towards him.

The love balls rolled gently inside her and she closed her eyes for an instant, clenching her teeth against the tremors which travelled along her nerve-endings.

'Don't take it so hard, Maggie – you know how I always like to win.'

Maggie opened her eyes and looked directly at Alexander. From the look in his eye she could tell he wasn't talking about the cards. And he was well aware of the nature of her discomfort, if not of its source.

'Are you all right, Maggie?' said Antony.

She smiled gratefully at him and nodded.

'Are you dealing another hand, or shall we move to the next table?'

The disgruntled voice of another customer made Maggie jump and she passed him an apologetic smile.

'Bets please,' she murmured, forcing herself to concentrate.

She felt, rather than saw Tourell's approach several minutes later. He walked up behind Alexander and placed his hand lightly on his shoulders.

'Are you distracting my staff?' he smiled, winking at Maggie as she caught his eye.

Alexander's back stiffened visibly and he shrugged slightly, so that Tourell was obliged to break contact with him. An expression passed swiftly across Tourell's face and Maggie frowned. If she didn't know these two men, she would have interpreted their behaviour quite differently. She knew it couldn't be, but the expression, so quickly brought under control by Tourell, had seemed to her to be one of pain.

'Considering you poached her from me I think I'm being quite civilised, Tourell.'

Tourell laughed softly.

'Touché, Alex. How are you, Maggie?'

Maggie stared at him, surprised by the warmth in his voice, not knowing what to say. Tourell's eyes darkened and the smile faded slightly. Slowly walking round to her side of the table, he placed a hand casually on the nape of her neck, beneath her hair.

Conscious of everyone's eyes on her, Maggie suppressed her instinctive shiver. She dared not turn her head to look at Tourell for fear of revealing the strength of her reaction to his touch. Instead she stared fixedly at the cards she was shuffling and willed him to leave, for now.

She could feel his breath, warm against her cheek as he murmured.

'I'll see you later, Maggie,' adding, so low that only she could hear, 'you received my gift, I see.'

How could he tell? Maggie's face flamed scarlet as she thought of the love balls inside her. Then he ran a finger lightly over the black orchid she had pinned to the front of her dress and she felt foolish. Of course.

She turned to him and smiled, sucking in her breath as she saw the look in his eyes. They were dark, turbulent with desire, and she knew that he *did* know that she was wearing his gift, and that he would reward her, in time.

Tourell turned away and left her, striding back towards the private room without so much as a backward glance. Maggie's hands were shaking as she dealt the cards. Alexander's anger was a palpable force around her, and she dared not look up.

Worse, she knew that she did not care what he thought of her. Her only concern was to get through the night so that she could be with Tourell.

Antony fiddled with his remaining chips and watched the scene unfolding in front of him. Maggie was acting

139

like a startled fawn and her uncharacteristic clumsiness worried him. He didn't know what Tourell had said to her, but it had had the effect of sending her into a mental spin.

Alexander sat, rigid backed, in the seat beside him, bathed in a cold fury. And Carla stood to one side, her usually pretty face made ugly by the unconcealed gloat she directed at Maggie.

Maggie misdealt the cards and one of the customers, a bull-necked individual with mean eyes, swore loudly at her. Antony was amazed to see that Maggie's normal *élan* seemed to have deserted her. She mumbled an apology, appearing to be near to tears as the man blustered on. Antony was on the verge of leaping to her defence when a woman appeared in a flurry of bright blue chiffon and Estee Lauder's White Linen perfume.

'What's the problem, Maggie?'

Maggie shook her head.

'I'm sorry, Cyn, I guess I made a mistake.'

'A mistake! Hundreds of pounds at stake and *she* says she's *sorry*!'

Cyn had obviously summed up the situation at once and she smoothed the agitated customer's ruffled feathers whilst at the same time arranging a relief dealer and gathering Maggie against her substantial side.

Antony watched in wonder as Cyn bore Maggie away, moving on an invisible cloud of capability.

'Who was that?' he asked Alex as they disappeared through a staff door.

Alexander threw his remaining chips down on the table and leapt to his feet.

'Where are you going?'

'Out.'

Alexander passed a ten pound note to Carla.

'Get yourself a cab back to the club.'

The girl pouted, but obviously realised it would be

best not to object. Antony clenched his jaw, trying desperately hard to deal with the situation in a way which Alexander would accept.

'I take it you don't want me to come with you?'

Alexander glanced at him, then quickly looked away again.

'No.'

Antony felt like thumping the table. Alexander on one of his jaunts was the last thing he needed. Knowing that the other man was waiting for him to humiliate himself even further by remonstrating with him, Antony forced himself to turn away, shrugging his shoulders.

'Fine. I'm not ready to leave yet.'

He sensed Alex pause, but he did not turn around. His eyes rested on the door through which Maggie and Cyn had disappeared. His interest pricked, he moved away before Alexander, leaving the other man standing.

Let Alexander do his worst – tonight Antony was in the mood to explore other avenues.

Chapter Ten

'Don't let him upset you – he's all hot air and no balls,' Cyn reassured Maggie as they reached the rest room.

Smiling gratefully at her, Maggie lowered herself gingerly onto one of the hard, moulded plastic chairs. Cynthia wasn't to know that it wasn't the dissatisfied customer who had unnerved her. How could she explain that it had been the pressure of having Alexander's intense gaze on her while Tourell played havoc with her already overwrought senses that had made her so jumpy?

She wrapped her unsteady hands around the warm cup of coffee Cyn passed her. The other woman sat down opposite her and Maggie could feel her curious eyes on her from across the table. Her own eyes flew up in surprise as Cyn unexpectedly reached across and tucked a recalcitrant lock of hair behind her ear.

'Maybe you're overdoing things, keeping up two jobs?' she queried softly.

Maggie shook her head, unembarrassed as Cyn's fingers lingered against the soft skin of her cheek. The contact was tentative, but significant. Any other time Maggie knew she would have been glad to respond, but there was only one person who could quench the fire which raged within her tonight.

'Do you think it might be possible for me to watch the private game?' she asked.

Cyn withdrew her hand, a hint of regret reflected in her clear blue eyes.

'I don't see why not,' she smiled, signalling that she did not mind Maggie's rejection.

Maggie smiled at her with genuine liking and rose. Impulsively, she leaned across the table and pressed her lips against Cyn's soft-skinned cheek. She smelled of face powder and expensive perfume.

'Oh – I'm sorry . . .'

They both looked round in surprise as Antony appeared unexpectedly in the doorway. His initial expression of surprise soon turned into a wide grin as the two women broke apart.

'I was trying to find Maggie,' he explained, looking directly at Cynthia.

'Well you've found me,' Maggie remarked drily, noting the interest which had lit up Cyn's eyes. 'Cyn, this is Antony. Antony – Cyn.'

Feeling like a rare fillet steak at a vegetarian dinner, she retreated to the door on the other side of the room. Antony had not moved from the opposite doorway and he and Cyn were simply staring at each other. Maggie could feel the sudden tension in the room and was pleased for them as she quietly closed the door after her.

Cynthia stared at the beautiful young man who had appeared in the doorway and allowed the delicious *frisson* of attraction to ripple through her body. He was almost young enough to be her son, and yet she had no doubts that he too was experiencing the feeling which crackled between them.

He was tall, over six feet, and well muscled, wearing a smart, dark coloured suit with a plain, dazzlingly white shirt and purple bow-tie. But what he wore was unimportant, he was the kind of man who wore his clothes, not the other way round.

The harsh, fluorescent lighting shone on his hair, emphasising the natural gold highlights. Cyn hadn't noticed him before; next to the other blond man he had been overshadowed. Seeing him now, alone, she wondered why.

'Fancy some coffee? It's from a machine but if you close your eyes you'd never know.'

Antony smiled and nodded, moving further into the room now that she had given him permission to do so. Cyn liked the way he walked, he was loose-limbed and relaxed whilst still giving the impression of strength. She watched as he helped himself to coffee from the vending machine and brought his steaming plastic cup to the table.

'You're not supposed to be out back here, you know,' she said without much conviction.

Antony grinned.

'I was looking for Maggie. She seemed upset. Shall I take my drink back into the casino?'

Laughing, Cyn shook her head.

'The caterers would have a fit if they saw you on the floor with that thing!'

Anthony regarded her quizzically over the plastic rim of his cup.

'So – where do we go from here?'

Cyn watched his strong, brown-skinned throat ripple as he drank and shivered.

'There's a private game on upstairs – maybe you'd like to join?'

Antony put down his cup and appeared to consider for a moment.

'Will you be there?'

Cyn shrugged with feigned nonchalance.

'I usually put in an appearance when the table's short.'

'You play?'

She nodded.

'Then would you mind if I just watched you?' he asked, his voice husky, sending delicious thrills up and down her spine.

Cyn made up her mind suddenly.

'All right, Antony, you follow me – you can be my lucky mascot tonight.'

She stood up and moved towards the door through which Maggie had disappeared. Antony followed her, admiring the rhythmic roll of her full hips as she walked. He smiled to himself. Lucky mascot. He liked the sound of that.

Maggie was hot. Her eyes smarted with the effects of the smoke and her lungs ached in protest. Her back ached from the hours she had spent standing in high heels and her vulva throbbed with the after-shocks of yet another minor climax.

Beside her, Tourell kept his eyes on the game, his cards held effortlessly in a fan with his left hand. As far as Maggie could tell, he was winning, but she couldn't concentrate for long enough to be certain. Besides, winning or losing, Tourell's demeanour never seemed to change.

Looking at him now, she saw that his eyes were hooded, his expression unreadable. He had what her father would have called a good poker face. A thin cigar was burning in an ashtray beside him, to his left, next to a tall glass of iced mineral water.

Maggie was sure that to the casual observer it might have seemed that there was no connection between them. Tourell never looked at her, not so much as a glance, let alone speak to her. All his concentration appeared to be focused on the cards.

Only she knew that beneath the table, his right hand caressed the sensitive area on the inside of her knee. Removing it briefly, Tourell lay down a fifty pound note and took another card. His fingertips began to describe small, symmetrical circles over the soft silk of Maggie's stockings, edging further up her leg.

There was no sound in the room save the steady rhythm of a dozen people breathing the acrid air. Under the stench of tobacco, Maggie could just detect the faint, delicate aroma of Cyn's perfume across the table. She and Antony had joined them just as the current game was starting.

Anthony wasn't playing himself, Maggie noticed. He sat next to Cyn, his chair very slightly pulled back, like her own. He was watching Cyn, his expression intent, as if he was trying to memorise every inch of her face.

Cyn appeared at first glance to be concentrating on the game. Her soft, plump hand which held the cards trembled slightly, though and her eyes flickered almost nervously, betraying her response to Antony's nearness.

Maggie caught her breath as Tourell brushed the backs of his fingers lightly across the crotch of her panties. She was thankful that the lighting in the room was so dim for she knew that the lacy material was wet, bearing witness to her continued arousal.

Fighting against the urge to close her eyes, Maggie felt his forefinger breach the barrier of her thin knicker elastic and slip into her heated flesh. Immediately, he found the chain which linked the two love balls still buried deep within her, and caressed it.

The balls clicked together and Maggie coughed slightly in an instinctive attempt to mask the sound. Tourell's lips curved upward, but still he did not look at her. Instead, he nodded at the man across from him to make his move, whilst at the same time his knuckle pressed against her swollen bud.

The atmosphere around the table was thick with tension as the stakes were raised. As far as Maggie could tell, there were only really three players left in the game; Tourell, Cyn and the man sitting on the other side of Antony. He was a broad-faced, thuggish looking character whose numerous heavy gold rings flashed every time he moved his hands. From across the table, Maggie could see he was sweating profusely, though she had no way of knowing whether it was from the heat or the tension.

The two players who had already withdrawn had not left, they were watching the remaining play intently. Maggie's nerve-endings prickled with an awareness of the tensions in the room, but she was too absorbed in her own, very different tension to think too much about it.

Tourell's bony knuckle was moving rhythmically back and forth over her exposed clitoris, overriding the discomfort of the surfeit of stimulation she had endured and urging her body to yet higher peaks of pleasure.

As if from a distance, Maggie saw Cyn lay down her cards with a gesture of good-natured defeat. A new hand was dealt and she almost wept with frustration as Tourell removed his hand from her pulsing body to take his cards. A residue of her juices glistened on his knuckles under the dim lights and Maggie's mouth went dry.

Surreptitiously glancing at the other people in the room, she was relieved to see that no one seemed to have noticed. All eyes were on the big man sitting next to Antony as he fanned out his cards. He frowned slightly and there was an almost palpable increase of tension around the table.

The man to Maggie's right shuffled forward in his seat. Cyn glanced from Tourell to the other man and back again, her expression troubled. Only Tourell remained impassive, waiting patiently for the man to make a move.

Maggie expelled her breath on a litle sigh of relief as he resumed his fondling of her heated flesh. This time, though, as his hand slipped under the elastic of her panties, he slipped his first and second finger inside her. The love balls were moved higher, pressing against the neck of her womb so that she felt full, as if she might burst apart with the pressure.

Tourell's thumb flicked against the hard, slippery button of her clitoris and Maggie clenched her teeth tightly to stop herself from crying out as her arms and legs grew heavy with anticipation.

The man opposite finally made his play, placing his cards face up on the table, close to the pile of currency which had been building throughout the evening. His eyes narrowed as he regarded Tourell, though not before Maggie had seen the gloating triumph he had tried to conceal.

Tourell did not immediately react. Beneath the table, his thumb circled relentlessly round and round on Maggie's pleasure bud while the two fingers he had immersed inside her played with the love balls. The effort of appearing outwardly calm and in control made Maggie's head swim. Her lungs hurt as she fought against the loud sighs which were straining to escape through her lips.

The silence in the room was oppressive now, to break it would be sure to draw attention to herself. Wriggling discreetly in her seat, Maggie spread her thighs wider and bore down on his thumb pad. The heat was spreading now, coating the nerves of her thighs, calves, feet and curling through her belly like good malt whisky.

Her tongue felt swollen, her lips tender as the lips of her vulva swelled around Tourell's moving fingers. The room seemed hazy, the faces around her madly out of focus, unreal. Feeling totally detatched from the proceedings, she watched as if from a distance as Tourell slowly lay down his cards.

A collective gasp rose up from the table and all eyes turned to the man opposite. Despair chased disbelief across his features and his shoulders slumped.

'You bastard!' he hissed through his teeth.

Maggie saw the two doormen move swiftly forwards so that they were standing, one either side of the loser. The man didn't look at them, but his whole demeanour showed that he realised they were there. He seemed to be about to say something, but thought better of it, choosing instead to scrape back his chair and leap to his feet.

He raised his finger and pointed to Tourell.

'One day . . .' he whispered.

Then he shook his head, defeated. Turning away, he made for the door, the doormen in close attendance.

'Bear down.'

Tourell's voice was husky in her ear and Maggie obeyed him without a thought. She bore down, pressing her tender flesh against the palm of his hand. Oblivious to the murmur of relieved conversation now that the man had left, Maggie wriggled so that she could grind her small scrap of womanly flesh against the unyielding strength of Tourell's thumb.

Slowly, he began to withdraw his fingers, tangling them in the chain which connected the hard, metallic love balls which she had worn all evening. Feeling them begin to slip out of her, Maggie instinctively clenched her pelvic floor muscles. Tourell pulled gently on the chain ensuring that her action had the opposite effect.

The balls plopped softly into his palm as Maggie inadvertently expelled them. And that was when she came.

None of the gentle, yet regular orgasms had prepared her for this. Wave after wave of heat washed through her. Her mind was a fog, she forgot completely where she was, who she was with, who she was.

Spreading her thighs wide, she thrust her quivering flesh against Tourell's soaking hand, grinding her pulsating clitoris against the love balls which were still in his palm. She must have made some kind of sound, for suddenly Tourell's mouth covered hers, drowning her cries of ecstatic release.

His tongue plundered the heated recesses of her mouth, thrusting like a miniature cock against her tongue. Maggie clung to him, her head reeling as, at last, her orgasm faded, to be replaced by an all encompassing need to possess him.

Tourell broke away suddenly, expectedly. His eyes were almost black as they blazed down at hers, reflecting an emotion she did not understand. She had no time to reflect on it. As if through a tunnel, she heard a male voice remark:

'Wow, that was some kiss, Tourell. Are you in on this hand or aren't you?'

Tourell did not bother to reply. He took Maggie by the hand and hauled her to her feet. She tugged ineffectually at the hem of her skirt which had somehow become entangled in the waistband of her briefs and allowed Tourell to pull her through the door which led to his apartment.

His hand was hot and sticky with her juices. She could smell the sharp, potent scent of her sex heavy on the air between them. Her legs felt weak, barely able to support her and she stumbled as they reached the steps which led down to his door.

Tourell turned and caught her. Time stood still for an electrically charged moment as he held her in his arms and stared down into her still-glazed eyes. Then he lowered her down so that her bottom was resting on the harsh industrial carpet which covered the step.

With his weight leaning against her, the step above dug painfully into the small of her back. Maggie hardly felt it as Tourell bunched her skirt around her waist and ripped away her sodden panties. She wanted him, wanted him inside her, filling her, filling the space where the love balls had lain for the past evening.

His cock was thick and strong as it slipped easily into her. Maggie welcomed him in, wrapping her long legs tightly around his waist and urging him to drive deeper, harder. Her hands splayed against the damp fabric of his shirt, her palms absorbing the heat emanating from his skin.

Impatient with her clothing, he ripped away the bodice so that her full, creamy breast fell into his palm like ripe fruit waiting to be bitten. And he did bite, though gently, on the nipple which had swollen to be so hard it was painful. Drawing the surrounding area into his hot mouth, Tourell rolled the nipple round and round on the tip of his tongue until she could bear it no longer.

Crying out, Maggie tangled her fingers into the crisp thickness of his hair and urged him to raise his head. She wanted to watch his face as he came, to look into his eyes and see the extent to which he lost himself to her at the point of release.

A pulse was beating wildly in his jaw and Maggie pressed her lips against it, moulding his skull between her hands. His head was a beautiful shape beneath the thickness of his hair, his ears small and perfectly formed. Maggie dipped her head to lick delicately round the finely crafted whorls of one ear and he shuddered convulsively.

He was almost there, she could sense it, feel it in the increased urgency of his movements. He was looking directly at her, yet Maggie knew he was no longer seeing her, he had turned inward, reaching inside himself for some final impetus which she could not share.

Suddenly, he thrust even deeper into her, then lay very still as his seed travelled the length of his cock and, at last, was released. Maggie clung to him tightly, sensing the intensity of his climax, triumphant that she had been its cause.

They lay like that for several minutes, numbed with exhaustion, gradually floating back down to earth, to reality. Only it wasn't quite reality. When, at last, Tourell withdrew, he turned away from her while he straightened his clothes before helping Maggie to her feet.

Glancing down at herself, she saw her clothes were in tatters, one breast exposed, creamy white against the vulgar green fabric. To her surprise, Tourell put his arm around her shoulders.

'Let's find you something to wear,' he said softly, his voice almost hoarse with emotion.

Maggie leaned on him gratefully as they entered the apartment. Tourell guided her to the big, functional bed enclosed by a metal trellis covered in ivy. Maggie sank down gratefully on the practical cotton covers and closed her eyes.

She heard water running in the bathroom and Tourell's footsteps as he returned. Her eyebrows rose as she saw the large bowl he was carrying and the towel he had flung over one shoulder.

'Lie still,' he told her.

She had no trouble in complying, she felt exhausted. It was warm in the apartment and her eyes felt heavy, half closing as Tourell removed what remained of her dress. Unclipping her garter belt, he rolled down her stockings one by one and dropped them on the floor beside the bed.

When she was naked, he reached into the bowl and squeezed a large natural sponge. Maggie shivered as he touched it against the base of her throat and began slowly, gently, to wash her.

The warm, rose-scented water felt silky on her heated skin. It refreshed her, wiping away the sweat which had dried on her body, skimming gently over the tender peaks of her breasts and down to her stomach.

When he touched the sponge against the apex of her thighs, Maggie felt a trickle of warm water run along the sticky folds of skin and she shivered. Coaxing her legs apart, he washed her and dried her there before turning his attention to her legs and feet.

After he had dried between her toes, he made her roll over so that he could wash her back, lingering over the crease between her buttocks, making her skin stand up in goose bumps. When, at last, he had finished, he took the bowl and sponge away.

Maggie smiled wickedly as she saw the huge feathery powder puff he brought back with him, but lay absolutely still as he used it to powder her all over, from neck to toes. Glancing down at herself, she saw that she was covered in a fine white film of powder. The delicate scent of roses teased her nostrils.

Her eyes were so heavy now, so very heavy . . . she gave in and allowed them to close. She wondered, then, what had happened to Antony and Cynthia, her lips curving into a soft smile as she guessed.

She sighed as a silk sheet was wafted across her body,

followed by the weight of a satin covered duvet. She smelled the heady, woodsmoke aroma of Tourell's skin as he bent and brushed his lips briefly over her cheek. Then she slept.

Chapter Eleven

*A*ntony waited patiently for Cyn to play out her hand, confident that, for all her attempts at non-chalance, she was as eager to be alone with him as he was with her.

No one had arrived to fill the two vacant chairs where Maggie and Tourell had been. Maggie had been so aroused, he could still smell the slight, subtle smell of her hanging on the air. Goodness knows he knew her well enough . . . he smiled as he imagined what Tourell had been doing to her under the table.

Tourell. He was a cool individual, for sure. Throughout the game he had remained impassive, totally in control. He reminded Antony so much of Alexander. Maybe that was why the two men hated each other so much.

Antony frowned. He didn't want to think of Alexander, not tonight. Tonight he wanted to indulge himself in the hedonistic pleasures of a woman's body, to lose himself in soft, perfumed, feminine flesh . . .

He turned his attention back to Cynthia. She was older than he by a good dozen years, though her round face was smooth and unlined. Her hands, as she held her cards, were plump, the fingers short and dimpled. Her white skin looked soft and he itched to stroke his finger across her knuckles.

He liked the way she dressed, it said a lot about her personal style. The sleeveless, silky overblouse was cut in a loose, flowing style which reached mid-thigh. Its bright, kingfisher blue toned effortlessly with the lighter blue of the sleeves of the chiffon blouse she wore underneath.

Navy blue palazzo pants with turquoise swirls completed the outfit. On another woman it might have looked garish, on Cyn it was merely striking. She was, he mused, like an outrageously exotic bloom amongst a bouquet of genteel English roses. There was nothing understated about her, and nothing covert.

Everything about Cyn struck Antony as being generous, from the warmth of her smile to her abundance of flesh, to the promise in her direct blue eyes as she turned them on him. His breath caught in his throat and his cock swelled within the confines of his formal black trousers.

Leaning towards Cyn so that he could press his lips close to her ear, he whispered 'Let's get out of here.'

Cyn did not look at him, but the slight flush of colour which seeped into her cheeks told him she had heard. She started as she realised that everyone remaining round the table was waiting for her to make her move. Glancing at her cards, Antony saw that, if she played the correct strategy, she was holding a winning hand.

Glancing at each of her opponents in turn, Cyn shrugged.

'That's me finished, fellas.'

She lay her cards face down on the table with every appearance of regret. Turning a small, secret smile on

Antony, she pushed her chair away from the table and rose to her feet.

'My place or yours?' she asked Antony as they emerged into the public gambling hall.

Antony thought of the apartment at the Black Orchid Club. That was his home, the place he shared with Alexander. Neither of them had ever taken anyone else back there, not without the other's full knowledge and approval.

'Yours?' he asked huskily.

Cyn nodded.

'Okay. Buy me a vodka and tonic at the bar and I'll ring for a cab.'

The interior of the taxi cab smelt stale and musty and Antony opened the windows. Cyn laughed as a gust of cool air blew back her hair. Watching her, her face alight with the sheer joy of living, her generous mouth stretched wide in a smile, Antony felt a stab of desire, white hot, in his groin.

Impulsively, he reached out to her. Her soft lips parted sensuously under his as he probed her mouth with his tongue. She tasted of vodka and aniseed. Antony's fingers sank into the soft flesh covering her shoulders as he pressed her to him and excitement ricocheted along his nerves.

There was something about bigger women, a kind of all encompassing voluptuousness which he had always found inviting. Welcoming. Antony sighed against Cynthia's lips and her mouth curved into a smile. Tracing the strong contours of his shoulders with her palms she brought them down so that they were flat against his chest.

'Mmmm! You have a beautiful body Antony,' she said husikly.

He ran his forefinger from her throat down to the start of her cleavage, lingering there for a moment.

'So do you,' he whispered.

Edging his hand lower, he cupped one full, pendulous breast. It more than filled his hand, spilling over like some ungovernable rush of desire. Antony couldn't wait to feel the heat of her skin against his. Realising suddenly that the taxi had come to a halt, he regretfully let her go.

Cyn lived on the top floor of a delapidated Victorian town house which was part of a horseshoe shaped terrace. The interior of her flat gave the lie to the seedy outward appearance of the house. It was decorated in a myriad of jewel-bright colours; canary yellow curtains swathed across the twin windows, falling in extravagant, silky folds to pool on the pure white carpet.

A huge sofa covered in blood-red velvet, worn to pink in the centre of each cushion, dominated the room. The walls were covered in a cream and gold flock wallpaper which would have been more at home in a mock tudor pub than in a Victorian house. Yet somehow it didn't look out of place here, did not produce the cringe-making effect Antony would have pictured had someone else described it to him.

The scent of jasmine permeated the room as Cyn switched on the three lamps. Their combined light was not enough to dispel the lingering shadows and Antony felt as if he had been enclosed in a secret, sensual world, redolent of heady, feminine scents and latent promise.

Without a word, Cynthia poured wine into two expensive, cut-crystal glasses and handed one to Antony. The wine felt thick as it rolled across his tongue. A claret, he guessed, well matured and heavy with tannin. Taking another sip, he looked up at Cyn over the rim of the glass.

She was standing, sipping her drink, her eyes watching him. Antony felt a deep, primaeval tug in his belly as he saw that she was in front of a lamp, the light of which formed a nebula around her, showing the outline of her body within the light fabric of her clothes.

His mouth felt dry and he drank deeply, not objecting when Cyn automatically leaned forward to fill his empty glass. As she bent close to him, he was treated to a delicious glimpse of her cleavage, the depth of which he could only guess at. Her perfume enveloped him and he closed his eyes for a moment, drinking in the essence of her.

When he opened them again, she had moved away, but she was smiling, a small intrinsically feminine smile which endeared her to him.

'Why don't you sit down?' he asked her, surprised by the sound of his own voice. It was unnaturally thick, almost hoarse and he lubricated his throat again with the wine.

Cyn shrugged her shoulders slightly and moved slowly towards the sofa. Antony blinked as he realised that her outline was blurred, her features indistinct. He put down his glass and passed his hand across his eyes.

'Are you all right?' Cynthia's voice was soft, full of concern.

He laughed ruefully. 'This wine's heady stuff. Are you trying to get me drunk?'

Cynthia's hand was cool and soft as she stroked it across his forehead. She chuckled. 'On the contrary – I want *all* your faculties intact tonight!'

He reached up and ran his hand over her soft, short hair, tracing the outline of her skull and one perfect ear. Feeling the faint tremor which ran through her body, he drew her down towards him so that she was half lying across his lap.

Looking down at her serene face, Antony felt more sober than he had felt in his life. All his senses were razor sharp as he tuned in to Cynthia's reactions. She

159

exuded an aura of calm, though he sensed there was a turmoil of deeper feeling beneath the surface which mirrored his own.

Running the palm of his hand from her shoulder down her arm to her waist, he felt the ripples of firm, abundant flesh and was unable to hide his excitement. Smiling, Cynthia reached up and drew his head down to hers.

She kissed him slowly, languorously, as if savouring the taste of him. Antony drew her wine-rich tongue into his mouth and felt again that almost dizzying surge of emotion which had gripped him before. Holding her more tightly, he pressed the broad expanse of his chest against the yielding softness of her generous breasts.

He frowned as she gently disentangled herself.

'We'll be more comfortable in the next room,' she explained as she caught his expression, her voice barely more than a whisper.

Anthony needed no second invitation. Linking his fingers with hers, he rose and followed her through a door.

If the living room was a reflection of Cyn's exuberant public persona, her bedroom was surely an echo of the sensualist within. An enormous king-size divan left little room for any other furniture except for a slipper chair and a large, black laquered chest which appeared to double as a dressing table. Busy, oriental-style engravings were painted gaily across every surface of the chest, exhausting the eye.

Yet all this merited no more than a perfunctory glance. Antony's eyes were virtually riveted to the bed. A huge, quilted comforter, heavy with intricate embroidery in many coloured silks covered the entire surface. Cynthia moved to the bed and stripped it off to reveal cream silk sheets beneath a more conventional satin-covered duvet.

More conventional, that is, except for the colour. Like all the soft furnishings in the room, the cover was a deep, ruby red. Heavy, self-embroidered lengths of fabric were draped across the ceiling, falling in an extravagant waterfall of sumptuous curtaining to all four corners of the bed. Rose-tinted spotlights deepened the colour, drawing him in, enclosing him, womblike, as he sank down on the bed.

As he did so, he noticed the condoms placed discreetly within reach by the pillows and he smiled to himself. This was one lady who knew how to look after herself. He felt safe with her, not so much in a physical sense, but emotionally.

Cyn stood in front of him and slowly began to remove her clothes. Antony sat and watched, mesmerised as she pulled the overblouse over her head and began to unfasten the chiffon blouse beneath.

There was no hint of self-consciousness in her movements, no sense of false modesty. Cyn exuded a sense of pride in her body that Antony found powerfully erotic. His eyes widened as she opened the blouse and deftly unclipped the front-fastening bra.

Her lush, extravagant breasts spilled out as if with joy at being released from the confines of the bra. Antony felt hot. Her nipples were like two large, flat discs, hardening into tempting, elongated peaks before his eyes.

It was more than he could bear. With a groan of pure, unadulterated joy, Antony fell to his knees on the soft red carpet and reached for her. With something approaching reverence, he cupped the twin globes in his hands, caressing the silky smoothness of her skin, before running his fingertips lightly across their burgeoning tips.

Cyn moved slightly, brushing his cheek with her pale pink nipples and suddenly he was awed no longer.

Burying his face in the deep, moist crevice between them, he pressed her breasts either side of his face. The heady scent of her skin filled his nostrils as he turned his lips to kiss first one, then the other.

He couldn't get enough of the taste of her, covering each breast with frenzied, open-mouthed kisses so that they shivered beneath his lips. Knowing he could not hold off for much longer, Antony allowed himself an exquisite, shuddering sigh before drawing one enticing nipple into his mouth.

It tasted like the sweetest nectar as he suckled noisily on it, driven forward by some deep-seated, atavistic memory. As if from far away he heard Cyn's small, rhythmic gasps of ecstasy, recognising at once the cause of the sudden, convulsive movement which transmitted itself to him through her breast.

Antony could have wept for joy to know that at last he had found a woman who enjoyed having her breasts sucked so much that she could actually climax as a direct result. Shaking with barely suppressed excitement, he stood and enclosed Cynthia in his arms. Feeling how she trembled still, he lay her gently on the bed and quickly dispensed with the rest of her clothes.

When she was naked before him, Antony stood for a long time simply looking at her. Cynthia lay passively, gazing up at him through heavy-lidded blue eyes, pleased by his pleasure in her body.

There was nothing flabby about her bulk, rather the extravagant folds of flesh were firm, covered by healthily pink skin. There were no hard edges to her shape, no angles or sharp hollows. Antony pictured himself lowering himself on top of her, imagining how it would feel to sink into the soft, welcome cushion of her flesh . . .

'You're so beautiful,' he breathed at last, 'so very, very beautiful . . .'

She lifted her lightly freckled arms to him.

'Come and look more closely,' she invited huskily, moving her hips in small gesture of impatience when he did not respond at once.

'I like the view from here!' he protested, teasing her, making her wait.

Cyn made a small moue of disappointment and Antony lowered himself on the bed beside her. The nipple he had enjoyed so freely lay softly spent at the centre of her left breast. Its twin, though, still begged for attention, standing proud of the softer, lighter skin of her breasts.

Anthony smiled wickedly and traced its outline with the very tip of his forefinger. Pressing the pad of his finger gently against it, he watched as it flattened, then expanded again, growing harder still.

'Ohh . . . yes!' Cyn moaned softly, her eyes closing.

'You like that, don't you?' he murmured throatily against her ear.

She trembled as he dipped the tip of his tongue into her ear and flicked it lightly over the delicate scrap of flesh at its base.

'Yes!' she repeated, 'oh yes!'

He dipped his head then, as he knew she wanted him to, and slowly teased the tumescent nipple into the heated purse of his mouth. Lathing it gently with his tongue, he rolled and teased it, biting gently on the tip as Cynthia writhed with pleasure.

Circling the tip of her breast with his hand, he squeezed gently, forcing the nipple into sharp relief so that it was completely at the mercy of his lips and tongue. It had darkened to a deep, reddish brown now and it quivered against his tongue as he drew it again into his mouth.

He could play with her breasts forever, but he didn't want to make her come again, not yet. Regretfully, he smoothed her breast with his palm and let it go. He shook his head as Cyn touched the front of his trousers.

'No – I want you to lie absolutely still . . .'

His eyes roved freely over her body as he quickly stripped off his own clothes, dropping them in a disregarded heap on the floor. He noted how Cyn's eyes narrowed appreciatively as the rigid shaft of his cock sprang eagerly into view and his breathing quickened.

Kneeling to one side of her, he ran the fingertips of one hand from her throat to her navel, tracing the delicious undulations of her body. It had been a long time since he had been with a woman whose belly was anything other than tight and unnaturally flat. This almost lewd display of womanliness, this excessive fecundity, made his body tremble in anticipation.

The pale blonde hair which covered the fleshy mound of her pubis was surprisingly sparse. It grew in a neat arrangement of chevron stripes, meeting in the middle to form a thicker arrow which pointed down, between her legs.

Anthony pressed his lips against the tender crease and, as if he had turned a key in a lock, her thighs fell open to reveal her secret inner flesh. He felt her shudder as he passed his tongue delicately along the groove. She tasted sweet, her faint, feminine odour sending its unique message to the base of Antony's desire.

Not yet, he reminded himself with difficulty. He wanted this to last, wanted to eke out every *frisson* of pleasure that could be had from their coupling. Raising his head, he lay down alongside her and drew her into his arms.

He kissed the soft skin of her shoulder, licking the salty-sweetness of her skin as he explored her arm. There was a dimple at her elbow and he dipped his tongue into it, delighting at her involuntary shiver.

Licking away the fresh sweat from beneath her arm,

Antony kissed a trail down her side, squeezing and pinching gently at her unapologetic bulk until she writhed against him, pressing her body against the length of his in blatant invitation.

'I can't lie still any longer,' Cyn gasped, screwing up her face in a rictus of anguished ecstasy, 'Dammit, Antony, I want you inside me! Come inside me now!'

Antony's penis ached with need, he had no power to resist her entreaties. With a small groan of capitulation, he rolled her onto her back and reached for the condom by the pillow. Seconds later he was poised above her, balancing himself on his fists and toes so that he could take one last look at her.

His rigid shaft looked angry and red, its circumcised tip bobbing up and down, brushing against the exquisite softness of her skin. Cynthia drew up her knees, slowly and deliberately parting her thighs so that he could see what lay between them.

Her vulva was flushed rose pink, the moist folds of flesh still swollen from the earlier climax. Antony could see the tip of her clitoris protruding slightly from its protective hood and he lowered himself so that the very tip of his penis kissed it.

He did not object as Cynthia reached for him and guided him to the entrance of her body. Trembling like the young, inexperienced boy he had not been for so long, Antony slipped inside her.

Her accommodating sheath was very hot and very moist. Antony allowed himself the luxury of sinking into her, withdrawing slowly so that the most exquisite sensations feathered along the length of his cock. His testicles tingled in their sac, perspiration breaking out all over his body as he repeated the manoeuvre.

It was even better the second time and Antony felt a delicious warmth invade his limbs. Now, at last, he felt he could lay his full weight on top of her, if only for a moment. He closed his eyes, savouring the experience. Cyn was so warm. Embracing her was like sinking into a warm feather mattress, feeling the softness of her body yield so joyously beneath the hardness of his . . .

Antony felt an overwhelming sense of being enclosed by her, of being admitted to a secret place of feminine delight which was cushioned by Cyn's expansive flesh. Seduced by her all-encompassing voluptuousness, he slowly let his self-control slip through his fingers as the first stirrings of orgasm approached.

Cyn squeezed her knees against Antony's narrow hips and drew him further inside her. He was so strong, so gloriously virile! She had wondered whether he would be, knowing he was involved with another man. How wrong she had been to doubt it!

And he was so gratifyingly adoring . . . she moved slightly beneath him, urging him to plunge deeper into her, grinding her hips against his so that her clitoris was teased by each joyful thrust.

He was close to the edge now, she could feel his tension, sense his considerable self-control melting away. Sensing how much he enjoyed being surrounded by her body, she levered herself up so that she could roll him over onto his back, putting herself on top.

Antony's eyes opened in surprise, though their rhythm was barely broken. The sight of her pendulous breasts swinging softly above his face was too much. Sitting up, he clasped Cyn round the waist and buried his face between them.

Now she had the deep penetration she craved. Now she could rock back and forth on his lap, enjoying the feel of his lips and tongue and occasionally his teeth on her skin as she engineered their mutual pleasure.

Screwing up her face in concentration, Cyn stimulated the secret place which lay deep in the recesses of her body, using Antony's cock as a tool by which to achieve the culmination of her desire.

She threw back her head as Antony suddenly exploded inside her. Pressing his head harder against her quivering breasts, she ground her hips round and round, skewering herself on his pulsating shaft until, at last, she joined him at the peak, opening her mouth wide and letting out a howl of sheer triumph.

Together, they rolled sideways on the bed, rutting like mindless animals until there was nothing left in either of them but relief. Antony withdrew his rapidly deflating penis and disposed of his protective sheath. Then he crawled back into bed and they clung together, a mass of tangled limbs, the sweat drying on their skin as the cool blue light of morning chased off the night.

Chapter Twelve

Watching Alexander pace back and forth across the living room made Carla's eyeballs ache. It really was too much. She had waited patiently for him here and from the moment he walked through the door he'd been in a foul mood. She wondered why she'd bothered to wait, the amount of notice he was taking of her.

She stuck out her bottom lip and began to pick at her nail varnish.

'For Christ's sake stop that!'

Carla gaped as Alexander exploded at her. She'd thought he was oblivious to her presence, now it seemed he had merely been waiting for an opportunity to yell at her.

'What's the matter, Alex?' she asked, hearing the whine in her voice, yet unable to control it.

'Nothing's the matter – why should anything be the matter?'

'I noticed that neither Maggie nor Antony have come home yet,' she remarked slyly, looking up at him from beneath her lashes.

'It's early yet,' he snapped through gritted teeth.

He turned away from her and paced over to the window, but not quickly enough to disguise the flush which had crept under his skin. Shoving his fists into the pockets of his trousers, he kept his back firmly to her. The action caused the material to pull tight across the taut globes of his muscular buttocks and Carla smiled to herself.

Creeping up behind him, she slipped her arms around his waist and rubbed herself provocatively against him.

'Never mind them – I'm here, aren't I? Come to bed, Alex,' she coaxed, reaching round to rub the palm of her hand across the front of his trousers.

She gave a little cry of alarm as Alexander shrugged her off almost violently. Staggering slightly as she backed away from him, she was relieved when his hand shot out to steady her.

'Carla – I'm sorry . . . come here . . .'

She could not continue to pout with his lips moving so sensuously over hers. With a little sigh of triumph, she wrapped her arms around his neck and pressed her slender form against him.

He tasted delicious, a mixture of whisky and tobacco. Running her hands through his hair, she revelled in the soft, silky feel of it as it caressed her fingers. He was so tall, so strong . . . closing her eyes, Carla easily forgot his tetchiness, remembering instead how he had been when they first met. Before Maggie came back.

'I love you, Alex,' she murmured feverishly as his hands roved her body.

She felt his momentary tension and cursed herself for her stupidity. Alex hated her saying that. It was something he had never, ever said to her. And never would? Carla pushed the small doubt to the back of her mind, telling herself it didn't matter one way or another. With sex as good as this, who needed love?

Alexander slipped one arm beneath her knees and lifted her, as effortlessly as if she were a doll. She felt like a doll when he made love to her, he made her feel so precious, so fragile.

Except when Antony was around, of course. It was taking longer than anticipated to get rid of Antony and Carla knew, with the instincts of an alley cat, that Antony was a far bigger threat than Maggie.

Alex was laying her down now, lowering her onto the bed as if she were made of china. Feverishly, she helped him remove her clothes so that she could be naked beneath him.

He was still fully dressed in his shirt and trousers. She loved being alone with him like this, loved the feel of his clothing rasping against the softness of her bare skin. His lips and hands were working their way down her body now, making her nerve endings tingle with anticipation.

Yet there was something . . . Carla frowned as she realised that Alexander's touch was different, strangely impersonal. His kisses were almost half hearted, so that his love-making felt as though he were merely pressing the right buttons to make her respond to him rather than joining with her on a journey of delight.

Panicking slightly, Carla wriggled down the bed and began to unfasten his clothes. Alexander rolled onto his back and watched her, his expression inscrutable. Having dispensed with the buttons of his shirt, she pressed dozens of tiny kisses over his smooth, hairless chest, teasing his neat, brown nipples into hardness with her tongue before moving further down his body.

Trying to hide her growing unease, she slipped the metal hooks at the waistband of his trousers through their eyelets and drew down his zip. He lifted his hips obligingly as she eased them down, together with his miniscule black briefs.

Glancing briefly at him, she saw he was watching her impassively. It was hard to conceal her disappointment, but she thought she'd managed it.

It was obvious that her close proximity had done nothing to arouse him for his penis lay in lifeless misery against his thigh. Alexander must have known how she would feel, yet he made no move to touch her, or speak to her.

Undeterred, Carla set about trying to interest him. Running the palm of her hand lovingly along the limp shaft, she rubbed her nipples against his, kissing him deeply. Her tongue met no resistance as she probed his mouth, yet he did nothing to encourage her.

He simply lay there, staring up at her through blank eyes, totally passive.

Carla tried to ignore the stirrings of panic, kissing a path from his chin down his body, taking his determinedly flaccid penis into her mouth. She kissed it, she sucked on it, she rolled the tip on her tongue – nothing had the slightest effect – Finally, she gave up in abject humiliation. Raising her head, she caught Alexander's eye. He stared back at her without a word, though there was a dangerous glint in his eye. Surely it wasn't . . . amusement?

'Oh! You! You . . . how could you! You never wanted me in the first place! You . . .!'

Gathering up her clothes, she ran from the room, tears of humiliation pricking the backs of her eyelids.

It was almost daylight when Antony let himself into the flat. Knowing that the scent of Cynthia's body still clung to him, he tiptoed to the bathroom and turned on the shower.

As the warm water cascaded over him, he recalled the sensation of Cyn's naked skin against his and shivered. Glancing down, he saw that he was hard again.

He grimaced. Having made love to Cyn twice more after the first, delicious joining, he was amazed that his body had any energy left in reserve.

Cyn was a true voluptuary, he reflected as he towelled himself dry. She had given herself to him so freely, with such generosity of spirit, he was certain that the memory of this night would be one he would cherish for a very long time. Maybe he could even repeat it. Cyn had made it clear she was willing, though typically of her, she had also very firmly *not* put any pressure on him.

Who knew when they might have need of each other again? Opening the airing cupboard, he took out fresh cotton boxer shorts and climbed into them. God, he was tired! Bone weary. All he wanted now was to curl up with Alexander by his side.

As soon as he stepped into the darkened bedroom, Antony knew that Alexander wasn't asleep. He was breathing evenly enough and his back was turned towards him, but there was something about the tension in his limbs which gave him away. Frowning, Antony slipped beneath the covers.

'Alex? Are you awake?' he whispered.

When he didn't reply, Antony folded himself, spoon fashion, against his unwelcoming back. The familiar warmth of his skin drew Antony closer and he closed his eyes as he breathed in the beloved scent of him.

Where had Alex been tonight? Antony pushed the thought away, knowing he was never likely to get an answer if he should ask. Whereas he, he would volunteer the information of his tryst with Cyn. He liked things to be out in the open, he had never been able to match Alexander for game playing.

What did it matter what either of them had been

doing tonight? They were both here now, together. On an impulse, he levered himself up and pressed his cheek against Alexander's in a gesture of tenderness.

He froze as he felt the moisture on Alexander's cheek.

'Alex? Alexander, what is it?'

Concern sharpened his voice and he rolled Alex onto his back so that he could see his face. The normally cool blue eyes stared back reproachfully at him. The well sculpted, bronzed face was blotchy, streaked with tears. Antony was not sure what shocked him more; that impassive, in-control Alexander had been crying, or that he had allowed Antony to see.

Without thinking, he reached out and traced his fingers along the tracks of his tears, noticing how Alex flinched away. Antony shook his head, more in wonder than bewilderment. Bending his head, he rested his forehead against Alexander's for a moment.

'Tell me?' he whispered.

Running the tip of his tongue along the salty stains on Alexander's face, Antony drew back and waited with outward calm for Alex to respond.

He could see the dilemma raging in Alexander's eyes as he sought to gather his dignity about him. Suddenly, he seemed to give up.

'I didn't think you were going to come back,' he said simply.

Antony was careful not to show his surprise. Emotion vibrated in the air between them and he sensed that what he said now could have a bearing on the rest of their relationship. That knowledge passed between them like a small jolt of electricity. Antony shook his head, close to tears himself.

'You thought that *I* would leave *you*?' he whispered.

Alexander did not move, but the look in his eyes said it all. Antony reached out for him and drew him into his arms, cradling his head on his shoulder and rocking him slowly back and forth as he wept.

And as daylight began to stream through the curtains, the sounds of the wakening street filtering up from the pavements outside, Antony knew that all that he desired was within his grasp. That the man now sleeping contently in his arms had a chink in his emotional armour which could be breached, given time and love. Time and love. Antony smiled and kissed the top of Alexander's golden head. He had plenty of both of those to give.

Maggie lay in that disorientating state between sleep and wakefulness and tried to hold on to the dream she could feel escaping her. She had been lying on her back on a beach, yes, that was it. A wide, deserted beach which swept in a grand arc around a bay, fringed with palm trees. The sand was white, super-fine as it ran between her fingers.

She was naked, the sun caressed her exposed skin, warm enough to make her sleepy but not hot enough to burn her. She could hear a lone bird singing wistfully in one of the trees above her. That, and the ceaseless ebb and flow of the sea was all that she could hear.

Her eyes were closed and she felt safe, contented in her isolation. She must have been lying like that for some time for her arms and legs felt heavy, as if she had been sleeping. One arm was flung out at right angles to her body, the other was bent above her head. Her legs were parted and the sea was lapping gently at her hairless mons, tickling deliciously at her exposed labia and teasing her slumberous clitoris.

Opening her eyes, Maggie looked down to see Tourell's dark head between her thighs and she knew that she had only been half dreaming.

He must have sensed that she had woken for he

raised his head for long enough to grin wickedly at her before going back to his self-imposed task. Maggie stretched her spine, unconsciously rearranging her arms into the position she had adopted in her dream.

Tourell's skilful tongue was playing havoc with her equilibrium. It soothed the tissues which had been stretched by the love balls the night before whilst at the same time managing to inflame her. She could feel the stickiness adhering to her inner thighs and wondered how much was due to her arousal, Tourell's saliva or their combined emissions from before . . .

She moaned softly as Tourell began to focus his attention on her hardening nub. Reaching down, she massaged his scalp rhythmically, loving the feel of the soft crispness of his hair beneath her fingers. He was flicking his tongue quickly back and forth over that sensitive scrap of flesh, teasing it out of hiding before pushing it back again with the tip of his tongue.

After a few moments, Maggie began to protest, unable to bear it if he sent her towards the peak only to deny her at the last minute one more time.

'Please! Oh Tourell, stop torturing me! What . . .?'

She gasped as she felt his fingers pressing gently against the rose of her anus. Something cool and hard insinuated itself past the protective sphincter and worked its way up her back passage.

Maggie frowned as she tried to decide what it was he had inserted inside her. It felt like . . . beads, yes, like a string of beads . . .

Tourell began to rotate the very tip of his tongue slowly round and round on the surface of her clitoris. His touch was so light, barely there, it drove her wild as she tried to press herself against him, needing a harder, firmer touch now.

He would not let her increase the pressure, instead he kept up the slow, relentless rotation until pleasure came close to the verge of pain and Maggie was begging him to let her have her release. She could not reach her climax, it shimmered behind her closed eyelids, just out of her reach.

Her anal passage spasmed as the thing he had insereted into her began to move. Slowly, with such exquisite precision, Tourell drew the beads from her body. First one, then another slipped from her bottom.

Maggie lost all control. She couldn't bear it. Her head thrashed from side to side as, at last, Tourell lashed her throbbing clitoris with his tongue whilst at the same time pulling the string of beads slowly from her body.

As soon as her orgasm started, he lifted his head and she was aware of him watching her as she came, smiling as, with the last bead drawn from her body, a rush of hot fluid poured from her and soaked the sheets beneath her.

Maggie opened her eyes in anguished horror as she realised that she had wet herself.

'I . . . I . . . oh!'

She broke off on a half-sob, half-sigh as Tourell cupped his hand over her hot sex, letting the combination of arousal and urine soak his skin. Pressing the flat pad of his forefinger firmly against the tiny mouth of her urethra, he applied enough pressure to undermine Maggie's frantic attempts to hold back the flow.

She cried out as she lost control and her bladder emptied itself. Smiling at her, Tourell bent his head and ran the tip of his tongue around the tender inner skin of her parted lips. Only when she relaxed enough to kiss him back did he let go of her sex to smooth back the hair on her forehead in an odd gesture of approval.

Maggie felt uncomfortable lying on the wet sheets. As soon as Tourell raised his head, she made for the bathroom and turned on the shower. Her cheeks burned with shame and she held her hands to them, pressing the coolness of her palms against the heated skin.

How could he engineer her humiliation like that? Maggie tried to ignore the thrill of remembering as hot water cascaded over her face and body. Slowly, as the water washed away all trace of her shame, a slow, burning anger took hold of her.

Who did he think he was, taking her beyond the brink of pleasure whilst still holding back an essential part of himself? Only Alexander had ever managed to remain immune to her for this long. Maggie had no intention of allowing Tourell to repeat the path she had taken with Alexander. Agreement or no agreement, if he wanted her again it would be on her terms.

She gasped as the shower curtain moved and Tourell joined her under the spray. He gave her no time to protest, pushing her gently but firmly against the tiled wall of the shower cubicle and placing his hands on her waist.

Maggie could feel his cock pressing insistently against her back, pointing up her spine. The warm water ran in a ceaseless waterfall between them. Tourell's skin glided like silk against the mound of her buttocks, inflaming her.

Compliant, she allowed him to lift her onto his rigid shaft, whimpering softly as he slid into her with ease. Bracing herself with both palms placed flat against the wall, she lifted her face to the spray, allowing it to run over her closed eyelids and into her open mouth.

Tourell was like a sturdy tree, his feet planted solidly shoulder-width apart as his strong cock and arms took the weight of her. As the moment of his crisis approached, he bent her over so that she was leaning forward from the waist, her long wet hair streaming with water, brushing the floor of the shower cubicle.

Maggie felt the flow of his seed mingle with the spray

of the shower and she straightened, leaning heavily against him and turning her head so that she could rub her cheek against the wet mass of hair on his chest. He was breathing heavily in her ear, though, despite his exertion, he still stood firm.

It was Tourell who turned off the shower, Tourell who wrapped first Maggie, then himself in big, white towels. Then he picked her up and carried her back to the bedroom.

The soiled sheets had been stripped from the bed and spirited away to be replaced by fresh. They sank together onto the bed and Tourell pulled her almost roughly into his arms.

'Leave Alexander – come and live here, with me.'

His outburst was so unexpected, Maggie did not know what to say. She stared into his intense blue eyes and shook her head.

'I . . . I can't . . . I . . .'

She had been about to say that she needed time to think, to assess the situation from a distance, but Tourell interrupted.

'Has he corrupted you so thoroughly? Did you really think I would be willing to share you?' He shook his head. 'No, Maggie, I'm not a generous man.'

The last was said with such quiet conviction that Maggie knew he was serious.

'What do you mean?' she asked softly.

Tourell sat up, regarding her intently so that she could be under no doubt that he meant what he said.

'If you want this . . . thing we have discovered together, there must be no one else. Only me, Maggie. That will have to be enough. Those are my terms – all or nothing.'

Butterflies fluttered in Maggie's stomach as she realised what it was he was saying.

'Good old-fashioned monogamy?' she joked feebly.

Tourell did not smile. She shook her head.

'I don't know. Please – don't misunderstand,' she reached out for him as he turned angrily away. 'Perhaps you don't know me well enough . . .'

'Oh, I think I do,' he replied silkily.

He reached under her towel and cupped his hand possessively around her sex. Maggie shivered, closing her eyes momentarily as she imagined how it would be if, having known him, she was never to see him like this again.

Suddenly, he was brisk. 'How involved is Alexander with the running of the Black Orchid Club?'

Maggie frowned, confused by the sudden change of subject. 'Well, he's . . . quite involved,' she said vaguely as she thought of his influence over Antony. Did that influence extend to business matters too? 'Of course, Antony is the owner . . .'

'In name, maybe,' Tourell dismissed Antony with an impatient gesture.

'Has Alexander invested money in the club?'

Maggie shook her head.

'I really wouldn't know. He has a say in the hiring and firing and I have heard Tony talking things over with him.'

Tourell's lips twisted into a bitter smile.

'Of course.'

Maggie felt defensive of Antony suddenly.

'They're very close. It's not all one-sided, you know, in fact I would say that Alex needs Antony just as much as Antony relies on Alexander.'

Tourell fixed her suddenly with a brilliant blue gaze which defied her to look away.

'And you, Maggie – where do you fit in?'

For a moment she didn't know what to say. That she was the third corner of the triangle? She shifted on the bed uncomfortably.

'I'm there because I want to be,' she replied firmly, aware as she spoke the words that Tourell would not like them.

A small pulse beating in his jaw told her that she was right. He seemed to be about to say something, then thought better of it, surprising her with a smile.

'Would you like some coffee?'

'I . . . yes I would.'

'OK. Leave it to me.'

'Do you have something I could wear?' she asked, glancing down pointedly at the towel.

Tourell opened a chest of drawers. Maggie took the clean blue jeans and white shirt he passed to her.

'Will these do?'

She nodded and watched him dress in black Levis and a checked shirt. Maggie couldn't explain it, but she felt a sudden, urgent need for some space of her own, so she waited for him to move to the kitchen area before she stirred and began to dress herself.

'Help yourself to anything else you need,' he called over his shoulder.

The jeans were ridiculously big round her waist, so Maggie rummaged around in the chest for a tie to use as a belt. Her fingers struck something hard and she peered into the drawer to see what she had come across.

It was a photograph of a man and a boy. The man was obviously a younger version of Tourell. He was staring moodily into the camera, the little boy in his arms, though he couldn't have been more than three or four, mimicking his expression.

So Tourell had a son. Maggie closed the drawer, refusing to allow herself to wonder about him. There was nothing unusual, after all, in a man of Tourell's age having a past of which he never spoke. Tucking the white shirt into the jeans, she followed her nose to the kitchen area where a jug of fresh coffee was percolating.

No one would guess what had taken place in this apartment between them, Maggie mused as they stood opposite each other, sipping mugs of coffee. The absence of windows made it impossible to tell whether it was night or day. For the first time Maggie realised that there were no clocks in the house.

She frowned. What kind of man chose to live in a subterranean apartment where the normal constraints of time had no place?

'I ought to go,' she said abruptly.

'Really?' He sounded mildly disappointed, though he smiled congenially at her. 'Are you free over the weekend? I'm going to the country for a few days – would you like to come?'

The invitation was as unexpected as it was tempting. It was as if Tourell had picked up on the direction of her thoughts and had decided to alter her opinion of him. Stranger still, in view of her earlier anger, Maggie found she wanted to go with him. Wanted to see him on home ground.

'I'd like that,' she said, all vestige of her former mood gone.

'Good. Can you get away at eight on Saturday morning? Good – I'll pick you up. If the weather's fine we could stop *en route* for a picnic.'

He smiled at her then, an open, almost disingenuous smile which sent a thrill of pleasure down Maggie's spine. And suddenly monogamy seemed like it could be a viable option after all.

Chapter Thirteen

*A*ntony brought Alexander breakfast in bed the following morning. Sitting on the end of the bed, he watched Alexander eat, sure that there was more to be said between them than they had managed the night before.

Alex drank the orange juice and gave every appearance of enjoying the hearty cooked breakfast Antony had made. He ate in silence, a frown of concentration etched between his brows, as if there was nothing in his mind save the devouring of his breakfast.

Knowing him so well, though, Antony detected the lines of tension around his eyes and ached for him. It wasn't until he had poured himself a second cup of coffee that Alexander exploded.

'Dammit, Antony, how *could* you spend the night with a woman like that?'

Antony hid a smile, knowing that it would enrage Alexander if he appeared at all amused by this uncharacteristic display of insecurity.

'A woman like what?' he enquired innocently.

'She was so . . . so *womanly.*'

This time Antony did laugh. Knowing that Alex, when he occasionally felt the need of a woman always chose those with slim, boyish figures, he realised what was upsetting him. Cyn's voluptuousness would have no appeal to Alexander and it obviously frightened him that it held an attraction for Antony.

'I *like* women, Alex,' he said softly. 'I like *people*. All kinds of people, big, small, fat, thin, old, young . . . it's never seemed to bother you before.'

Alexander remained silent and Antony leaned forward to touch his hand.

'You've always known I'm more "bi" than you, Alex,' he pointed out gently. 'But it's not important, any more than your occasional flings have been important, not really. It's you who I love.'

Alexander stared back at him and suddenly he looked very young, very vulnerable. Antony took the tray off his lap and laid it carefully on the floor beside the bed. Climbing in beside Alexander, he took him into his arms.

He was naked beneath the covers, his healthy, tanned skin smooth and warm under Antony's fingers. Smoothing the skin of his arms, he caressed the tightly sinewed limbs, enjoying the sensation of strength beneath the softness.

An emotion far deeper than lust made him press his lips against Alexander's forehead. Suddenly, Alex pulled away and wrestled him easily onto his back on the bed. Antony quickly overcame his surprise. From the look in Alexander's eyes he could see that the old Alex was back.

Regretting, fleetingly, the passing of the vulnerability he had been allowed to glimpse earlier, Antony nevertheless welcomed the familiar *frisson* of excitement that shot through him.

'Love?' Alexander mocked, holding Antony's wrists

easily above his head. 'What does this have to do with love?'

He smiled as he saw the pain flash across Antony's features.

'You didn't *ask*, Tony, that's the crime here. You didn't really think you could hurt me by screwing someone else, did you? Did you?'

Antony winced as Alexander's nails dug painfully into his wrists.

'No,' he whispered, willing to play along.

Nothing, certainly no amount of denial from Alex, could take from him the knowledge that Alexander was not nearly as invulnerable as he liked to have him believe. If he needed to disguise the true nature of his feelings, that was all right. Antony *knew*, and he was happy.

Smiling serenely at him, Antony felt a small, petty surge of triumph as Alexander leapt up.

'You think you'll be smiling in a little while?' he asked conversationally.

Antony lay passively on the bed and looked up at him. Whichever way you looked at it, Alexander was a beautiful animal. Rearing up over him now, unselfconsciously naked, his powerful body looked as if it had been sculpted in bronze. Feasting his eyes on its perfect symmetry, Antony felt his penis rise and grow hard in tribute to Alex's beauty.

Alexander saw and his lips twisted into a cruel smile. His own cock was rigid, standing proud, straight up from his loins as he went over to the cupboard in the corner of the room.

Shivering slightly with apprehension, Antony lay still and waited to see what Alexander's demonic imagination had in store for him this time. His eyes widened as Alex turned and he saw that he was holding a length of dyed leather thonging.

Advancing on him, Alexander smiled again. He was winding the thong around his fists, pulling it tight as if he was about to strangle him. Antony held his breath. Not even for Alex would he go that far – life was far too precious to be toyed with.

He was acutely relieved when Alexander looped the leather thong at the base of his penis. Working quickly, he wound the thong around Antony's balls, passing each loose end along the line of his groin and across the tops of his legs.

Antony groaned softly as he pulled the leather tight and his scrotum was stretched into two separate sections. Then he began to wind the thong around his swollen cock-shaft, criss-crossing it so that it looked as though he had encased it in a leather latticed cage.

Knowing now that Alexander was intent on humiliation tonight, Antony bit his lip as he reached the bulbous tip and paused. Caressing the velvety skin with the pad of his thumb, Alex played with him, smearing the little teardrop of fluid which oozed from the crease across the surface of his penis.

Antony's cock twitched in its cruel restraint and, smiling, Alex bent his head and licked the now purple helmet. Antony groaned, sure that if he had not been restrained in such a way, he would fast be approaching his crisis. As it was, he concentrated hard on breathing deeply, trying to override the urgent signals being sent to his brain, for he was sure that, if he should ejaculate now, he would damage himself.

Alexander lifted his head and gave him an approving smile. He looked almost apologetic as he bound the cock-tip as he had the stem and passed the loose threads of the leather thong under Antony's body.

Rolling him over, he tied the two ends of the leather thong together so that Antony's shaft was bound, if not painfully then firmly, to his belly.

Antony breathed a sigh of relief. From the zealous light in Alexander's eyes he had expected far worse than this. This though, was actually quite pleasurable. It forced him to wait, but since he was confident that Alexander would eventually release him so that he could climax, he was happy to play along.

Inflamed, it seemed, by Antony's passivity, Alexander landed several sharp slaps on his naked buttocks, using the flat of his hand. It stung, but not unpleasurably so and Antony moaned, pressing his face into the softness of the pillow.

Alexander's hands roved lovingly over his muscular cheeks, prising them apart so that the puckered brown entrance to his body was exposed. Running a feather-light caress from the base of his bound scrotum along his perineum, Alex stopped short of that sensitive place, jumping over it and continuing instead to his coccyx.

That fleshy pad over the bony base of his spine had always been one of Antony's most ticklish spots and he squirmed as little tremors of sensation feathered along his spine.

'Turn over.'

Alex had left his arms unbound, so Antony levered himself up and did as he was asked. Alexander's eyes were bright, his cheeks flushed with suppressed excitement. Looking down at himself, Antony saw that his penis was struggling to break free of its bonds and a dark red flush was spreading from his groin area across his stomach and down his thighs, a silent, rosy plea for release.

Suddenly, Alexander strode from the room. Antony frowned as he heard a tap running in the bathroom and Alex returned holding a large, wet sponge. Holding it above Antony's bound body, he squeezed slowly.

Antony gasped as a trickle of warm water hit his skin. It ran in little rivulets into the thick covering of pubic hair and tickled against his flattened testicles. His cock softened a little in reaction to the sudden flow of water against it, bringing him relief from the constriction caused by the thong.

Alexander saw his expression of relief and smiled.

'Enjoy it while you can, Tony,' he whispered, discarding the sponge and lying full-length against Antony's side. 'The effects will soon wear off and you'll grow hard again. Even harder than before, after I've finished with you.'

He fastened his mouth on his and kissed him deeply, drawing Antony's tongue into his mouth and sucking gently on it while his hands rubbed and pinched his flat, brown nipples to hardness.

'Think, though,' said Alex quietly, drawing away a little so that he could see the effect his low, hypnotic voice was having on Antony, 'think what will happen as the water dries. The leather will shrink, grow tighter . . . yes!' he laughed softly as he saw the realisation dawn in Antony's eyes and they opened wide in horror. 'That's right – it will cut into your vulnerable flesh, cut off the blood supply to that beautiful rod . . . Oh Antony, how will you bear it?'

He kissed him again and, in spite of his unease, Antony kissed him back, wrapping his arms about his shoulders and holding him close. Raining kisses over his face in feverish desire, Antony allowed Alexander to arrange him as he chose, opening his eyes to find himself lying beneath the other man's strong young body, his vibrant cock bouncing softly, just inches from his face.

Antony drew it eagerly into his mouth, tasting the musky saltiness of it as he ran his tongue along the silky skin of its underside. Playing his fingers along the rough skinned purse which held his testicles, he pressed his fingers firmly against the delicate wall of

Alexander's perineum and felt his cock twitch convulsively in his mouth.

Closing his eyes, Antony relaxed his throat and allowed him to penetrate deeper. He groaned as Alexander suddenly pulled away.

'Kneel up.'

Alexander's voice was hoarse, rough with passion and Antony scrambled to do his bidding. He winced as the drying leather pulled on the delicate skin of his cock, turning his back on Alexander and pushing his arse into the air.

Alex did not waste any time. Lubricating his anus with fragrant oil, he slipped easily inside. Antony took him in with a little cry of joy. The ecstasy of feeling Alexander's shaft moving back and forth in his body provided an exquisite counterpoint to the increasing pain created by the rapidly drying leather thong.

When he had finished, Alexander withdrew and rolled Antony roughly onto his back. Inspecting the leather, he must have realised that it was close to cutting into him, for he produced scissors and snipped it away.

The relief of having his penis released once more was so acute that Antony felt tears spring to his eyes. His penis and scrotum felt as though they were on fire, the blood now flowing back into them, searing him.

Glancing down at himself he saw that he was fully erect again, though his shaft was a fiery red, the circumcised tip an angry looking purple. He cried out in pain as Alexander's hand enclosed him. Then he replaced his hand with his lips and gently drew the abused flesh into the wet, warm cavity of his mouth.

Antony felt he would swoon with bliss as, gradually, the pain turned to a white-hot pleasure. Under Alexander's gentle ministrations his cock came to life again. All sensation was restored, only clearer, more acute than before.

Alex licked and sucked and lathed the rigid flesh until Antony did not know whether to beg him to stop, or to beg him to go on. He could feel the seed gathering at the base of his cock and he enmeshed his fingers into Alexander's hair so that he would not pull away and deny him.

When he came it was with an explosion of ejaculate that hit the back of Alexander's throat and flooded his mouth. On and on it went, the nectar of life pumping out of Antony's body until he groaned, weak with exhaustion.

Kissing him, Antony tasted himself on Alexander's tongue, the sour-sweet taste mingling with the salty tang of sweat and tears. Emotion running high, they clung to each other, damp, sated bodies pressed close, limbs intertwined, mouths and lips and tongues enmeshed.

And Antony knew, without a shadow of a doubt that this was how he wanted it to be. Alexander might seek to control, to punish, to humiliate, but that ultimately, this – this loving – was what he wanted too.

Maggie could not stop thinking about the weekend. Nor could she remove from her mind Tourell's ultimatum. If she wanted him, then she would have to turn her back on her chosen lifestyle and her quest for sensual experience would be at an end.

Would that be so bad? In Tourell she had found a lover who could satisfy and surprise her, couldn't he be enough?

Maggie got up from her desk, giving up all pretence of working and moved restlessly to the window. Below her the city sang its muted song, the constant movement of the traffic and pedestrians creating an eternal tableau of everyday life. Did anyone ever look up at the innocuous converted warehouse where she stood, looking down from the penultimate floor, and wonder what might go on inside?

A headache was beginning just behind her eyes and Maggie massaged it with her forefingers.

'Let me do that for you.'

She tensed as Alexander's voice sounded softly from across the room.

'Alex! I didn't hear you come in!'

He raised an eyebrow at her and she failed in her attempt to keep a blush from stealing into her cheeks. Knowing that he would have noticed, she turned her face back to the window.

'I was just thinking how strange it is that no one *out there* has any idea what goes on in here.'

'Not really,' he disagreed, his voice now close to her ear. 'Most people have neither the wit nor the imagination to guess. If they care at all.'

His fingertips were firm as they unerringly found the spot at the core of her headache and began to skilfully massage it away. Maggie closed her eyes and leaned into his body.

'Mmm, that feels so good!'

She felt him smile as he touched his lips to her earlobe.

'Something's been making you tense. Is it working at the casino?'

Maggie stiffened and moved away from him.

'No, I . . . it's just that it makes me feel uneasy, spying on everybody. I mean, the other croupiers, Cyn – they've become my friends.'

Alexander's mouth tightened as she mentioned Cyn and she flinched from the venomous expression which passed across his eyes. His smile seemed forced as he took a seat by the window.

'Tell me about Tourell.'

Maggie's throat felt dry as she reluctantly took the seat opposite him.

'Shall I ring for some coffee?'

'If it makes you feel better,' he replied perceptively.

Maggie jumped up, glad of a brief stay of execution. Which was ridiculous, she told herself as she ordered coffee and sat down again. Alexander was merely asking her to report back, as she had agreed to do. So why did she feel as though she was tiptoeing across a minefield?

'What do you want to know?' she asked, resigned to fulfilling her obligation.

'Does he live on the premises?'

Surprised by the seemingly innocuous question, Maggie answered at once.

'Partly, though he has a house in the country. He's invited me there this weekend, he . . .' she trailed off, embarrassed.

To her relief, Alexander merely nodded.

'Yes, it's in the Cotswolds. You'll like it.'

Their eyes met then and Maggie was uncomfortably aware that Alexander knew how involved she was becoming with Tourell. She jumped as there was a knock at the door.

Taking the tray of coffee and biscuits, she poured in silence, waiting for Alexander to make the next move.

'If he's taking you to the country I suppose it's safe to assume that he lives there alone?'

It hadn't occurred to Maggie that Tourell might be married, or living with someone.

'I would think so.'

'How many nights a week does the big game take place?'

'I'm not sure, certainly there's been one every night I've been on duty.'

'And Tourell plays every time?'

191

She nodded.

'Does he win? Stupid question. Of course he wins.'

Maggie looked at Alexander curiously. She couldn't understand his bitter hatred of Tourell which was made all the more intriguing by Tourell's reciprocal interest in him. There was obviously something between the two men, something very personal . . . had they been lovers, perhaps?

'Antony is planning to set up another interview day fairly soon,'

Maggie jumped as she realised Alexander was speaking again and that he had completely changed the subject.

'I'm sorry, what did you say? We're taking on new men?'

'That's right. I take it that you're only going to the country for the weekend?'

He was smiling at her and Maggie had to force herself to smile back, to act normally.

'Of course. Let me know which day and I'll put it in my diary.'

She turned away, reaching across her desk for her diary. Sensing Alexander rise and walk over to her, Maggie tensed, holding her breath as he cupped her chin in one palm and turned her face towards him. It was impossible to avoid his eye and Maggie forced herself to meet it boldly.

Even now, after all this time, she was moved by the sight of his beauty. His smooth-skinned face was tanned, graced by the most perfectly symmetrical features she had ever seen on a man. His startlingly blue eyes were framed by thick, dark lashes which often concealed his thoughts. His mouth, beneath a straight, aquiline nose, was beautifully drawn with firm lips which advertised his basic sensuality.

It was easy to see why so many men and women,

herself included, found him irresistible. Not just because of his physical perfection, though admittedly that was the initial lure. But because the strength of his personality oozed from every pore, his formidable self-control evident in every flicker of his eyes.

Maggie felt powerless to resist as he slowly bent his head and moved his lips seductively over hers. No one had ever kissed her the way Alexander kissed her. He had no need to touch her in any other way, a few minutes of having his mouth toying with hers and she was wet, willing to cross any barriers with him – as she had, so many times.

His eyes looked sad as he broke away and stared down at her.

'It was a mistake to send you away from us Maggie,' he said softly.

Taken aback by the unexpected admission, Maggie jerked her head away from him and shrugged. 'You found a replacement for me quickly enough.'

It irked her that she was incapable of disguising from him the extent of her bitterness at that fact. Alexander smiled.

'You mean Carla? She's left.'

Maggie blinked in surprise. Carla was gone?

'When?'

'Early this morning. She never really fitted in, Maggie. Not like you.'

He kissed her again, this time drawing her to her feet so that he could hold the soft length of her against the masculine strength of his body. Maggie could feel his erection pressing into the soft flesh of her belly and felt an answering need stirring within her.

She shivered as he ran his hands feverishly up and down her sides.

'It doesn't have to end, Maggie. Antony loves you. He missed you while you were away.'

His voice was hypnotic, seducing her mind as his hands and lips played havoc with her body.

'You belong here, darling Maggie . . . *I* love you. You know that, don't you?'

She nodded, hardly able to believe the words he was pouring, like warm honey in her ear. Liquid heat was spreading outwards from her stomach, and she felt herself weakening, falling under his spell as she always had.

Closing her eyes as he ran his lips up and down her neck, she tried to block out the sound of Tourell's voice, but it clamoured to be heard, ringing in her ears as if he were standing beside her.

'Only me, Maggie, all or nothing . . .'

She whimpered, the sound coming from deep in her throat. Alexander felt the vibration of it before the sound escaped from her lips and he drew away.

Scanning her eyes, he acknowledged her withdrawal from him and, with a small, regretful smile, he picked up her hand and raised it to his lips. Then he turned and walked away.

Maggie watched him walk across her office, his sleek shoulder muscles rippling under his shirt and she felt a pang of premature regret. If she was to accept Tourell's offer she would never again be able to run her hands over those muscles. Nor would she be able to put the new interviewees through their sexual paces, even if it were for the benefit of the Black Orchid Club and its members.

Alexander turned at the door.

'Look out for Tourell,' he cautioned, his tone grudging, as if he was reluctant to tell her, but felt compelled.

'What do you mean?' Maggie asked, dreading the answer he would give.

Alexander shrugged his magnificent shoulders and gave a small smile.

'He hurts people. Even strong people like you.'

Again, there was that small half-smile. Then he disappeared through the door, leaving Maggie staring after him. That was a case of the proverbial pot calling the kettle black, she mused to herself. But she couldn't shake off the heavy feeling of impending disaster that Alexander's words had invoked.

And she knew, without doubt, that they would follow her through the weekend.

Chapter Fourteen

Maggie watched from the window of Antony's apartment as Tourell drove into the car-park. The car was black and low slung, the personalised number plates concealing its age. Her stomach muscles cramped with nerves as he parked and killed the engine.

'I'd better go – I don't want him to have to come inside.'

Antony, who had been waiting with her, nodded and picked up her suitcase. They took the lift, emerging into the bright summer sunshine just as Tourell climbed out of the car.

Maggie felt Antony tense beside her and she glanced from one man to the other. Both faces were set and hostile as they nodded a curt greeting and Antony passed Maggie's bag to Tourell. Sure that this was further evidence that Tourell had been Alexander's lover before Antony, Maggie said goodbye quickly and slipped into the soft leather bucket seat of Tourell's car.

'Is Alexander not in?' he asked her as he eased the car out of the tight parking space.

'He went out early this morning,' she replied, noticing how Tourell's mouth tightened.

It had been obvious to Maggie that Alexander had gone out deliberately to avoid meeting Tourell and she had to admit that she was glad. The atmosphere between Tourell and Antony had been bad enough, if Alex had been there . . .

'You're looking very lovely today,' he remarked after a while.

Glancing down at the bright blue button-through sundress with its large, scarlet blooms, Maggie smiled.

'Thank you. You said something about a picnic . . .?'

His tense face relaxed into a smile.

'There's a hamper in the boot.'

Maggie relaxed and lay her head back on the leather head-rest. Tourell leaned forward and pushed a disc into the CD player and the easy music of Tchaikovsky filled the car.

It was a beautiful day, the sun filtering through the glass so that Maggie was bathed in a gentle warmth. Tourell was a competent driver, his brown hands relaxed on the wheel as they sped west, leaving the city behind them.

Looking at him sideways, Maggie ran her eyes approvingly over the smooth line of his profile. She had never seen him dressed in anything other than a formal tuxedo, other than for that short period before she had left a few days before. Today he was wearing blue jeans and a sky blue, short-sleeved shirt, open at the neck.

Even his hair looked more relaxed, curling slightly around his ears and above his collar, as if he had recently stepped from the shower. Thinking of the shower made Maggie remember the one they had shared in the apartment. She flushed with remembered ecstasy and, at that moment, Tourell glanced her way and their eyes collided.

He wasn't smiling now and his eyes burned into hers like blue ice, boring into her mind. Maggie felt her mouth run dry as she read the blatant sensual challenge he was throwing her and, between her thighs, her most intimate flesh tingled and swelled.

It seemed as though they had been gazing at each other for ages, yet it could only have been for a split second for Tourell quickly returned his attention to the road ahead. The easy atmosphere that had surrounded them before though, had been banished, leaving in its wake an electric tension which sent ripples of awareness travelling round Maggie's body.

She tried closing her eyes, enjoying the warm sun on her bare skin and allowing the beautiful music to fill her mind. Still, she was acutely aware of the man driving silently beside her.

At length they turned off the motorway and drove deeper into the countryside. Maggie looked about her with interest, delighted with the verdant, rolling hills and picturesque hamlets through which they travelled.

The pace was more leisurely now and Maggie was aware of Tourell's every movement, the play of every muscle and sinew as he operated the clutch and brake. Occasionally when he changed gear, his knuckles brushed lightly over Maggie's cotton-covered thigh. It was an innocuous enough contact, but Maggie could still feel his fleeting touch long after it had gone.

The music finished and Tourell made no move to replace it. A heavy silence enclosed them, increasing Maggie's tension so that she felt as though she would scream if she didn't speak soon. And yet, when she tried to, the words would not come, sticking in her throat as they had many years before when she was a tongue-tied adolescent.

When, at last, Tourell broke the silence, the sound of his voice made her jump.

'I know of a place near here which would be ideal for our picnic. Are you ready for a break?'

'Yes, I . . . it would be nice to stretch my legs,' she replied, wondering why her tongue seemed to want to cleave to the roof of her mouth.

A few minutes later, Tourell pulled off the main road and parked the car in a large, gravelled car-park. Maggie hid her disappointment when she saw that there were several cars parked there. She had hoped that Tourell would take her somewhere more discreet, somewhere out of the way where they could be alone.

Lifting a large wicker hamper and a blanket out of the boot, Tourell locked the car and took her by the arm. They began to walk at a leisurely pace, following one of the designated pathways. They passed several other picnickers – families and young lovers, strolling arm in arm. Further away a small family group were struggling to launch a kite.

Maggie stopped to watch, shading her eyes against the glare of the sun as the kite was caught in an eddy of wind and flew up, up, up into the blue sky. The brightly coloured plastic dipped and danced for a moment, then the breeze dropped and it plummeted to the ground.

Turning to Tourell, Maggie saw that he was watching, not the kite, but her. She stared at him and everything around her slipped out of focus as leaping tendrils of desire caught her in their grip. Her legs felt heavy as he took her arm and urged her to walk on. Feeling as though she was wading through treacle, Maggie hoped fervently that Tourell knew of somewhere quiet: that he intended to assuage the need which she knew must be obvious to him.

Heading towards a ridge to their right, Maggie was relieved to find that, once over it, there were a multitude of hummocks and sheltered spots where they might picnic unobserved. Stopping in a dip just below the path, Tourell put down the hamper and spread the blanket on the ground.

Sitting down, Maggie glanced about her. They were surrounded on three sides by a dense growth of gorse, heavy with yellow blossoms. The grassy path ran behind them, slightly raised so that anyone passing would have to look down to see them.

Tourell stretched out beside her and opened the lid of the hamper. Maggie's mouth began to water as she watched him unload fresh, crusty bread, and soft, runny brie. There was champagne and two long-stemmed glasses to drink it from plus, inside the hamper, Maggie could see a veritable feast of summer fruits.

The champagne hissed gently as he dispensed with the cork and poured it into the glasses. The tiny bubbles fizzed on her tongue and coated her throat as she sipped the cold liquid greedily. Tourell refilled her glass as soon as it became empty and they both sat in silence for a while, sipping their champagne and bathing in the benign, late morning sun.

Tourell looked relaxed, giving no sign that he felt the tension which Maggie was unable to shake off. The sunshine warmed his skin to a golden colour and his dark hair provided a striking contrast as it curled round his ears. A piquant dart of desire ricocheted through her with unexpected speed and she closed her eyes briefly to savour it. He seemed to be in no hurry and she was prepared to wait, for now.

They were on their second bottle of champagne before Tourell turned his attention to the food. Cutting the French loaf into slices, he larded one with soft cheese and passed it to Maggie. She hadn't realised how truly hungry she was until she began to eat.

There was something so carefree about eating in the open air. Breadcrumbs fell unregarded on the dry grass around them as they washed down the feast with yet more champagne. Abandoning her glass, Maggie lay back on the blanket, folding one arm behind her head as a pillow.

The sunshine and the champagne combined to make her feel drowsy and she closed her eyes. Bird-song reached her ears, carried on the breeze and she could hear the gentle chirrup of a cricket close by in the long grass. All her perceptions seemed heightened, receptive to the least variation.

'Would you like some fruit?'

Tourell's voice was soft in her ear, as if he too was loth to disturb the peace which surrounded them. Maggie nodded and turned her head to watch him, using her forearm to shield her eyes from the glare of the sun.

She smiled as she saw the huge punnet of ready hulled strawberries and a little glass pitcher of cream. Her smile slipped off her face as Tourell caught her eye and she recognised the expression in his. His eyes were dark, reflecting back her own tightly controlled tension.

He wanted her, she thought with a little start of happiness, he wanted her just as ferociously as she wanted him. She held her breath as, dipping one, small strawberry in the cream, he leaned across and pressed it between her teeth.

As Maggie swallowed the sweet, succulent pulp, Tourell kissed her, tasting the fruit on her lips. Her arms came up around his neck and she arched her body invitingly against him. She welcomed the touch of his fingers against the bare skin of her throat and chest as he traced small circles lightly with his fingertips, working his way to where the first button of her dress was sited.

It seemed as if she had waited for so long for him to touch her, now she hardly dared move in case he stopped. He was in no hurry, caressing her skin with protracted tenderness so that her entire body began to tremble with desire.

Briefly, it crossed her mind that someone might happen upon them as they walked across the downs, but somehow she could not bring herself to care enough to try to stop him. Unfastening all the buttons of her dress, he gazed down into her eyes before sitting up beside her. Opening the sides of her dress, he arranged them either side of her, as if he was unwrapping a birthday present.

Maggie shivered slightly as a warm breeze kissed her naked skin, bringing goose bumps up on her flesh. Slowly, almost reverently, Tourell unclipped the fastening of her bra and peeled the separated cups away from her breasts. Then he untied her white cotton panties and slowly pulled them up, between her buttocks, brushing along the exposed skin of her pubis before casting them aside.

Lying absolutely still, Maggie watched as he turned his attention to the picnic basket. There were the strawberries, a bunch of small, seedless green grapes, ripe, purple plums, a bunch of long, firm bananas and downy peaches. When he turned back towards her there was a wicked glint in his eye which set her pulse racing.

Tracing a leisurely path across her body with the flat of his hand, Tourell kissed her again, his tongue probing the inner recesses of her mouth, drawing a yearning response from hers. As his hand closed over one full breast, she stretched, like a cat in the sun, arching her back and pointing her toes.

Raising his head a little above hers, Tourell murmured against her lips,

'Don't move.'

'Why?' she whispered.

He smiled, smoothing his hand down the side of her body and polished her hip-bone under his palm.

'Trust me,' he murmured, running the tip of his tongue along the inside of her lower lip which quivered under his touch.

Maggie could feel the excitement curling in the pit of her stomach. His cool, firm lips brushed across her temples, his fingertips playing, feather-light, across her breasts and down to the gentle undulation of her stomach. The backs of his fingers stroked along the hairless crease at the apex of her thighs, teasing her until Maggie's breath began to come in short, rapid gasps.

'Lie still,' he told her, moving away.

Maggie lay motionless, arms by her sides, squeezing her thighs tightly together in a fruitless attempt to ease the yearning ache caused by his careless caress. She could hear voices carried on the soft breeze and wondered for a moment what she would do if someone came across them.

She could hear Tourell emptying the picnic basket, heard the clink of plates and glasses and the soft hiss as he opened yet another bottle of champagne. It was a soothing sound, this languid activity taking place at her side while she lay, naked and aroused under the blue, blue sky.

Eventually, she was lulled into a half doze by the incessant song of the crickets and the caress of the warm, comforting rays of the sun. She almost forgot they were in a public place, in the open air.

'Here – have another strawberry.'

Maggie opened her mouth obediently and Tourell placed the soft, cream soaked fruit on her tongue.

'Do you like fruit salad? Peaches . . .?'

The slice of peach flesh was cold and juicy against her tongue. Maggie gasped as Tourell began to lay the slices of fruit in the crease beneath her breasts. Taking his time, he arranged them so that they lay in a neat semi-circle beneath either one.

Next, he pressed a small, sweet grape between her teeth. The flavour burst into her mouth as she bit into the firm flesh. She laughed delightedly as he balanced the entire bunch of grapes at the apex of her thighs. It felt cool and heavy, the point of the triangle of fruit pressing down, between her legs.

Tourell gently coaxed her thighs slightly apart so that several of the smooth-skinned globes rested against her moisture-slicked labia. Maggie held her breath, wondering what he would do next. She gasped as she felt a soft fruit held against the hard tip of one nipple.

Slowly rolling the fruit between his finger and thumb, Tourell crushed it on the hard nub and Maggie could smell the sweet, distinctive scent of strawberries as the juice ran slowly down the slope of her breasts.

He crushed another on her other breast, followed by another and another on each, until her breasts were awash with strawberry juice which trickled into her armpits and down to the top of her rib cage where it mingled with the peach juice which had already dried in a sticky film on her skin.

'Open your mouth,' he murmured, his voice thick.

Maggie obliged and felt a trickle of thick, cool, double cream drip onto her tongue. Swallowing, she shivered as he poured it into the well of her throat and down, over the sticky mess of strawberries on her breasts.

'Again.'

This time a few well-placed drops of champagne fizzed on her tongue before trickling across her stomach, welling in a pool in her navel. Tourell rubbed a firm, ripe plum against her lips, allowing her to bite into it. Her tongue darted out to catch the juice which trickled over her chin and Tourell bent his head to catch the drops she missed with his.

They kissed, slowly, their tongues entwining amidst the fruit and the cream and the champagne. Suddenly, Tourell tensed. Maggie held her breath as she heard what he had heard, voices, coming closer. His lips were still on hers, stopping her from asking him to cover her. She waited, expecting any moment to hear a shocked exclamation, an affronted cry.

The voices paused, very close, then they receded slowly and Maggie released her pent up breath as she realised they had gone.

'We must stop,' she murmured half heartedly as Tourell moved away.

He had made no attempt to cover her, if those people had chanced to look down and seen them . . . Maggie tensed as she heard him chuckle.

'Stop? When we've only just begun? Now, let me see . . . we have the strawberries with the champagne . . .'

He dipped his fingers into the mixture as he spoke then held them against Maggie's lips. In spite of herself, she felt compelled to draw each of his fingers into her mouth in turn, sucking them clean.

'And we have peaches and cream . . .'

He repeated the motion with his other hand.

'Now . . . the bananas. Yes, here they are. I like to eat my bananas with honey. Don't you?'

His voice was low and hypnotic, seducing her. Maggie was puzzled for a moment and then she felt the soft, firm fruit of a peeled banana stroking against her thigh.

'No!'

He merely chuckled at her shocked cry and nudged gently at her closed thighs with the fruit. Maggie felt a wave of shamed excitement as her legs opened, seemingly of their own accord and her swollen labia parted to allow him access to the innermost recesses of her body.

'Tourell!' she whispered, shocked, 'please . . . I can't . . . Oh!'

The soft, firm banana slid easily into her honeyed passage, filling her with its soft, pulpy flesh until at last her body closed around it.

'Mmm!' Tourell murmured softly, placing a kiss on the top of her shoulder, 'you must see yourself.'

Slowly, Maggie looked down at her naked, sticky body. Her breasts were streaked with pink juice, rivulets of thick, white cream still running in slow, viscous trickles down her breasts and onto her stomach. Levering herself up onto her elbows, she could see the grapes, some crushed now between her legs, their spilt juice glistening on her inner thighs. Though she could not see it, she knew her vulva bulged, full of fruit, and she lay back on the blanket with a small, anguished cry.

Tourell kissed her, tenderly, behind one ear before brushing his lips down to where the champagne had dried in the tender dip at the base of her throat. With exquisite slowness, he licked the strawberry juice from each breasts, drawing her nipples into his mouth one by one and suckling them until they stood, twin peaks of aching desire, glinting in the sunlight.

Maggie's stomach muscles contracted as he turned his attention to her navel, lapping at the thick cream which had pooled there before running his rough tongue down to the edge of the shaven triangle below. The grapes tumbled, disregarded, to the ground as he nuzzled the soft mound and kissed down further, between her legs.

Her thighs spasmed involuntarily as she felt his tongue probe the entrance to her womb and his lips touched the sensitive skin of her perineum. She could feel the firm flesh of the banana, softened now by her feminine moisture, gradually being expelled from her body.

Obeying her natural instincts, Maggie bore down and felt the fruit slipping out of her. As it emerged from her body, Tourell sucked some into his mouth, treating it as if it were the finest caviar. Maggie turned her head away as he brought some up to her lips, but the combination of his insistent fingers at her lips and the sudden, inexorable pressure which was building at the core of here proved too much.

The mixture did indeed taste like honeyed fruit and Maggie did not protest when Tourell once again put his head between her legs. The last of the banana slipped out of her and he held her labia apart as he probed inside her with his tongue.

Maggie could hold back no longer. With a stifled cry, she let go the sensations which had been building steadily all day. Her climax burst from her in wave after pleasurable wave, each one peaking higher than the last. Tourell pressed his lips against her pulsing vulva, drawing out her pleasure so that she writhed beneath him in uncontrollable ecstasy.

It seemed as though hours had passed since they first arrived on the Downs. Tourell re-fastened Maggie's bra and dress over her sticky skin and cradled her in his arms while the after-glow raged through her like a forest fire.

She could feel the hard length of him straining to break through the heavy denim of his jeans and, as she had before, she wondered at his self-control. Yet when she reached out a hand to caress him, he stopped her, standing and pulling her to her feet instead.

'We have a whole weekend ahead,' he said in answer to the question in her eyes.

Maggie shrugged slightly and bent to pick up her sodden panties, but again, Tourell stopped her.

'For me,' he said huskily, 'leave them off this weekend. Be open to me.'

Maggie shivered as the seductive words fluttered against her ear and she began to help him clear away the picnic. It took mere minutes. As they moved away, Maggie looked back at the hollow over her shoulder.

There was no evidence of the debauchery which had taken place on that spot, nothing left behind to show they had been there. Nothing, that is, except a pair of white cotton panties, discarded in the long grass.

Chapter Fifteen

*T*ourell's house was a far grander affair then anything Maggie had envisaged and for a moment as they drew into the driveway, she was lost for words.

Having slept for much of what had remained of the journey, she felt quite drowsy when Tourell killed the engine and turned to look at her.

'*This* is your house?' she asked stupidly.

His mouth twisted into a smile.

'Well, I haven't brought you to a hotel.'

It was big enough to be a hotel, Maggie thought privately as she climbed out of the car and stood looking up at it.

Standing three storeys high it was built of mellow local stone with a vast number of many mullioned windows. Double oak doors were framed by creeping ivy above three well-scrubbed stone steps which swept in an arc at the base.

'Do you live here alone?'

'I have a house-keeper and gardener who live in the annexe. They're away this weekend, though,' he added, catching her expression, 'I asked Mrs Lyons to prepare the rooms and stock the freezer before she left.'

He took her hand when she didn't seem inclined to move and urged her up the steps to the front door.

'You don't come here often then?' she asked as he turned his key in the lock.

'What makes you ask that?' he responded, walking quickly inside and deactivating the sophisticated alarm system their arrival looked set to trigger.

Maggie was too busy looking around her to elaborate. The entire house appeared to have been redecorated recently for everything, from the wallpaper to the light fittings, looked new. The pungent smell of new carpets pervaded the place. Only the furniture seemed as though it had been in the house a while; all of it was dark and heavy and looked to Maggie's untrained eye as though it was in keeping with the age of the house.

'Come through to the sitting room,' Tourell told her. 'You can explore later if you're interested, but really I only use a small number of rooms.'

The sitting room was surprisingly cosy considering the draughtiness of the hallway, though it was still colder inside than out. Glancing approvingly at the warm peach and green colour scheme, Maggie began to relax.

'Do you think I could take a bath? I'm feeling a bit sticky.'

He smiled wickedly at her.

'Maybe we should let you ferment!' he laughed at her look of distaste. 'Up the stairs, first bedroom on the right. There's a bathroom attached. It should have everything there you need.'

'What will you do while I'm gone?'

He shrugged.

'Organise dinner. Make up a fire in here.'

'In the middle of summer?' she was incredulous.

'We'll need it after dark. These old houses don't hold the heat. Don't be long.'

Maggie smiled and walked slowly out of the room, aware of his eyes on her body.

The bedroom was comfortably masculine, the bathroom a sybaritic delight. An enormous, claw-footed Victorian bath, raised on a plinth like an altar dominated a room which was carpeted in plush cream carpet. A stained-glass window almost covered the wall above the bath and Maggie stared in amazement at it. It was unlike any stained-glass window she had ever seen.

The central figure in the window was a woman, creamy skinned and sloe-eyed, her long, dark hair tumbling down across her naked shoulders in vibrant disarray. There was a flush to her pale cheeks and her ruby-red lips were parted slightly to show small, perfect teeth through which the tip of a tiny pink tongue could just be seen.

She was half lying, half sitting on a blood-red *chaise-longue*, naked, save for one foot which, incongruously, was still wearing one shiny black court shoe. The foot which was wearing the shoe was balanced precariously on the floor, the woman's bare heel rising up, out of the shoe, as if it was about to fall off.

The other leg was bent at the knee, the foot resting on an embroidered cushion at the base of the *chaise* and her plump thighs were parted to reveal a tantalising glimpse of the dewy pink flesh between them.

One arm was flung in an evocative gesture of abandonment above her head whilst the other lay across her lap, her hand buried within the warm, wet folds of her labia. Maggie marvelled at the exquisite detail, the astonishing subtleties of colour wrought by the artist. Cold glass had been transformed into a living, sexual woman.

Maggie could feel her own nipples growing hard as

211

she gazed at the glass lady's rosy peaks, her own mouth growing dry as she contemplated the expression on her face. That the woman was near to crisis was evident from the softness of her features; the slackening mouth, the hooded, unfocused eyes.

Feeling the moisture gathering between her own legs in empathy, Maggie dragged her eyes reluctantly away and turned her attention to running the bath. The absent Mrs Lyons had obviously taken care to ensure that there would be a plentiful supply of hot water.

Maggie sat on the side of the bath and peeled away her sticky dress as the bathroom filled with steam. There was a large glass flagon by the ornate taps, filled with varying shades of bath crystals. Lifting out the stopper, Maggie caught the scent of roses and poured a measure into the swirling water.

Immediately, the water began to hiss and foam and the room was filled with the heady floral fragrance Maggie had grown used to encountering at Tourell's apartment.

Glancing down at herself, Maggie saw that her skin was stained with juice; pale pink strawberry and yellow peach, clear grape and smears of thick, white cream, dried to a flaky crust. Between her legs she still felt as though she was oozing mashed banana and she grimaced.

Sinking into the hot, rose-scented water was sheer bliss. Allowing her hair to fan out, Ophelia-like around her head, Maggie lay back and closed her eyes.

It was a large bath, big enough for her to stretch out without her toes touching the far end. Feeling the water buoying her up, Maggie let her arms and legs float for a while as she soaked away the fruit salad Tourell had created on her body.

Recalling the sensation of his hands and lips on her body, lapping at the soft fruits, Maggie shivered with delight. Opening her eyes, she encountered the sensual, knowing gaze of the woman in the stained-glass window and she was once again transfixed.

Had Tourell commissioned this piece expecially? It was certainly a work of art, quite unlike anything Maggie had ever seen before. The woman looked so real, so *alive*, Maggie could almost imagine herself cupping those full, ripe breasts in her hands and teasing the rosy nipples to hardness before reaching lower . . .

Maggie ran her hands over her own breasts, surprised to find her nipples were already erect. Gazing at the woman who watched over her, Maggie ran her hands slowly over her slippery, wet skin, enjoying the feel of the familiar contours of her own body.

Edging her hand between her legs, she found a slipperiness there that had nothing to do with the fragrant water. Her clitoris was already a hard nub of expectation and she teased it gently with the pad of her forefinger.

Was this how the model had felt when she was posing for the artist who had created the stained-glass window? Maggie rubbed herself slowly, enjoying the gradual onset of desire as it crept through her limbs.

Spreading her legs wider, she moved the tiny button of pleasure rhythmically back and forth in silent communion with the glass lady. Gradually, she felt her own eyes droop as the woman's did, felt the heat steal into her cheeks as her lips parted.

It started slowly, so slowly, like the ripples of the tide as it washes up the beach. Maggie's mouth opened wide as the ripples became waves and the waves grew bigger, sweeping her away to the plane where nothing is real save the physical, to the realm where sensation reigns supreme.

Afterwards, she felt rejuvenated and she smiled at the woman in the window. She was still intent upon her own pleasure and Maggie felt absurdly sorry for her, unable as she was to reach fulfilment.

Impatient, suddenly, Maggie pulled out the plug and reached for a towel, eager to rejoin Tourell downstairs. She didn't bother to dress, merely strapping herself in a dry towel, leaving her hair lying wet against her bare shoulders.

Opening the sitting-room door, Maggie saw that Tourell had, true to his word, made up a fire in the grate. He was sitting in an armchair in front of it, a tumbler of whisky by his side. His eyes were closed and he did not react as Maggie softly closed the door behind her.

A haunting melody was playing on the stereo and Tourell had rested his head against the high back of the chair, stretching out his legs in front of him. Watching him for a moment, Maggie noted the rhythmic rise and fall of his chest and realised that he was sleeping.

Disappointment quickly gave way to glee as she thought how she could waken him. Creeping across the room, she began to unfasten his shirt, her touch feather-light, her breathing deliberately shallow.

He did not stir as she reached the bottom button and exposed his chest. It was an attractive chest, broad and well-muscled without a spare inch of flesh. The hair that covered it was thick and black, curling wildly around his flat, brown nipples and arrowing down across the flat plane of his belly to disappear into his jeans.

It gave Maggie a thrill to have him here, vulnerable in front of her. If it had not been certain that he would soon waken, she would have taken her time, explored every inch of him with fingers and tongue . . . as it was, she knew she must act fast.

His belt was easy to undo and slip through its loops. The button at the top of his jeans was stiff and Maggie cursed silently as she struggled with it. Something about the quality of his breathing told her that he had woken, but glancing at him, she saw that he had not opened his eyes. She smiled to herself.

The button gave, at last, after which it was comparatively easy to slide down the zip. He wasn't wearing underwear, a fact that sent a small *frisson* of delight racing along Maggie's nerve-endings. She was unsurprised to find he was hard already as she took his cock into her hands and bent her head.

Her wet hair fell onto his belly, showering him with little droplets of water. She felt his stomach muslces clench involuntarily and she smiled as she opened her mouth and enclosed him.

His cock seemed to swell and fill her mouth as she ran her tongue lovingly along the shaft, tickling the sensitive area where the shaft met the vulnerable sac at its base. He shuddered as she moved her mouth slowly up and down, tantalising him.

There was no doubt that he was awake now and Maggie allowed the towel to fall away from her still-damp body so that he would be tempted by the soft, pink skin offered to him. She was not disappointed. Groaning softly, Tourell ran his palms down her back, following the line of her spine as she bent over him, moulding the shape of her upturned buttocks.

Suddenly, unexpectedly, he delivered a sharp, stinging slap to her unprotected bottom. The shock made Maggie cry out, so that his cock slipped out of her mouth. She tried to straighten up, but Tourell's arm came down across her back, pressing her down so that she was lying across his lap, her head and shoulders dangling helplessly towards the floor.

He held her still, ignoring her struggles as he slapped her again. This time the sound of his palm against her tender flesh seemed to echo round the room and Maggie began to protest.

'Let me up! Tourell . . . Oh!'

Ignoring her, he smacked her again, then again, soothing the stinging flesh each time with the palm of his hand before bringing it down again. Maggie's cries of indignation very quickly turned to soft sighs as the heat travelled through her body.

She writhed against Tourell's lap as her flesh shivered under his touch, the rough denim chafing the tender skin of her stomach. His cock rested comfortably in the flattened valley between her breasts and she was aware of its potent presence even while her entire attention seem focused on the pleasurable pain radiating out from her poor, spanked bottom.

It was some seconds before Maggie realised he had stopped smacking her. His fingers were cool as they travelled over her buttocks and between the twin globes. Maggie tensed as his fingertips traced the shape of the tattoo which nestled on one side of her cleft.

'A black orchid,' he breathed.

Maggie closed her eyes as she recalled the day she had been badged as a member of the Black Orchid Club. The memory of the fear as she entered the tattooist's shop, joined inexorably with that other, sweeter memory of the first time she had been aroused by the sight of another woman's body, unlocking deep and secret desires which, ultimately, had been the key to her liberation . . .

She sighed as Tourell's fingers continued on their journey, sinking slowly in to the sweet, honeyed warmth of her vulva. Her clitoris pulsed with an echo of her earlier climax as his fingers brushed teasingly against it.

Suddenly, he took hold of her upper arms and lifted her bodily to her feet. Maggie saw the urgency in his eyes and felt a thrill travel through her. Straddling him, she guided his shaft inside her, balancing herself with her palms against his shoulders.

Penetration was so much deeper this way, with Tourell's cock head touching the very neck of her womb. Maggie felt the perspiration break out all over her body as he gathered her to him with his arms about her waist and began to rock her gently back and forth, his head pressed hard against her naked breasts.

Cradling his head in her hands, Maggie encouraged him to take one aching nipple into his mouth. The compelling tug of his lips at her breasts set up an answering pull deep in her womb and she began to rise up and down on his lap, drawing him in so that she felt the friction caused by his penis moving against the silky internal skin. Every ripple reverberated in her head so that she could think of nothing else but the movement of his body within hers.

The skin of her bottom felt sore as she bounced lightly on his unzipped jeans, the moisture from her body seeping into the heavy fabric. She did not resist as Tourell bent her back over his arm and let go of her breast. Reaching behind her, she balanced her hands on his knees, watching through heavy lidded eyes as his gaze raked her body, open to him now, his cock buried deep within her.

She threw back her head as he pressed her clitoris with his thumb and rolled it within its skin. Wet hair streaming down her naked back, Maggie lifted one hand and reached behind her so that she could feel the joining of their bodies. His cock was soaked with her juices, slippery to the touch.

Cupping his hair-roughened testicles with her hand she squeezed, gently kneading them between her fingers as his breath began to come in short, gasping bursts. And as he neared his climax, Maggie came, crying out his name in a frenzy of triumphal joy.

Tourell wrapped her legs about his waist and buried his face in the damp valley between her breasts. Holding her to him, he pressed them against either side of his face, moving his head from side to side as his own orgasm began to subside.

Maggie ran her fingers through his hair over and over, raining kisses on his forehead, on the top of his ears, anywhere her lips could reach.

It was a long time before either of them felt inclined to move.

Later they ate defrosted beef stroganoff in front of the fire, both wrapped in towelling dressing gowns. Tourell's hair was still damp from his shower and it curled rebelliously on his forehead and around his ears.

He appeared to be relaxed and Maggie felt disinclined to talk. For the first time since they had met she felt comfortable with him. She frowned at the thought.

'What is it?'

He picked up on her change of expression immediately and Maggie glanced ruefully at him, not sure that she liked being this transparent. What she saw in his eyes made the breath catch in her throat and her mouth and lips dried.

How she could have imagined for a moment that she could be 'comfortable' with him she did not know. He was like a sleeping tiger, acquiescent, for now, but still deadly. Maggie let the atavistic shiver of apprehension run through her body, facing it, converting it into desire.

'You remind me of Alexander sometimes,' she blurted.

She hadn't meant to say it, but as the words escaped her lips she knew that it was true, Tourell did, on occasion, remind her very much of Alex.

He raised an eyebrow at her, though he didn't reply, merely smiling enigmatically. Encouraged by his lack of censure, Maggie could not contain her curiosity.

'You know each other well, don't you? You and Alexander? Were you lovers once?'

She could see by his face that she had managed to surprise him. For a moment, he looked quite stunned, and Maggie began to feel foolish. Throwing back his head, he roared with laughter.

'Lovers? I'm sorry to disappoint you, Maggie, but I don't swing that way. But you're right, I do know Alexander. Speaking of whom, tell me about the trip you were sent on not so long ago.'

Seeing that Tourell was not about to give her any more information, Maggie settled back into her seat and tried to focus her mind. It still made her uneasy, carrying information back and forth between the two men about each other. So far she had managed to keep them happy without divulging anything of substance about either of them, but still she was no nearer knowing why they each wanted to know about the other than she was before.

'Antony was thinking about setting up a hotel,' she revealed grudgingly.

'Something along the lines of the Black Orchid Club?'

'That's right, except the hotel wouldn't be for women only, rather it would cater for couples. I thought it was a very good idea,' she continued, her enthusiasm for the apparently forgotten project unabated. 'It would give both men and women a chance to act out their fantasies in a controlled environment.'

'So why isn't Antony going ahead with the idea?'

Maggie shrugged.

'I honestly don't know. Alex must have mooted some kind of reason why it isn't a good idea.'

'Why do you think it's Alexander who's thrown a spanner in the works?' Tourell asked her reasonably.

'I don't know for sure. It's just that Antony was so keen on the idea to start with, he'd even gone as far as drawing up a business plan for the bank. But Tony wouldn't do anything without Alexander's approval and when they called me back from my trip, Antony's enthusiasm had definitely waned.'

'But yours hasn't?' he prompted shrewdly as Maggie chewed on her lower lip.

'As I said, I think it's an excellent idea. I'd hoped to have a chance to set it up.'

Tourell leaned slightly towards her, though he did not reach out and touch her as she expected. Instead he spoke softly, so that his sweet breath caressed her cheek.

'You could do it yourself.'

Maggie looked towards him, surprised.

'Without Antony and Alexander?'

He shrugged and sat back in the seat, his expression amused.

'Why not? You're obviously capable of making a go of it and there's no reason why you couldn't present a business plan to the bank.'

Maggie smiled cynically.

'What bank is going to give me money to set up what they would almost certainly regard as a den of iniquity?'

Tourell shrugged again, the bored expression which crept over his face telling her plainly that he had tired of the subject.

'A private investor then. Whatever. But I didn't bring you here to talk business.'

Maggie grinned wickedly.

'Oh? And what did you bring me here for?'

His eyes passed slowly over her body in blatant assessment.

'To fuck you. In every way possible, as often as you can take it.'

Maggie's eyes opened wide at the crudeness of his statement. A rush of fluid between her legs told her that her body wasn't offended, and her mind . . .? It was simply a question of changing up a gear.

With a smile spreading slowly across her face, Maggie crept along the settee and into Tourell's waiting arms.

Antony woke up to find the bed empty beside him. Reaching for his robe, he went through on soundless, bare feet to the living room and saw Alexander staring out of the darkened window.

He paused. Alexander was naked, his golden skin made silver by the moonlight streaming through the unshielded window. His dark blond hair look grey, his broad, powerful shoulders sweeping gracefully from his long, strong neck.

The finely sculpted lines of his back tapered into his neatly indented waist, the harmonious swell of his buttocks with the delectable shadow between melting into hard, hair-roughened thighs. Even his calves were shapely, as if moulded from clay be expert hands. A perfect Adonis, standing motionless in the moonlight.

'Alex?' Antony whispered.

Alexander did not turn, though a sudden tension in the way he held his head betrayed that he had heard.

'Can't you sleep?'

Antony walked slowly to the window and put his hand on Alexander's shoulder. The skin was cool and dry, silky smooth and irresistible to the touch. Antony could feel the tension in him and waited, knowing that eventually he would speak.

'He's trying to destroy me,' he said at last.

Antony did not need to ask who, Tourell had been a tangible presence between them for weeks.

'Why would he want to do that?' he asked reasonably.

'Why not?'

Alexander's voice was barely more than a whisper, yet there was no discernible emotion there, merely a flat monotone. Antony frowned, worried for him.

'You've got to stop this, Alex, it's taking over our lives.'

Alexander turned his head and Antony was shocked by the flatness in his eyes.

'Maggie is with him this weekend. How can you sleep, knowing that?'

Antony shrugged and dropped his eyes. 'Maggie is a free agent,' he mumbled unconvincingly.

Alex gave a short, harsh laugh. 'He's using her to get closer to me.'

Antony sighed. 'Would that be so bad?' he asked gently, flinching away from the look of fury Alexander darted at him. 'All right, I understand. But I can't see the point in losing sleep over it.'

'I'm going down there tomorrow,' he said, as if he hadn't heard.

'Going down . . . but why? What would be the point in a confrontation?'

Alexander turned away from the window and Antony gave an inward sigh as he saw the implacable resolve written on his beloved's face.

'All right. I'll come with you. Only do you think we could get just a couple of hours sleep first?'

Alexander smiled for the first time, a smile that lit up his face and made Antony remember why he would travel to the ends of the earth with him. Or, at least, to the Cotswolds to confront Tourell.

Chapter Sixteen

Maggie awoke to a cacophony of bird-song. Opening her eyes, she squinted against the sunlight streaming across the bed, only gradually becoming aware that she was alone.

Her hand snaked out to touch the indentation in the feather mattress where Tourell had slept beside her. It was cold. Frowning, she tried to remember whether he had said anything about his plans for the morning the night before. She smiled. Whatever Tourell had said the night before, it was nothing to do with the morning. And everything to do with how he had intended for them to spend the night.

Yawning, Maggie sat up in bed. She felt sore and sticky, so she hauled herself to the bathroom and ran a bath. The glass lady looked down kindly on her as she soaped away the excess of the night and lay back to soak in the water.

Tourell had proved himself a tireless lover. He had that rare combination of attributes; the stamina of youth combined with the experience of an older man. Maggie shivered at the memory of his hands and mouth on her body, in her body, driving her to the point of hysteria with his insatiable demands.

Her entire body felt pleasurably sore as she patted herself dry with a soft towel. Dressing quickly in a short black skirt and hot pink halter-necked blouse, Maggie brushed out her hair and tried to imagine what the day would bring.

The kitchen was empty when she found it. Alarm chased through her – surely Tourell wouldn't have left without so much as a word? Looking out of the window, she was relieved to see him sitting at a table on the paved terrace. He looked relaxed, dressed in denim jeans and a white shirt, a dark red silk tie knotted loosely at his throat.

His eyes skimmed her body appreciatively as she went out to join him.

'You're awake at last!' he smiled. 'How do you walk in those ridiculously high-heeled shoes?'

Maggie sat down, not sure whether he was expecting an answer. Glancing at him, she saw that he was laughing at her.

'Croissants?'

He passed her a covered bowl filled with flaky golden croissants, still warm from the oven. Maggie took one and broke it apart, smothering it in pure butter and strawberry jam.

'Hmmm! This is delicious!' she announced, trying to catch a trickle of melted butter which was rolling down her chin with the tip of her tongue.

'Have another,' he offered, pouring her a cup of strong black coffee.

Maggie ate until she had sated her appetite, sitting back in her seat with a small groan of protest when he offered her a fourth.

'No, my skirt feels tight already!'

Tourell's eyes narrowed in a way she was coming to recognise.

'Perhaps you should take it off.'

Maggie laughed, a little nervously.

'What, here? In the garden?'

Tourell shrugged and swept his hand around them.

'There's no one here but ourselves.'

'Yes, but . . . I can't!'

Maggie felt foolish. How could she explain that the idea of being out in the open like this inhibited her? That after all that she had done to him, allowed him to do to her, she felt embarrassed at the thought of sitting in the garden with him without her skirt.

'What do you have on underneath?'

'Just my pants,' she shrugged self-consciously, suddenly remembering that he had asked her to leave her pants off during this weekend.

Darting a glance at him from beneath her lashes, she was relieved to see that he appeared to have forgotten.

'No stockings, your legs are bare?'

She nodded, feeling the heat creeping inexplicably into her cheeks.

'What colour are your panties?'

'Black.'

'Bikini briefs or camiknickers?'

'They're . . . they're thong style. Black lace at the front and a thong at the back . . .'

She could not believe she was having a conversation about her knickers in the middle of a sunny country garden on a weekend morning such as this.

'Ah. So even as we speak, there is a fine strip of fabric nestling between your delectable buttocks, pressing deliciously against the tight little hole which you so loved me to penetrate with my tongue last night.'

Maggie blushed to the roots of her hair. She had indeed enjoyed the sensation of his tongue pushing

225

into her anus as his fingers filled the silken sheath of her vagina, opening her and tormenting the tight, hard bud of her clitoris as it strained against his thumb. But somehow, out here, his words seemed so incongruous, so shaming . . .

Tourell was smiling, making no secret of the fact that he was enjoying her discomfiture.

'Take off the skirt, Maggie,' he said, almost gently. 'It's hardly more than a scrap of fabric anyway. What possible difference could it make to your modesty?'

There was a note of command in his voice which Maggie found infinitely thrilling. Silently, she stood and wriggled her hips as she slid down the skirt, stepping out of it and kicking it under her chair.

'Very nice,' Tourell said softly as his eyes lingered on her lace-covered pubis.

Maggie sat down, conscious of the coldness of the cast-iron seat against her bare thighs. Tourell picked up the coffee pot and poured them both another cup.

'Of course,' he said conversationally, 'I shall have to punish you for wearing knickers in the first place.'

Maggie sat very still. The sounds which had surrounded her in the garden receded as the blood rushed in her ears. So he hadn't forgotten his edict and her disobedience to it had displeased him. He was going to punish her.

Very slowly, Maggie raised her eyes to his. His pupils had dilated so that they almost covered the irises and he was watching her intently. Suddenly, unexpectedly, he smiled.

'Would you like to see the garden?'

Maggie blinked at the change of subject, forcing her mind to emerge from the sensual fog which had been slowly invading it, and to concentrate.

'I have a wonderful gardener,' he was saying, pushing back his seat and standing. 'He's a genius when it comes to knowing exactly where a plant will best thrive and what conditions it needs to make it grow. Come, let me show you the rose garden. It's one of my favourite places.'

Maggie stood up, pulling ineffectually at the hemline of her halter-necked top as a cool breeze touched the bare skin at her midriff. She could imagine the sight she presented in her spindly high-heeled sandals, wearing nothing but a bright pink top and a pair of black lace thong briefs. Anyone coming up behind her would receive a startling view of her rear end.

'There's no one else here but us, Maggie,' Tourell assured her, as if reading her mind.

He held out his hand to her and Maggie moved forward uncertainly. His fingers were hard, yet warm as they closed over hers. Pulling her closer to him, she was supremely aware of the innate maleness of him, the combination of musk and woodsmoke that scented his skin, the warmth of smooth skin over hard muscle.

They walked along a narrow pathway which meandered through several flower beds, towards a screen of leylandi bushes some metres away from the terrace. A wooden archway connected the two halves of the hedge. As they walked through it Maggie's hair caught on a frond of overgrown clematis, making her falter.

Turning, Tourell saw her predicament and stopped to disentangle her. His fingers were gentle in her hair as he pulled the plant out of it. Maggie stood absolutely still, aware of a yearning ache beginning deep in her womb. More than anything, she wanted him to reach for her, to crush her in his arms and hold her against the hard wall of his chest.

She could have reached out herself, made the first move, but something stopped her. An awareness, an intuitive perception about his mood told her that he would not welcome her advances at this juncture.

There was a sense of control about him, an aura of power which Maggie was loath to dispel. He had said he intended to punish her for her minor transgression. She shivered, eager to find out what form his reprisal would take. Confident that his aim was as much her pleasure as her humiliation.

It was glorious, being able to trust him enough to agree to play such deliciously decadent games. And yet he was still enough of an enigma to her for there to remain a small, thrilling sense of danger . . .

He smiled slightly, tucking her hair over one ear as he smoothed it off her face. They walked on, the path sloping downwards now as they travelled through several raised beds, winding their way through a series of secret gardens, each hidden from the last.

Maggie was entranced by the garden. There were so many fragrant corners and secret places, so many ways for lovers to conceal themselves. They passed a summerhouse, moss-covered and rickety with age. For a moment Maggie thought that Tourell was going to stop and take her into its shady interior, but no, he urged her on, his grip on her elbow slightly tighter now, his face set and tense.

Casting a regretful glance over her shoulder at the summerhouse, Maggie walked beside him, struggling now to keep up with his longer legs. It wasn't easy to walk on the uneven pathway in her impractical sandals, and several times she stumbled, once twisting her ankle slightly so that she cried out in pain.

Tourell's step never faltered, he merely hauled her up, saving her from further injury, and virtually frog-marched her through yet another archway. To Maggie's relief, his steps slowed as they passed through it. She gapsed as she looked around her.

They appeared to have arrived at the farthest boundary to Tourell's land for the garden laid out in front of them was walled on three sides. On the wall facing them, seats had been cut into the stone at regular intervals and two almost identical statues were set in a recess at each side.

In the centre of the wall there was a small, green-painted door, heavily padlocked. In line with this, half-way between the door and the archway where they now stood, there was a sturdy wooden pergola, circular in design with an intricate carving of a bird at its apex. Radiating out from the central pergola, there were six narrow pathways, one of which led to the green door, one to the archway. Each of the remaining four led to the four corners of the walled garden, to a smaller pergola.

And everywhere Maggie looked, there were roses. Roses in bud, roses in bloom, roses shedding their petals over the elderly pathway. The garden was a riot of colour; pinks mingled with blood-red and orange, yellow interspersed with exotic purples and blues. Hybrids with speckled petals and pure white double-headed blooms, so heavy their stems were bending under their weight.

And the smell. The air was heavy with perfume as Maggie slowly walked ahead of Tourell, down the three steps which led into the rose garden and along the narrow path to the central pergola. It made her head ache as the heady scents mingled around her, competing with each other for prominence.

Intuitively, she stopped beneath the pergola. It was providing support for a climbing rose and Maggie reached up her hand to touch the satiny, soft petals of the delicate, pale pink flowers.

Tourell caught her hand in mid-air and caressed the fragile span of her wrist. Lowering her upturned eyes slowly to his, Maggie felt her pulse quicken as she saw the naked desire written on his features.

Above her head, the wooden structure criss-crossed in an intricate lattice to the centre. Where each strand of wood met, Maggie saw there was a large metal ring screwed securely into the apex. Her mouth dried as Tourell produced a skein of fine, white rope and looped the end up, through the ring.

Instinctively, she tried to pull out of his grasp, but he was too strong for her. He smiled wolfishly as he wound one end of the rope around her wrist so that her arm was tied to the metal ring above her head.

Standing back, he admired his handiwork for a moment before raising a quizzical eyebrow at her.

'Your other arm?'

He was giving her a chance to retreat, to refuse to participate. Reassured, Maggie slowly held out her free arm. Basking in his approving gaze, she watched as he wrapped the rope around her wrist and brought it up to join the other one above her head.

Even in her high heels, Maggie found she had to stretch up, balancing precariously on the balls of her feet. The skin beneath her arms pulled, close to the edge of discomfort. Tourell walked slowly round her and she turned her head to watch him, her bare skin tingling where his eyes raked her body.

The tension between them added to the heady, almost surreal atmosphere. Maggie could feel her stomach muscles knotting with apprehension as Tourell caught her eye and stared at her, unsmiling, for a full minute. Her eyes widened as he leaned over into the garden and pulled a cane from the dark, moist soil.

It was a garden cane, long and thin with gnarled bumps at intervals along its length. Maggie watched with horrified fascination as Tourell took out a clean, white handkerchief and carefully wiped off all traces of soil. A small cry of alarm escaped her lips as he suddenly wielded it through the air, once, twice, as if testing its flexibility. As if wishing to leave her in no doubt as to his intentions for the cane, he hit it twice against his denim-covered thigh, nodding as he heard the dull thwack of contact.

It was all too much for Maggie.

'Tourell, I . . .'

The words dried on her tongue as she saw his expression. It was dark and forbidding, his normally sensual mouth hardened to a thin, uncompromising line.

'It would be a pity to have to gag you,' he said thoughtfully. 'I'd prefer to hear your cries. But if you persist in talking . . .'

Maggie shook her head, whether to confirm she would remain silent, or whether to protest further, even she did not know. Tourell smiled again and her blood ran cold.

'It would be interesting to blindfold you, though. It would add to your pleasure if you didn't know what was coming next, don't you think?'

As he spoke he unknotted his tie and wound each end around his fists, pulling it tight between them. Approaching Maggie, he scanned her wide eyes and smiled. Maggie could not look away from him, could not so much as utter a sound for her mouth had dried and her lips felt parched.

Unexpectedly, Tourell dipped his head and ran the tip of his tongue along the line of her lips. They parted slightly as he placed a tiny kiss at the corner of her mouth before moving away, leaving her wanting.

Approaching her from behind, he placed the tie over her eyes and fastened it securely at the back of her head. It was too narrow to plunge her completely into darkness, and Maggie was glad of the two parallel, thin strips of light at top and bottom, even though she could not actually see anything.

231

She flinched as the cane whistled through the air, so close to her that she felt the quick draught as it passed. Tourell chuckled.

'Ah, Maggie! I'm going to enjoy this so much!'

He placed two fingers at the base of her throat and caressed the soft skin in the dip between her collarbones. Maggie was breathing very shallowly, her entire body held taut in readiness for the inevitable pain.

The whistle of the cane alerted her to its imminence seconds before it made contact with one exposed buttock. She howled, shocked by the intensity of it. Tourdell's hand passed across her bottom, caressing, soothing, before he brought the cane down again, this time on the other side.

Maggie cried out again, her body swaying as she tried to twist out of his reach.

'Stop! I can't . . .'

She felt Tourell's breath against her face.

'Shut up,' he said mildly. 'The only time you speak is to say "thank you", or to beg me to hit you again.'

Maggie could barely hear him, her entire consciousness was focused on the searing heat which had invaded her behind. With the heat came a sharper, more piquant sensation which intrigued her.

'Please . . .' she whispered.

Tourell ran his finger down the side of her cheek, passing it along the edge of her soft bottom lip before replying.

'Please what?'

Maggie groaned softly, unable to retrieve her self-possession.

'Please hit me again.'

The words whispered over her lips, like a benediction. It was almost a relief when the cane whooshed through the air again and landed squarely across her buttocks.

This time the pleasure followed hard on the heels of the pain and Maggie had no hesitation in thanking him. Hot tears seeped through the tie which covered her eyes and rolled down her cheeks. Her lips parted of their own volition, her mouth, her body opening up to the sweet pleasure/pain Tourell was inflicting upon her.

The rose-scented air seemed to have stilled around her. She started as Tourell rubbed a flower against her cheeks, crushing the petals so that their scent was released, making her head spin.

'Tell me how you feel,' he whispered.

Maggie sagged a little in her restraint.

'I . . . I feel very hot. My bottom is burning, little waves of heat travelling through me . . . on fire . . .'

'And are you wet? Let's find out, shall we?'

He thrust his hand roughly between her legs and squeezed her black lace covered pubis, pushing the material deep into the swollen folds of skin. Maggie writhed on his hand, begging him without words to pleasure her.

Tourell brought his hand up to her face and smeared her lips with the evidence of her arousal.

'You *do* like it, don't you?' he commented silkily.

His voice changed, becoming business-like as he rested his hands on her bare waist.

'Now, lets have a look at these, shall we? See what pleasure your gorgeous breasts can bring.'

Maggie gasped as he suddenly yanked up the halter-necked top and her breasts tumbled free into the scented air. Her nipples hardened instantly and she groaned as Tourell pinched them cruelly between his fingers.

'Lean forward.'

She obeyed him automatically, shuffling her feet back so that her bottom was thrust into the air, her breasts dangling freely. Tourell squeezed and kneaded them.

'Beautiful, so soft and pliable . . .'

He swung them slightly from side to side, letting them go so that they shivered under their own weight. Maggie gasped as he delivered two sharp slaps to their undersides and her tender flesh rippled.

'If only you could see them, Maggie! They quiver so beautifully, the nipples so pink and hard and tempting . . .'

He slapped them again and Maggie writhed, wriggling her bottom which then promptly received the same treatment.

'Please . . .!' she groaned, not knowing what it was that she pleaded for, only that she was desperate for release.

Tourell's response was to pick up the cane and begin tantalising her with it, flicking her with light, teasing strokes whilst fondling her unencumbered breasts with the other hand.

'God, you're beautiful,' he breathed and Maggie felt a surge of gratification at the betraying tremor in his voice. He wasn't so unaffected then.

'More,' she breathed, inciting him with a twitch of her hips, 'more, then I want you to take me, like this . . .'

Antony glanced at Alexander with concern as they drew up outside the house. He had hardly said a word all the way and now his mouth seemed fixed in a grim line and his mind was somewhere Antony could not reach.

There was no reply to the bell.

'Maybe they've gone out?' Antony suggested hopefully.

Alexander shook his head.

'I know where they'll be.'

Striding round the side of the house, Alexander

unlatched the gate and began to walk through the garden.

Maggie cried out with relief as Tourell finally pulled off her sodden briefs. She could hear him drawing his belt through the loops of his jeans, hear the zip travelling downward and the muted creak of the denim as he pushed them down.

His cock was hard and hot as it passed across the sore skin of her bottom. Maggie spread her legs eagerly, desperate to feel him inside her, filling her to capacity.

Reaching round her waist, Tourell took hold of her breasts and thrust himself with unerring accuracy into the wet, welcoming gate to her body.

Antony had to hurry to keep up with Alexander as he walked purposefully through the myriad of gardens within a garden. He gained a fleeting impression of colour and scent and rich, loamy soil, but he did not have time to look around him.

Alexander obviously knew where he was heading. Antony almost cannoned into him as he came to a standstill beneath a rose-covered archway. Then he saw what Alex had seen and he sucked in his breath.

There was Maggie, suspended from a pergola in the centre of the rose garden, naked save for a pink top which had been pushed up around her neck and her impossibly high heels. She was blindfolded. Her breast were swinging freely, jerking in time to the rhythmic thrusts of her body.

Antony recognised Tourell instantly. Maggie was facing them, but Tourell's legs could be seen planted firmly on the ground either side of her hips while his hands spanned her waist. He was pumping his hips back and forth as his cock plunged in and out of Maggie's writhing body. Antony felt his own cock harden and swell in response and he glanced at Alexander.

Tourell had clearly spotted them, for he and Alex had locked eyes across the few metres which separated them. To Antony's relief, Alexander's eyes were bright, not with fury, but with passion.

'Go and suck her breasts, Tony,' he whispered.

Antony needed no second request. Moving soundlessly, he approached the couple and sank to his knees.

Maggie gasped as one breast was taken into a hot mouth. Tourell was still behind her, so she knew it could not possibly be him who was now lathing her nipples with his tongue. There was a second man in the garden with them.

'Who . . .? Oh!'

Her protest was cut off mid-sentence as the second man put his head between her legs and began to lick eagerly at her exposed clitoris. Suddenly it didn't matter who it was, so long as they made her come.

It didn't take long. Seconds after Tourell withdrew, spilling his seed all over her upturned buttocks, Maggie ground down hard on the unknown man's tongue and her own climax overcame her.

Tourell rubbed the semen into her abused flesh as if it were a soothing balm until Maggie, spent at last, slumped, her entire weight supported by the metal ring in the roof of the pergola.

She was barely aware of the strong, gentle hands which untied her and swept her up, carrying her back to the house. But they were familiar hands, and Maggie felt safe and protected.

It wasn't until they reached the bedroom and she was laid on top of the bed that she opened her eyes and found herself staring into Antony's smiling grey eyes.

'You! What . . .?'

'Ssh! I'll explain everything while we bathe.'

'Where's Tourell?' Maggie asked as she watched Antony fill the bath with water.

He waited until she was submerged up to her neck before climbing in with her.

'Don't worry – he's downstairs.'

'Is Alexander here too?'

Antony put out a hand to restrain her as she made to leap out of the bath.

'They're best left alone – they have a lot of talking to do.'

'Don't you mind?' she asked curiously.

Antony frowned slightly, puzzled by her question.

'Mind? Why should I mind?'

Maggie felt the colour seeping into her cheeks.

'Well, I . . . I would have thought that if Tourell had been with Alex before you . . . what's so funny?'

Antony was laughing, comprehension on his face.

'You thought they were lovers?' he asked, passing her the soap and working up a lather on his chest.

Maggie nodded, perplexed.

'Maggie, Alexander is Tourell's *son*.'

'His son?'

Antony laughed again, delighted with her surprise.

'I thought you'd realised.'

Maggie shook her head, struggling to come to grips with this new information. Tourell – Alexander's *father*? It seemed impossible, and yet . . . little things came back to her. The curious sense of familiarity when she first saw him, the photograph on his bedside cabinet . . . the inexplicable flashes which had reminded her of Alex. Thinking about it, everything did have a curious sense of credibility. Some things still bothered her, though.

'But why did they want me to spy on each other?'

Antony shrugged.

'I wouldn't mind finding that out for myself,' he admitted.

They left the bath and dried themselves. Maggie noticed Antony's gaze on the beautiful glass lady and saw his erection. She smiled. Any other time and she would have been glad to relieve him of it, but right now she wanted to know what was going on.

Alexander and Tourell were sitting in the living room. Both hid their emotions well, though the hostility in the room was far milder than either Maggie or Antony had expected.

'Why did you bring me here?' she asked Tourell without preamble.

He smiled at her, offering up his hands in a placatory gesture.

'Not purely for the reasons you assume.'

'But you did expect Alex to follow us?'

He dropped his eyes for a moment. When he raised them again, Maggie saw that he was trying to be honest with her.

'Alex and I had so much to sort out between us. It's been many years since we've been alone together.'

Maggie turned to Alex and saw that he was watching her warily.

'Is that why you sent me to the casino? Because you wanted an excuse to approach Tourell?'

Alexander did not reply, merely looking away from her and picking idly at a loose thread on a cushion. There was a heavy silence for several minutes. Then Tourell rose and, walking over to Maggie, he said gently,

'You're angry, Maggie, and so you should be. You might well feel used, but believe me, no one meant for you to get hurt.'

Maggie moved away from him, folding her arms across her body. Glancing at Antony out of the corner of her eyes, she saw that he was frowning, torn between supporting her and going over to Alexander.

'And did it work, this ridiculous subterfuge?'

Tourell glanced at Alexander, who studiously avoided his gaze.

'It might,' Tourell said wearily.

Maggie decided it was time for her to leave.

'Where are you going?' Tourell caught her arm as she headed for the door.

She looked down at it pointedly and he let it go.

'I had hoped you'd stay here, with me,' he said softly.

Maggie looked at him incredulously. After all that had happened, he thought she would stay?

'Or you could come back to the club with us.'

It was the first time Alexander had spoken and Maggie was surprised by the defiance of his tone. Looking from him to Tourell, she saw the antagonism that lay between them and her heart went out to them both.

Both offers were tempting, in their way. Her relationship with Tourell was new and exciting, but his demand that she be faithful was not one which filled her with joy.

Living with Antony and Alexander had opened her eyes to so many new experiences, she was sure that she could be happy with them for a while longer. But a whole world was waiting out there, beyond the three corners of their *ménage à trois*.

Suddenly, Maggie knew exactly what she was going to do.

'I'm sorry,' she said decisively, 'but I've decided to go it alone. Tourell – remember you said I would be quite capable of setting up and running a hotel on my own? Well, I agree with you. I know it was your idea originally, Alex, but since you seem to have lost interest . . .?'

She left her sentence unfinished, inviting him to protest. He stared intently at her for a moment, then he shrugged his shoulders and waved a hand at her.

'I wish you luck, Maggie.'

She turned her attention to Tourell. He looked disappointed, but his smile was regretful rather than heartbroken.

Maggie felt light-hearted suddenly. With one last smile at the room at large she walked out and ran upstairs to pack her bag.

'Can I come in?'

She turned in surprise as Antony appeared in the doorway.

'Of course.'

He watched her for a moment, waiting until she had zipped up her case and glanced at him expectantly.

'You're serious about the hotel?'

She nodded.

'Would you consider a partnership?'

Maggie could hardly believe her ears.

'Have you discussed this with Alexander?'

Antony glanced towards the door and smiled.

'Alex isn't a problem,' he replied enigmatically.

'What about the club?'

'I thought I could still live there, with Alex. Your hotel would be another interest, that's all. What do you say?'

Maggie considered for a moment. Antony's expertise would be an invaluable asset to her. She could grasp her independence without entirely breaking her ties with the club and the two men who ran it. She smiled.

'OK,' she held out her hand. 'It's a deal!'

Antony took her hand in his and they grinned at each other. Simultaneously, they moved together, their lips colliding in a kiss to seal the deal. In slow motion, they sank as one onto the big double bed.

BLACK
lace

NO LADY
Saskia Hope

30 year-old Kate dumps her boyfriend, walks out of her job and sets off in search of sexual adventure. Set against the rugged terrain of the Pyrenees, the love-making is as rough as the landscape. Only a sense of danger can satisfy her longing for erotic encounters beyond the boundaries of ordinary experience.

ISBN 0 352 32857 6

WEB OF DESIRE
Sophie Danson

High-flying executive Marcie is gradually drawn away from the normality of her married life. Strange messages begin to appear on her computer, summoning her to sinister and fetishistic sexual liaisons with strangers whose identity remains secret. She's given glimpses of the world of The Omega Network, where her every desire is known and fulfilled.

ISBN 0 352 32856 8

BLUE HOTEL
Cherri Pickford

Hotelier Ramon can't understand why best-selling author Floy Pennington has come to stay at his quiet hotel in the rural idyll of the English countryside. Her exhibitionist tendencies are driving him crazy, as are her increasingly wanton encounters with the hotel's other guests.

ISBN 0 352 32858 4

CASSANDRA'S CONFLICT
Fredrica Alleyn

Behind the respectable facade of a house in present-day Hampstead lies a world of decadent indulgence and darkly bizarre eroticism. The sternly attractive Baron and his beautiful but cruel wife are playing games with the young Cassandra, employed as a nanny in their sumptuous household. Games where only the Baron knows the rules, and where there can only be one winner.

ISBN 0 352 32859 2

THE CAPTIVE FLESH
Cleo Cordell

Marietta and Claudine, French aristocrats saved from pirates, learn their invitation to stay at the opulent Algerian mansion of their rescuer, Kasim, requires something in return; their complete surrender to the ecstasy of pleasure in pain. Kasim's decadent orgies also require the services of the handsome blonde slave, Gabriel – perfect in his male beauty. Together in their slavery, they savour delights at the depths of shame.

ISBN 0 352 32872 X

PLEASURE HUNT
Sophie Danson

Sexual adventurer Olympia Deschamps is determined to become a member of the Legion D'Amour – the most exclusive society of French libertines who pride themselves on their capacity for limitless erotic pleasure. Set in Paris – Europe's most romantic city – Olympia's sense of unbridled hedonism finds release in an extraordinary variety of libidinous challenges.

ISBN 0 352 32880 0

BLACK ORCHID
Roxanne Carr

The Black Orchid is a women's health club which provides a specialised service for its high-powered clients; women who don't have the time to spend building complex relationships, but who enjoy the pleasures of the flesh. One woman, having savoured the erotic delights on offer at this spa of sensuality, embarks on a quest for the ultimate voyage of self-discovery through her sexuality. A quest which will test the unique talents of the exquisitely proportioned male staff.

ISBN 0 352 32888 6

ODALISQUE
Fleur Reynolds

A tale of family intrigue and depravity set against the glittering backdrop of the designer set. Auralie and Jeanine are cousins, both young, glamorous and wealthy. Catering to the business classes with their design consultancy and exclusive hotel, this facade of respectability conceals a reality of bitter rivalry and unnatural love.

ISBN 0 352 32887 8

OUTLAW LOVER
Saskia Hope

Fee Cambridge lives in an upper level deluxe pleasuredome of technologically advanced comfort. The pirates live in the harsh outer reaches of the decaying 21st century city where lawlessness abounds in a sexual underworld. Bored with her predictable husband and pampered lifestyle, Fee ventures into the wild side of town, finding an an outlaw who becomes her lover. Leading a double life of piracy and privilege, will her taste for adventure get her too deep into danger?

ISBN 0 352 32909 2

THE SENSES BEJEWELLED
Cleo Cordell

Willing captives Marietta and Claudine are settling into an opulent life at Kasim's harem. But 18th century Algeria can be a hostile place. When the women are kidnapped by Kasim's sworn enemy, they face indignities that will test the boundaries of erotic experience. Marietta is reunited with her slave lover Gabriel, whose heart she previously broke. Will Kasim win back his cherished concubines? This is the sequel to *The Captive Flesh*.

ISBN 0 352 32904 1

GEMINI HEAT
Portia Da Costa

As the metropolis sizzles in freak early summer temperatures, twin sisters Deana and Delia find themselves cooking up a heatwave of their own. Jackson de Guile, master of power dynamics and wealthy connoisseur of fine things, draws them both into a web of luxuriously decadent debauchery. Sooner or later, one of them has to make a life-changing decision.

ISBN 0 352 32912 2

VIRTUOSO
Katrina Vincenzi

Mika and Serena, darlings of classical music's jet-set, inhabit a world of secluded passion. The reason? Since Mika's tragic accident which put a stop to his meteoric rise to fame as a solo violinist, he cannot face the world, and together they lead a decadent, reclusive existence. But Serena is determined to change things. The potent force of her ravenous sensuality cannot be ignored, as she rekindles Mika's zest for love and life through unexpected means. But together they share a dark secret.

ISBN 0 352 32907 6

MOON OF DESIRE
Sophie Danson

When Soraya Chilton is posted to the ancient and mysterious city of Ragzburg on a mission for the Foreign Office, strange things begin to happen to her. Wild, sexual urges overwhelm her at the coming of each full moon. Will her boyfriend, Anton, be her saviour – or her victim? What price will she have to pay to lift the curse of unquenchable lust that courses through her veins?

ISBN 0 352 32911 4

FIONA'S FATE
Fredrica Alleyn

When Fiona Sheldon is kidnapped by the infamous Trimarchi brothers, along with her friend Bethany, she finds herself acting in ways her husband Duncan would be shocked by. For it is he who owes the brothers money and is more concerned to free his voluptuous mistress than his shy and quiet wife. Alessandro Trimarchi makes full use of this opportunity to discover the true extent of Fiona's suppressed, but powerful, sexuality.

ISBN 0 352 32913 0

HANDMAIDEN OF PALMYRA
Fleur Reynolds

3rd century Palmyra: a lush oasis in the Syrian desert. The beautiful and fiercely independent Samoya takes her place in the temple of Antioch as an apprentice priestess. Decadent bachelor Prince Alif has other plans for her and sends his scheming sister to bring her to his Bacchanalian wedding feast. Embarking on a journey across the desert, Samoya encounters Marcus, the battle-hardened centurion who will unearth the core of her desires and change the course of her destiny.

ISBN 0 352 32919 X

OUTLAW FANTASY
Saskia Hope

For Fee Cambridge, playing with fire had become a full time job. Helping her pirate lover to escape his lawless lifestyle had its rewards as well as its drawbacks. On the outer reaches of the 21st century metropolis the Amazenes are on the prowl; fierce warrior women who have some unfinished business with Fee's lover. Will she be able to stop him straying back to the wrong side of the tracks? This is the sequel to *Outlaw Lover*.

ISBN 0 352 32920 3

THE SILKEN CAGE
Sophie Danson

When University lecturer, Maria Treharne, inherits her aunt's mansion in Cornwall, she finds herself the subject of strange and unexpected attention. Her new dwelling resides on much-prized land; sacred, some would say. Anthony Pendorran has waited a long time for the mistress to arrive at Brackwater Tor. Now she's here, his lust can be quenched as their longing for each other has a hunger beyond the realm of the physical. Using the craft of goddess worship and sexual magnetism, Maria finds allies and foes in this savage and beautiful landscape.

ISBN 0 352 32928 9

RIVER OF SECRETS
Saskia Hope & Georgia Angelis

When intrepid female reporter Sydney Johnson takes over someone else's assignment up the Amazon river, the planned exploration seems straightforward enough. But the crew's photographer seems to be keeping some very shady company and the handsome botanist is proving to be a distraction with a difference. Sydney soon realises this mission to find a lost Inca city has a hidden agenda. Everyone is behaving so strangely, so sexually, and the tropical humidity is reaching fever pitch as if a mysterious force is working its magic over the expedition. Echoing with primeval sounds, the jungle holds both dangers and delights for Sydney in this Indiana Jones-esque story of lust and adventure.

ISBN 0 352 32925 4

VELVET CLAWS
Cleo Cordell

It's the 19th century; a time of exploration and discovery and young, spirited Gwendoline Farnshawe is determined not to be left behind in the parlour when the handsome and celebrated anthropologist, Jonathan Kimberton, is planning his latest expedition to Africa. Rebelling against Victorian society's expectation of a young woman and lured by the mystery and exotic climate of this exciting continent, Gwendoline sets sail with her entourage bound for a land of unknown pleasures.

ISBN 0 352 32926 2

WE NEED YOUR HELP . . .
to plan the future of women's erotic fiction –

– and no stamp required!

Yours are the only opinions that matter.

Black Lace is the first series of books devoted to erotic fiction by women for women.

We intend to keep providing the best-written, sexiest books you can buy. And we'd appreciate your help and valued opinion of the books so far. Tell us what you want to read.

THE BLACK LACE QUESTIONNAIRE

SECTION ONE: ABOUT YOU

1.1 Sex (*we presume you are female, but so as not to discriminate*)
Are you?
Male ☐
Female ☐

1.2 Age
under 21 ☐ 21–30 ☐
31–40 ☐ 41–50 ☐
51–60 ☐ over 60 ☐

1.3 At what age did you leave full-time education?
still in education ☐ 16 or younger ☐
17–19 ☐ 20 or older ☐

1.4 Occupation _____

1.5   Annual household income
      under £10,000   ☐   £10–£20,000   ☐
      £20–£30,000   ☐   £30–£40,000   ☐
      over £40,000   ☐

1.6   We are perfectly happy for you to remain anonymous;
      but if you would like to receive information on other
      publications available, please insert your name and
      address

      _____

      _____

      _____

      _____

SECTION TWO: ABOUT BUYING BLACK LACE BOOKS

2.1   How did you acquire this copy of *A Bouquet of Black Orchids*?
      I bought it myself   ☐   My partner bought it ☐
      I borrowed/found it   ☐

2.2   How did you find out about Black Lace books?
      I saw them in a shop   ☐
      I saw them advertised in a magazine   ☐
      I saw the London Underground posters   ☐
      I read about them in _____
      Other _____

2.3   Please tick the following statements you agree with:
      I would be less embarrassed about buying Black
      Lace books if the cover pictures were less explicit ☐
      I think that in general the pictures on Black
      Lace books are about right   ☐
      I think Black Lace cover pictures should be as
      explicit as possible   ☐

2.4   Would you read a Black Lace book in a public place – on
      a train for instance?
      Yes   ☐   No   ☐

SECTION THREE: ABOUT THIS BLACK LACE BOOK

3.1   Do you think the sex content in this book is:
      Too much ☐   About right ☐
      Not enough ☐

3.2   Do you think the writing style in this book is:
      Too unreal/escapist ☐   About right ☐
      Too down to earth ☐

3.3   Do you think the story in this book is:
      Too complicated ☐   About right ☐
      Too boring/simple ☐

3.4   Do you think the cover of this book is:
      Too explicit ☐   About right ☐
      Not explicit enough ☐

Here's a space for any other comments:

SECTION FOUR: ABOUT OTHER BLACK LACE BOOKS

4.1   How many Black Lace books have you read? ☐

4.2   If more than one, which one did you prefer?

4.3   Why?

SECTION FIVE: ABOUT YOUR IDEAL EROTIC NOVEL

We want to publish the books you want to read – so this is your chance to tell us exactly what your ideal erotic novel would be like.

5.1 Using a scale of 1 to 5 (1 = no interest at all, 5 = your ideal), please rate the following possible settings for an erotic novel:

Medieval/barbarian/sword 'n' sorcery ☐
Renaissance/Elizabethan/Restoration ☐
Victorian/Edwardian ☐
1920s & 1930s – the Jazz Age ☐
Present day ☐
Future/Science Fiction ☐

5.2 Using the same scale of 1 to 5, please rate the following themes you may find in an erotic novel:

Submissive male/dominant female ☐
Submissive female/dominant male ☐
Lesbianism ☐
Bondage/fetishism ☐
Romantic love ☐
Experimental sex e.g. anal/watersports/sex toys ☐
Gay male sex ☐
Group sex ☐

Using the same scale of 1 to 5, please rate the following styles in which an erotic novel could be written:

Realistic, down to earth, set in real life ☐
Escapist fantasy, but just about believable ☐
Completely unreal, impressionistic, dreamlike ☐

5.3 Would you prefer your ideal erotic novel to be written from the viewpoint of the main male characters or the main female characters?

Male ☐   Female ☐
Both ☐

5.4 What would your ideal Black Lace heroine be like? Tick as many as you like:

Dominant	☐	Glamorous	☐
Extroverted	☐	Contemporary	☐
Independent	☐	Bisexual	☐
Adventurous	☐	Naive	☐
Intellectual	☐	Introverted	☐
Professional	☐	Kinky	☐
Submissive	☐	Anything else?	☐
Ordinary	☐	_____	

5.5 What would your ideal male lead character be like? Again, tick as many as you like:

Rugged	☐		
Athletic	☐	Caring	☐
Sophisticated	☐	Cruel	☐
Retiring	☐	Debonair	☐
Outdoor-type	☐	Naive	☐
Executive-type	☐	Intellectual	☐
Ordinary	☐	Professional	☐
Kinky	☐	Romantic	☐
Hunky	☐		
Sexually dominant	☐	Anything else?	☐
Sexually submissive	☐	_____	

5.6 Is there one particular setting or subject matter that your ideal erotic novel would contain?

_____

SECTION SIX: LAST WORDS

6.1 What do you like best about Black Lace books?

_____

6.2 What do you most dislike about Black Lace books?

_____

6.3 In what way, if any, would you like to change Black Lace covers?

_____